Children of the Neon Bamboo

B. GLYNN KIMMEY

CHILDREN OF THE NEON BAMBOO

B. GLYNN KIMMEY

Cover Design - Khafid Wahyudi (Kating Egepe)
Internal Design - David Woods
Final Edit and Management - Chloe Harrison

Printed in the United States of America

WELCOME!

Hey, C'mon in. Let me walk you out back to the pool, and we'll get comfortable.

Yep, you've come at the perfect time—sun going down, light breeze, not too cold, not too hot. If I do my job right, you'll be motivated to make this next summer the best you've ever had, relish it like the last slurp of a tropical snow cone, wear it like your oldest, favorite t-shirt, luxuriate in it like the California sun.

Yeah, I'll have you ready to cruise the coast into an eternal sunset, radio up, wind in your hair.

Maybe it will re-energize your soul and make you feel like you're at an old red-roofed, wood-paneled Pizza Hut and you've just stepped back from the *Teenage Mutant Ninja Turtles* on the arcade to see that your Mountain Dew has been refilled and that your friends glow with joy, watching the cheese stretch two feet from the greasy pan.

What? I have flashes of ambition.

Take a seat.

Yeah . . . Mikey's little creative studio here and its inspiration first climate can be a little rough around the edges, but I think it'll work just fine for this story, maybe even help with the mood, add a little flavor, add a sense of creative gravitas, add a feeling that this is where you belong, sitting here listening to this story and reflecting on our curious world.

Unless you want to glide a convertible down Highway 1 through the Florida Keys, this is about as good as it gets.

Either way, you're gonna need me to loan ya a better shirt though.

And, yes, this pool-turned-nature-reserve is an acquired taste, but once you get it, you'll wonder why everyone doesn't have one.

Anyway, the summer of 19 motherfuckin' 90, when me and a Vietnamese rock star embroiled Fort Smith, Arkansas in chaotic international intrigue—a martial arts showdown at a combination sex shop/Dungeons & Dragons supply store. The ol' tale as old as time.

But for better or worse, I'm gonna tell it the way I prefer to tell it: with all my favorite parts. The real story, the good stuff, the inspiration, the invigoration, is all in the personalities and the aesthetics.

The colors, the mood, the feel, the zeitgeist, the atmospheric hues that created it all. The commercial vibrancy. The clothes. The cars. The movies. The music. The video games. The road trips. The air. The LIFE.

Often with little interest, I've watched cultural and artistic tides ebb and flow. But they meant something to somebody, somewhere. The one in this story, it's mine. It's what I've got. I'm proud and thankful for it. Maybe it's not your place, but I bet you have a place. Maybe a pumpkin patch on Halloween or a snowy

Christmas by the fire—your favorite ambiance when all is right in the world.

I'll get to the high stakes adventure when I get to it. The cross-country car chases over ancient samurai swords, the intersection of Filipino-knife-fighting experts, black-market antiquities traders, Japanese-jazz-fusion aficionados and off-the-grid-refugee gamecock fighters. But, that stuff can wait until you're in the proper mindset.

Don't worry—I'm gonna tell it, no gory detail spared.

What? We can get this over real quick if you want, a minute or two. All the big stuff that happened, if compressed down to the crucial moments, would span about three hours, give or take. Isn't there a quote that's like, "Life is made up of years that mean nothing, and moments that mean everything?" Someone distinguished said that.

You can piece the major points together from newspaper articles, can't you? You wanted an in-depth version, yeah?

So, if you're here for this, let's do it. And for you, I'm gonna get experimental, take my story craft to the next level, focus on getting you in the right mood for receiving. Any story is half teller and half listener. For you to perceive this one in totality, to feel it like it was felt back then, for you to understand the big night, the big moment, the final hurrah, you need to be in contact with the artifacts of the time.

Ergo, I've brought a box of peripherals, some tokens of the era to string your mind, body, and soul with vaporous webs of tone, aura, and color.

Hey, you came to me. I'm not getting paid. Supply and demand. Leverage. Business school stuff. And, like it or not, the old fashion griot, the oral storyteller, is a dying art. We've gotta adapt to a new world. A straightforward, simply told story won't cut it in this age when everyone carries a dopamine casino in their pocket.

To understand the story in all its glory, the feelings and the emotions, you really have to put them in context of the entire summer, and to really get the summer right, you have to feel the spirit. Otherwise, it's just another 1980's style action story. Otherwise, it's just the cliche tale of young boys caught in the crossfire of a multi-generational quest for priceless treasure. Otherwise, it's just a rare glimpse at how the Eastern Illuminati discretely manage their most important disputes.

Oh, I better get that shirt. The clothes make the man, they say. If your clothes feel right, other things start to fall into place.

And we're talking about Polynesian inspired geometric and abstract designs if you really want to nail the vibe. It wasn't exactly the iconic 80s Memphis style,[1] nor was it 90s grunge. There was a transitional phase. Hold tight...

I've even got some records ready to put on in the background. You might be surprised how musical this tale is.

If you change your mind and aren't feeling it after all, go watch a reality show about a husband-and-wife team who remodel and flip houses or something. You have my permission. The last thing I want to do is force a story on you when you're not in the mood.

1. No one knows this aesthetic by its creator's name, The Memphis Group. But look it up; you'll immediately recognize the triangles and terrazzo pastels. Think of an early 90s Taco Bell.

Waste of your time and mine. Don't worry about me, never had a problem entertaining myself.

You sure? Okay.

What are the chances? Of all the stars, planets, space, and matter in the galaxy, you are here, made of star stuff, pondering and smiling at the thought of a unique, brief instance that may not even be real, a phantasm of gratitude that you and only you could ever truly appreciate, an uncommunicable dose of pleasure. Maybe it's one joke, one mannerism, a brief recollection from the past that, even when alone, brings a gleam to your eye and causes one corner of your lip to twist up in thanks, a nod to the little things in life.

Despite the death, it's not a sad story. I owe it to them to tell it. They'd all be proud of how it turned out. They did the best they could with their time, and they wouldn't be selfish enough to expect someone to be resentful on their behalf.

I brought that little desk out here to set down an ashtray, notepad, drinks, or what-have-you.

Ah, drinks!

What would you prefer? One can't sit down for a good story on an evening like this without a drink. If you're in the mood for a soft drink, Pepsi or Mountain Dew. This story is unequivocally Pepsi culture. I mean, I should be the official spokesman for Pepsi/Frito Lay. Speaking of which, I could go for a bag of Doritos right now. Cool Ranch. Nacho Cheese wouldn't jive tonight.

If you feel like beer: Milwaukee's Best. "The Beast."

Now if you want both sweet and alcoholic, we can make you something I like to call the "Key Largo Sunset."

I've obviously had my fair share, but I won't stop you from ordering a pizza if you're in the mood. We may be on the outskirts of town, but we're within delivery range. Deep dish, extra cheese, pepperoni or mushrooms optional.

Savor your beverage.

The characters, though. The vibes are a nice patina on the soul when I'm in a good mood, ephemeral atmospheres of nostalgia and déjà vu, but the characters . . .

They touch a different part of my soul, the admirer of the enduring human spirit. Singular individuals moving forward without the validation of consensus, living free on their own terms, but not shirking responsibility when it's time to fight or sacrifice. The Brave. The Free.

When my back is against the wall, when I don't think I have what it takes, when I feel like giving up, their spirits guide the way through darkness like neon lights piercing a cyberpunk fog.

Haha—You comfortable? All right, let's get started.

MOM'S ACOUSTIC TOUR

"Hard Road" - Super Hang-On OST

Let's see, I graduated 6th grade from Woodrow Wilson Middle School in suburban Glendale, California. Nothing special there. Normally, I would have done what every other 12-year-old in my era did during the summer: hung around, having as much fun as possible. Bicycling to arcades, sitting around eating popsicles while watching Nickelodeon, MTV, and the same few VHS tapes over and over again. Friends' houses, grandparents' house, or my mom's apartment, the story would have been the same. I had already quit baseball, so there wouldn't be any of that, and I wasn't quite old enough to run with the skateboarding packs or go to teenage parties. Just the right age for killing time, doing whatever you feel like doing.

But noooo . . . my mom, the dear Chelsey Ann Regulski, and her boyfriend, Darrick, disrupted my summer plans by going on a summer-long acoustic tour up and down the western seaboard. By acoustic, I mean, acoustic guitar. They would sing and play a two-hour set in a song-swap fashion with heartfelt political and interpersonal commentary between songs. They even had a few duets. "Mad Hearts in an Imperfect World" was a particularly annoying song they co-wrote, through which I suffered their repeated rehearsals that could get a little testy, starting and stopping to correct the other's tone. At the time, I was thoroughly annoyed and disgusted, turning up the volume on my TV, trying to blot out the god awful racket. But looking back, it wasn't that bad of a song; while a little melodramatic, it was thoughtful and painstakingly crafted. Their music definitely wasn't something that would ever appeal to the kid I was or be a hit, or even popular for that matter, but I retroactively respect their effort and concern for the art form.

So while I was sailing around the Florida Keys with Vietnam veterans, my mom was hitting up all the chic, faux dive bars and the burgeoning coffee shop scene of the West Coast. A trip, I would bet, my grandfather was secretly subsidizing. Darrick, the BF, would say he was going to hustle and wash dishes, pick up aluminum cans, do whatever it takes to get from town to town, like a real-deal troubadour, an artist's artist, a Kerouac Woody Guthrie. He and my mom, a regular Bonnie and Clyde of the singer-songwriter circuit. The new breed of Echo Park heroes.

Singer-songwriters always have and always will think they are ushering in a new era of sophisticated yet from-the-heart songwriting. It's part of the job; it couldn't be any other way.

Darrick thought he was so cool, or post-cool rather, but I thought he was a jerk-off. He smoked cigarettes, which isn't something I'm particularly judgmental about, but it made me cringe the way he fastidiously worked the affectation of smoking into his pseudo-Irish, artist persona, looking out into the distance after every drag. He thought he was the reincarnation of James Joyce, lamenting that the plebes wouldn't get his Dylan-esque prosody in this degenerated artistic paradigm, his genius unappreciated in this flood of mediocrity. And, he thought he was better than my mom; she was lucky to be the one getting used by him on his ascent to greatness. Worst: he wore the stupidest hats to match his scarves and turquoise jewelry.

Now, most people in this story will get told in two lenses, how I saw them then and how I see them now through a, presumably, wiser and kinder lens. But not Darrick. Fuck him. I've stayed away from Irish poets and scarves ever since.

~

Ah, shit, now that I've said that, I feel bad about it. Annoying as he was, I wouldn't trade my problems for his. I must go to the nearest English department and find a brooding English major in highly stylized, anachronistic clothes and try to make amends.

What goes around comes around, I guess. I've gotten my share of nasty looks from the kids of women I've dated.

I'm not telling you about him because he'll come in and save the day out of nowhere. He's a reflection on my mother, the best way to show you where she was in life. But don't get me wrong, as hard as I can be on my mother, I love her. Despite all the demons she battles, she loves me and does the best she can. She's had a life of bitter compromises. I wasn't planned.

I never knew my dad. My mom was seventeen when she had me. From what I've gathered, he was some kind of artistic itinerant: musician, rock star, painter, taste maker, someone my highly aesthetic and impressionable teenager mother would have fawned over. Everyone was too embarrassed or ashamed to talk about it. If directly pressed, my mom would just say I was her big surprise. My family is and was cool enough not to give her too hard of a time about it.

For kids raised in L.A. in the 60s and 70s, my mom and uncle could have turned out much stranger. The Manson family, drugs, hippies, burn outs, Jesus Freaks, "the Co-ed Killer" Edmund Kemper, satanic cults. Damn near all of our icons of weird came from California at that time, the epicenter of the esoteric.

Consequently, taking care of me for the summer became the obligation of my grandparents. Complicating matters, my grandmother had moved back to her hometown of Van Buren, Arkansas eight months prior.

Grandpa was going to take me on a cross-country, bonding road trip and drop me off in Arkansas for Grandma to watch me for a couple months. Fun . . . I wasn't exactly happy about having my most valuable chronological real estate occupied by driving around a dork-mobile truck/RV hybrid or in Arkansas, which was the middle of nowhere to me.

Now you know. When I'm at the part where I'm hiding for my life in the middle of a rack of gay-bar black leathers, there will be no reason to stop the flow to wonder where my parents are and how could I get myself into such a mess.

Funny, now that I think about it, I need to ask mom how the tour went. That little phase of her life gets overshadowed. I bet it was a pain in the ass. I couldn't imagine trying to set up an acoustic tour. Props to them. It takes vast willpower to pick up the phone, take a lot more "no" for an answer than "yes" and then show up at these places and play for one or two serious fans, while the rest of the patrons wouldn't care if you died right there.

~

She hugged Grandpa, "Thanks, Dad. I love you."

"I love you too, sweetie. I know you all are going to knock their socks off," he said.

Mom told me good-bye with a hug and a kiss. Told me to wish her luck.

"Yeah, good luck," was all I said.

"You, Grandpa, and Grandma are going to have a lot of fun this summer," she said to me.

"Yeah, Mom, we will," I said.

"Say hi to Mom for me!" was her final statement before turning around.

I'm not sure why I was being short with her. I wasn't actively trying to antagonize her; I was, for the most part, cool with her being a free-spirited, non-traditional mother.

As she got in the van, Darrick was leaned up against the side, gazing off into the distant suburbs. Then he nodded at me as he got in the driver's seat.

Grandpa and I watched as they drove off. "I sure hope it works out," he said with less-than-perfect confidence.

THE POOL

You're judging. You wouldn't be the first nor the last person to talk shit about this pool. I'm pretty sure anyone who's seen it has made a snarky remark. The dark water. The windblown trash. The invasive, weed-like Pink Silk trees growing around the edge, fanning out, forming an Amazon-like canopy over the water.

Yeah, the pool disgusts the unaccustomed, the uninitiated, the close minded, those who can only handle one version, the platonic ideal of "a pool."

Yes, by conventional consensus about what a pool is, this one is repugnant. Compared to some sophisticated Miami ultra-modern architecture pool or an infinity pool at the edge of an Australian vista? Sure.

And everyone throws in their two cents about what Mikey should do to fix it up. That is until they've stuck around long enough to feel the enchantment...

Given time, you'll learn to appreciate if not downright treasure it. How much time? Depends on your personality and what magic you happen to witness.

First though, why is it like this? How did it get to be this way? He bought the house solely because the add-on family game center works perfectly as a live room for jamming and tracking drums. Besides, the pool is only a few feet deep anyway, so there's not much fun anyone could be having in it. Maintenance would be like $150 a month after an initial $1,000 investment to get it running. For someone scraping every penny he can to make his business go, it just doesn't make sense. He wishes it would just disappear. And various plumbers and landscapers have told him that filling it in will create more headaches. He's stuck with it.

He made the best of the situation and let nature take its course. An entire new ecosystem emerged. Frogs were the first to take over. Then Jason, a traveling semi-pro bass fisherman who was staying on the couch, took to the project and filled the pool with minnows, lily pads, and reeds, not to mention some crappie and catfish that didn't survive. After that, the race was on. The ecological community flourished. Bugs and minnows at the first level. Frogs and lizards next on the predation chain below snakes, and toward apex, occasional mammals like dogs and raccoons. But the coolest are the birds of prey—prairie hawks, owls, or crows—who dive bomb into the pool and soar away with a poor frog in its talons, bittersweet because you grow attached to the frogs, listening to them croon to their lovers with their baritone croaks on balmy summer nights.

Maybe one day the house will attract the American Bald Eagle it deserves.

And, it's got a long, beautiful history of artistic inspiration. The hard-cores around here say it's a shot of vitality, that no one has ever regretted jumping in the pool. Like the French Artists of the 1920s who thought African sculptures had secret powers, the creators around here believe that diving in the nasty pool invigorates intense creativity. Mike says he wrote an entire concept album after jumping in one evening, a midwestern gothic, spoken word/black jazz metal album based on a friend's experience living in a dilapidated trailer in the woods of Missouri and unsuccessfully trying to start a psychedelic mushroom farm.

Sometimes it gets a little weird. Sometimes it gets a little strange. Sometimes it gets a little bizarre, but like a lot of things in nature, the best stuff comes near the breaking point.

It can also be sublime. Look out on the pool and its exotic canopy with a cup of coffee on a rainy morning or walk around it on a nice spring afternoon.

It gives.

THE MOJAVE

"Atom Heart Mother Suite" and "Echoes" by Pink Floyd

Book rec: Mojave Mysteries Volume 1 by M.L. Berhman

A few days later, about 5 a.m., Grandpa dragged my groggy ass to his Toyota Galaxy camper, a pickup truck/motorhome hybrid.

We were headed up 395 to Death Valley. I barely remember it. Pillow against the window, I conked out while we moseyed along. He wasn't a fast driver to begin with, but, man, the Galaxy was pokey as hell.

See, Grandpa was into petroglyphs which are, by the strictest, most basic definition, rock carvings. But any North American petroglyph enthusiast is invariably talking about the kind left by Native Americans hundreds of years ago. Death Valley, California is probably the best place in the nation to look for them, so we were going to make our way up there for a couple days and back down into Joshua Tree before taking I-40 to Arkansas. Get a little bonding time in. Maybe teach me a few things about the natural world and have a little fun himself with his new petroglyph hobby.

Grandpa was a man of many hobbies and tinkerings, pretty good at all of them. He never committed to one long enough to be distinguished, but there's a lot to be said for milking a passion just until it gets tough and boring, optimization. He was a collector and trader, as well. He had an eye for first edition science fiction books and radio equipment. He would read various Thrifty Nickel type rags and the classifieds looking for hidden gems or inefficiently priced items he could flip.

~

The ride through the desert—momentary glimpses come back to me clear and vibrant like I am there, but most of the trip is wiped from my memory banks.

~

The health teacher, a huge football coach, walked over to his filing cabinet, picked out a manila file folder full of papers, said "Cousin Ronnie's dirt bike accident," and threw the folder into the air. He grabbed another, said "My sister's birthday," and threw it into the middle of the classroom with derision. Then he grabbed a hand's worth of folders full of paper, and while flinging them up into the air he yelled, "John Wayne Comancheros movie quotes! How many touchdowns Roger Staubach threw in Super Bowl Thirteen." He took a long look at us all, making sure he had our eye contact. "Gone!" Then he began to pantomime smoking a joint. Fingers at his lips, he made an inhaling sound then, theatricality increasing, he tossed some more folders into the air. "Memories. The things that make up your life. Each time you do drugs, you're tossing away part of your identity."

I haven't followed his advice to the T, but I can't say I disagree. I would expand what he was considering drugs to include alcohol, caffeine, nicotine, stress, and concentration on newer things in life. Time is ruthless. And nothing in this world is free.

I said all that to explain why I don't remember every part of the trip. I've been hard on this noggin, and I wasn't exactly a savant memory god to begin with.

I do remember some things though. We had two big Death Valley stops. And, I've talked to a serious petroglyph enthusiast to get some of the names right. Swansea was the first.

Hot and bored the moment I stepped out of the truck, I reluctantly walked the mile or so to the petroglyph site.

In a brown and tan ice chest he'd had since the early 70s, Grandpa, for my sake, kept soda and glass-bottled lemon-lime Gatorade. I had my first one finished 20 yards into our hike. He took the glass from me and put it into his pack while telling me about how rocks and fence posts can be broken by the expansion of salt crystals. I still don't understand that.

We made it to the site. I took one look, acknowledged their coolness then found a big rock to sit down against, the closest thing resembling shade. He spent what seemed like forever sketching in his notebook; it was probably only thirty minutes. He saw me with my head in my hands and gave me another Gatorade, before taking some pictures.

We walked back to the car. He could tell I wasn't having fun. To cheer me up, he said if I was a good sport, we'd stay in a hotel, even though I hadn't toughed out one night in the camper yet. This got me to cooperate. He knew how much I like hotels.

The next spot out around Cosa Springs had some thousand-year-old Native American habitation sites. After the walk there, it took me about five minutes to take everything in. I thought I was really being tough having to put up with him walking around analyzing the ruins all afternoon. He found a tarantula and showed me how to locate their eyes, smaller than pinheads in a place you wouldn't expect. Cool Grandpa. I wasn't too appreciative, but not disrespectful either. I did my best not to complain, but it wouldn't have taken a body language expert to tell I was ready to go.

On the way to the hotel, we stopped at a little Old-West themed diner where I scarfed down some cheeseburgers, onion rings, a milkshake, and Pepsi. I probably had the waitress refill my soda at least three or four times I was so famished from sitting in the heat.

I was fat and happy as we cruised up to the Atomic Inn. It felt great to turn on the TV, grab the remote, and jump on the southwestern, Native American themed thin comforter, the kind only found in hotels. I was relieved to be back in my element, my happy place. And standard issue, with-commercials cable TV just tastes a little better at hotels for some reason—always has, always will.

He let me sleep in as long as I wanted. He had already snagged the small soaps and shampoos. Grandpa was the kind of guy who never put on cologne in his life, never spent a cent more than he had to on toiletries, stretching a single-use Bic razor out over a week.

Once I was up and around, say 9 o'clock-ish, we headed back down through Death Valley, taking dirt roads, the beautiful, fierce Panamint mountains to the west. I was relaxed, just taking it all in.

We made it to the Mojave National Preserve to do a little hiking. I remember cooking in the heat and what my Grandpa looked like. Socks too high. Baggy khaki shorts. Skin spots. Skinny limbs with a little potbelly. It wasn't exactly inspiring. I didn't like hiking. Still don't. I realize how cool, serene and in-touch hikers are, but it ain't me, babe.

The best part was camping for the night. We pulled the Galaxy off the main dirt road a little ways, beside a pile of boulders.

We got comfortable. He pulled out some lawn chairs and set up the radio.

His hand-built radio. Ignorant of the technical specs, I didn't appreciate it as much as I should have. I just kinda assumed every Grandpa built radios. A few years back I showed the radio to some hobbyist radio builders and they were thoroughly impressed.

They had a lot to say about it, but long-story-short, it's a superhet with a "Radio Frequency" (RF) stage, multiple "intermediate frequency" (IF) stages, and extras such as a "Beat Frequency Oscillator" (BFO) to receive morse, as well as "Band Switching" to receive long waves, an "S Meter" to measure signal strength, a "Q multiplier" to improve selectivity, and a "VHF Converter" stage to receive VHF FM, etc. all in the smallest possible dimensions, which was a feat in itself.

When the radio buffs saw it, they instantly recognized that not only was the builder a member of the tribe, but a master. I wish I could show it to you, but I put it up at Grandma's house. Packing it around with me in my car was going to get it broken. I wish I had a picture, but I don't. Next time I go back to California, I'll send you a pic.

After the long day of hiking, I was finally able to embrace the inherent spirituality of the Mojave, its beautiful mixture of open spaces and rocky precipices. Sitting there, chilling out, drinking a few more lemon-lime Gatorades, scarfing down some Snickers and a few packs of orange-colored cheese and crackers, I watched the sunset as Grandpa tinkered around getting his radio antenna set up on the nearby rock formation.

"Go ahead, fiddle with it, dial in a good frequency. With the antenna and our elevation, you should be able to pick up stations from here to Tokyo." He said as I turned the wrong knobs. He came down from the rocks to show me how to operate it, and sure enough it seemed like every FM band had a station. I settled on a college indie rock station that was playing some cool stuff I didn't recognize.

This is about where he started telling me about the mysteries of the Mojave, the reports of demonic satanic rituals, bodies found without hands, feet, or heads. A mothman-esque creature that steals from campsites. Giant reptiles that time forgot. And, more realistically, squatters, meth labs, and abandoned mineshafts that serve as cemeteries for poor souls murdered by L.A. weirdos or Las Vegas mobsters.

He had me spooked, but assured me no one would bother us, citing the relative infrequency of such events and that innocent campers don't really get taken. It was kind of scary, but a fun scary. I was pretty sure he had a gun somewhere in the camper, maybe even on his person, but guns were something he was touchy about. If I had to wager what his philosophy on firearms was, I'd say: necessary evil, not to be glamorized. Whatever. Point is, I was frightened enough to make things interesting and memorable but wasn't too scared to fall asleep.

I woke up in the middle of the night, and he was still awake, sitting in his fold out lawn chair looking up at the stars, listening to Art Bell's *Coast to Coast AM*, the classic late night paranormal talk show. Skinwalkers were the topic that night. Unfortunately, it's hard to find old broadcasts. They didn't record them all like they do in the digital era. Tape was expensive and space-consuming.

Falling asleep or driving, *Coast to Coast AM* is still the perfect late-night companion. My all-time favorite episode is the Ray Manzarek one where he talks about the formation of The Doors. Find an archived recording if you can.

It was a pretty cool experience under the desert stars with my grandpa. Simple as it was, it's one of my all-time favorite moments. I wonder what all he was thinking while he was sitting there all night. He was Grandpa. I loved him. The best friend I've ever had, but the idea that he may have led an interesting life before I was alive never once entered my thoughts. He might as well have just appeared when I was born.

It's funny. If you were to look at him and wonder how it would turn out for him, you wouldn't have gotten it right with a million guesses.

GRANDPA'S ALIEN ARC

Documentary: The Truth about the Philadelphia Experiment: Invisibility, Time Travel, and Mind Control by Reality Entertainment

"Did You Ever See a Dream Walking?"- Bing Crosby

All right, all right. I know you're dying to talk about it, that aborted fetus known as *Glitter Astern*, my book on UFOs.

Yes, I spent the better part of a year obsessed with the idea that Grandpa knew something about UFOs, unidentified flying objects, to be clear: extraterrestrials. If you want to get into the nitty-gritty, you can find my archived blogs from back in the late aughts, but I'm a little salty about it now and really don't feel like saying any more than what's necessary. The chapter is over. I am aliened out.

Back when I was doing the Santa Fe, New Mexico thing, I would often hear bombers flying overhead, subconsciously priming me the eureka moment when in a UFO documentary someone mentioned that Lockheed Martin's Skunk Works developed the stealth bomber from alien technology. Where had I heard of Lockheed Martin? I know that name. I know that name.

A fire burst forth!

Grandpa worked for Lockheed! An entire new universe unfolded in front of me. Grandpa knew something about UFOs.

It all came together right there. His appetite for science fiction, his employment, the research into petroglyphs, the ancient sites, his nightly listening of Art Bell, his copy of *Chariot of the Gods*, and our nights spent outside under the stars in UFO hotspots.

I was there for the 90s, completely, so I was predisposed for this kind of thing. Before 9/11 made the USA cool and trustworthy again, anxiety about the power and reach of the government permeated American culture. Conspiracy was fresh and interesting. The Cold War was over and we needed a new collective fear. Bob Lazaar, *The X-files*, Ruby Ridge, the Oklahoma City bombing, Waco, Branch Davidians, the fundamentalist Christian obsession with the End Times, Bill Clinton the Antichrist, etc.

The first three months of the project I was wild with enthusiasm, one of the "most alive" phases of my existence. I was living Indiana Jones and the Last Crusade, my grandfather guiding me from the grave to unlock the secrets of the universe. Me and Grandpa's names in the headlines, forever associated with cracking the code. "The Regulski Men Did It!" It felt good. The hope, the bright vision of the future. L.I.V.I.N., brother!

Grandma has storage spaces full of Grandpa's books that Mom and I make her keep. I read, reread, flipped upside down, turned my brain inside out searching through his science fiction monthlies, books on petroglyphs, archeology, and technology. I left no avenue unexplored, no possible connection unexamined.

Which included a deep dive into his employment at the massive defense contractor, subsequently giving myself a small education in aeronautical technology history. Grandpa was steadily employed at Lockheed from 1955 to 1985, right through their fascinating Skunk Works period where our best physicists and engineers were locked in a basement, working like the Free World depended on them, pounding coffee and smoking cigarettes trying to win the Cold War. They came up with some of the coolest things like the U-2 spy plane, SR-71 Blackbird and the F-117 Nighthawk, the first plane to incorporate stealth technology.

Interestingly, and unfortunately, I called, wrote, tried to find people, and no one would or could tell me exactly what he did there. Not even Grandma. He could have been anything from the bottom-of-the-totem-pole guy doing basic soldering or a key

Skunk Works player. He made too much money to be at the very bottom, but I just don't know and likely never will.

Doubts, denial, stubborn consistency, and ultimately resignation.

An alien plot to this story is just wishful thinking. There is a sliver of hope, but we may have to go with Occum's Razor on this one, and say he just liked the desert and esoteric things as ends in themselves without an overarching relationship.

I wasted a lot of time, but it was a great way to get to know more about my grandfather, a way to connect. And I learned other cool things, which I think I'll save for later.

Just another phase I went through. Remember what Winston Churchill said, "Success in life is going from one failure to the next with enthusiasm."

Everyone who says I should use my energy for more secure and reliable employment is probably right, but I've made peace with the fact my drum beats a little differently, not a lot of consistency but I go for some home run fills and have some oddly placed, yet interesting ghost notes.

BREAKING THE NEWS

The next morning we got up and were on our way. Arkansas, here we come. We took it slow, admiring the scenery as I surfed the radio. The New Wave songs— now a completely accepted part of our aesthetic past—blew his mind. Flock of Seagulls, The Smiths, The Cure, Depeche Mode, Pet Shop Boys, all that was weird, weird, weird to him. He didn't get anything that came after the malt shop era.

There was an ever-flowing scientific and historical commentary for every geography and town along the way, trying to expand my brain, inspire a sense of wonder, lay down neural frameworks that might come in handy in the future. Honorable endeavor for sure, but my interest waxed and waned.

We made lots of stops. Grandpa had to pee a lot. Prostates can be a bitch. Or maybe it was to apply hemorrhoidal ointment. Not sure. Who knows? He never mentioned his ailments. But Lucky for me, he would always let me grab a soda and candy each time. Or if I was real lucky there would be a Slush Puppy machine.

God, I'd trade all of Solomon's gold to be riding around with him right now. I'm a lucky, lucky man, regardless.

~

Buuuut . . . the vibe changed.

Somewhere in our detour through the epic, otherworldly, tan-and-brown dreamscape that is the High Plains of the Oklahoma panhandle near the Colorado border, my grandfather dropped the bomb, "You'll be staying at your Aunt Brenda's house." Wait, what? Surely someone told me this before, but somehow, somewhere this information didn't register. Too unlikely. Too horrific. My mind wouldn't allow me to face it.

"Are you kidding me?" exploded out of my mouth as I stomped the floor in an unusual-around-my-grandfather tantrum. "This is going to be the worst summer ever." I started feeling sorry for myself, scrunching my nose and pressing the back of my head into the seat.

"It's going to be all right. You'll be just fine," he said, trying to calm me. After that he just let me simmer down on my own, but the train of dramatizations about my unending cascade of misery and torture could not be derailed.

BRENDA

"American Girl" - Tom Petty and the Heartbreakers

Brenda Ann Harris, Aunt Brenda, my grandmother's younger, only sister, born in 1939, chain-smoking, foul mouthed, thrice-divorced, back to using her maiden name, ran her own hair salon, specializing in perms.

The tail end of the Vietnam War took her first husband, her precious Johnny, her one true love. No, he didn't get killed. He got deployed and decided not to come back to Arkansas; rumor has it he found someone else. "That fuckin army brainwashed him," I heard her say over a million times, insinuating that if he would have come home her life would have worked out perfectly. Or "My Johnny wouldn't do that." No one really knows what Johnny was like, but it's safe to say that at the time I thought anyone who would have married Brenda must've had a screw loose.

Her third husband, the biker, had left her in 1988. Not sure why. Her second husband from the early 80s, I barely remember him. He was a soft-spoken businessman. I think she dumped him for the biker.

She neither received nor gave any quarter.

For most of the time we shared on Earth together, I loved Brenda. But I knew living with her wouldn't be as comfortable as I was accustomed to. She didn't have a nurturing, parental bone in her body.

I feel ya, sister.

VAN BUREN, ARKANSAS

"There's Room Here for the Lonely"

*- Bogdonovich *Busted* Casey*

I'm sentimental about the place, but to a kid from L.A, Arkansas couldn't have been more backwater and unexciting.

Incorporated in 1845, named after Martin Van Buren, the first U.S. president born an American citizen, bordering Oklahoma, the town has always been a quick stop along the Arkansas River and, now, Interstate I-40, a place to get supplies or drop off mail on your way across the country. In 1990, it had a population of 14,000 people.

I had gone there when I was four or so, but barely remembered it. I knew we were getting close when I saw all the anthropomorphized pig bumper stickers. Razorbacks, unique moniker, I'll give it to them.

Van Buren had things. Video rentals, car washes, baseball diamonds, city pool, city park, grocery stores, tennis courts, lots of churches, thrift stores, antique stores, hardware stores. The old part of town, Main Street, has maintained its old-timey vibe so well they've covered the street in dirt and filmed westerns there.

You'd have to cross the river into the larger town of Fort Smith for things like batting cages, go-karts, putt-putt, movie theaters, and shopping malls.

But, Van Buren has two crown jewels: Paul's Bakery and Pizza Parlour.

Donuts, another culinary item with which I'm well acquainted. I've eaten donuts from one side of this world to the other—strip malls, mom and pops, upmarket delicatessens, you name it. And I'll say this: Paul's Bakery in Van Buren, Arkansas is by far the best in the world. Bangkok to Calgary.

Cape Town to Cairo. Detroit down to Houston. New York to L.A. There's pride in every American heart for Paul's Bakery.

And although I'm an unofficial spokesman for Pizza Hut, hangout in Van Buren for a week and you will undoubtedly have some Pizza Parlour. They serve a unique pizza, thinner, but not New York style either. I haven't had pizza anywhere that's the same. Their sausage and Canadian bacon are particularly different. I'm not into sausage on my pizza, but theirs is special; combine it with mushrooms.

Any way you slice it, Van Buren really isn't that crazy of a town. You may have to travel for certain things you want, but it has everything you need, and you can be anything you want there. Teenage methhead to the Ivy League. Some people from Van Buren think they are big-city urbane, while the kids in the next house over in the subdivision feel like they're right out of "A Country Boy Can Survive." Lots of variance in its own way. Not too dissimilar to most places around the world, I guess.

Once you started leaving the city limits, though, especially back then, you were indisputably in rural Arkansas.

~

Oak Crest Trailer Park down highway 64 to the east was about the last stop before civilization thinned. That's the trailer park my aunt Brenda lived in, where I'd be staying. As far as trailer parks go, it wasn't a bad one. Plenty of shade and people mostly took care of their humble properties.

BIG CHARLES WAYMIRE

I'm gonna throw you a little red meat to get you through the summer quotidian video game stuff. It'll keep you on your toes, keep you wondering when it will tie-in.

~

Big Charles Waymire, a hardworking Nebraska farm hand, enlisted in the U.S. Army just in time to catch the tail-end of the war in the Pacific. He ended up in D Battery 457 Parachute Artillery Regiment, 11th Airborne division, part of General Douglas MacArthur's big mission to take back the Philippines.[2] For jungle acclimation they trained at Fort Polk, Louisiana, before heading to Papua New Guinea. The division did some mop-up duty on Leyte without anything noteworthy happening.

Then, it was on to their big moment. An airborne drop into the main island of the Philippines, Luzon, a mountainous, treacherous jungle covered land that would need to be taken inch-by-bloody-inch. The fighting against dug-in, camouflaged machine gun nests was terrible but the evacuations were worse. Harassed by Japanese sniper fire, rain beat down on them as they tried to take the wounded down slippery, narrow trails. And if the American G.I.s weren't on a mountain, they were in a swamp.

Somewhere along their way across the island of Luzon, it was time for Big Charles's artillery battery to put down some roots and prepare for fire missions. And while changing socks he saw a young local lady, Rosalinde, struggling to repair a destroyed village.

While the rest of the men of his company took much needed rest after marching and forcing their 75mm howitzers through the jungles of the Philippines, the inspired Big Charles busted his ass to help clear out rubble, trying to impress her, and despite how hard Charles worked, she gave him no attention. Didn't even say a word to him. To her, he was just a horny soldier she'd

2. Also, interestingly, the relatively un-memorialized, un-aggrandized 11th Airborne was the home of Rod fuckin' Serling, the man behind *The Twilight Zone*. Like you didn't know that. God, we are lucky to have backs of such hard asses to stand on, molders of this wonderful modern world.

never see again after he left for the impending doom that would be the Battle of Manila.[3] Besides, the brutal Japanese occupation probably didn't create many romance-minded young ladies.

Soldiers are always quick to fall in love, always have been, always will be; it's part of the job. But they move on just as fast, forgetting about the object of their affections and finding new romantic fixations. Not Big Charles. After the god-awful painscape that was the Battle of Manila, he found a way to pass-off duty, find her, and help her family rebuild, testing the leniency of his chain of command, staying gone for as long as he could. Big Charles was loyal as a dog, showing off his farm-boy work ethic, sacredly laboring to rebuild their hamlet, asking nothing in return. By the time his battery had to move south to clear the remainder of the island, the Filipino family who had been living a nightmare the past five years were believers in Big Charles Waymire.

Once the island was liberated, the division came back through and bivouacked twenty miles from her hamlet. Despite torrential rain, for two more weeks Charles still found ways to spend all the time he could with her, cherishing every second because the future was bleak. The 11th's next assignment: airborne drop into the heart of the Japanese mainland. To a history buff, the subtext is obvious. But in case it's not, that's a suicide mission.[4]

But history worked out for Big Charles. Not only did he get a reprieve from the final fight, luckily for the young couple, the 11th was tasked to occupy Japan, then he angled to stay in Japan at the occupational finance office in the general headquarters. He wrote Rosalinde twice a week and visited every time he had a chance.

The real crazy stuff happens next.

3. A little public service announcement from me to you, a history lesson from the Artmeister, me doing my part to disseminate culture and knowledge of our past. The Battle of Manila: It was fucking crazy, the nadir of Japanese barbarism. Hell on Earth. The Japanese, as Jesse "The Body" Ventura would say, were buried-in like an Alabama tick as three American divisions—the 1st Cav, 11th Airborne, and the 37th Infantry, enclosed the city. The desperate, last Japanese soldiers were utterly brutal to the Filipino civilians. Rape, mutilation, mass murder, human shields. The long, bitter battle ended with thousands of Japanese blowing themselves and their Filipino captives up in a mass suicide. Some estimates have the Filipino death toll as high as 100,000. The Japanese general in charge of their army in the Philippines, Tomoyuki Yamashita, was hanged for war crimes early in 1946.

4. When weighing how to finish the war, the big brains at the War Department estimated that an invasion of the mainland would have cost two million American boys.

SETTLING IN

We pulled into Oak Park; young trees lined the road. It's not the worst kind of trailer park, the desperate kind that fills popular imagination. The fences stood straight and the yards were manicured and covered in kitsch.

We pulled the Galaxy alongside the road. I didn't know what to do. My enthusiasm remained low. Grandma's maroon '86 Toyota Corolla was in the driveway. Stick shift. These days I can't imagine a woman like that driving a standard. A relic of the past.

"Is she here or is she with her boyfriend?" I asked with the nastiest inflection on boyfriend. Gag.

"Be nice now. To her and him. Don't make a stink," Grandpa said.

"I don't know why you don't whip the guy's ass," I blurted out like a brat.

"Watch your language, young man," he switched to an authoritative tone.

"I don't get it."

"You will when you're older," he said, somewhat to himself.

We both sat for a moment, thinking of what to say next. He took it down a notch and tried to level with me.

"She's not getting any younger. She's done right by me and you and your mom and Kenny. It's time for her to have some time for herself." Grandpa wasn't even bitter about it, probably sent her money to make sure she was happy. My mom kept them worried, so I think they both liked the relief of a few lower-stress years.

I just kept my head turned away into the window.

"I'm just not that fun," he said.

"Sure you are."

Sitting there stewing, I didn't even notice her walk up. I was surprised as hell, recoiling with wide eyes, when she knocked on the window.

"Hi guys!" she said, waving at us and flashing her brilliant smile.

~

Karen Regulski, formerly Karen Harris. Born in 1938, Ft. Smith, Arkansas. At age twenty, she took a trip to Southern California with Brenda and her friends. There, she met a nice man in his late twenties, a smart, clean-cut, healthy veteran with a great job building the machines of a beautiful tomorrow.

In my idealized Syd-Mead-inspired modernist vision of the 50s, they met at some swinging Tiki Bar with a Jazz band playing in the background, and they danced on the sand under the stars. But I think the story is that one of Brenda's friends confronted Grandpa and forced a conversation.

1950s L.A., The Golden Decade. It was too much for an Arkansas girl to pass up. They were married within a year. It was the American dream. They bought a house in the fresh suburbs of Pasadena, watching its value climb. At twenty-two she had my uncle Kenny, two years later, my mom.

Regardless of any of the factors associated with good fortune, families are hard. She felt like treating herself after a thirty-year grind. There were winners and losers with my grandpa's nerdiness. Grandma could be seen as the loser, his kids and grandkids were the winners. My grandma never hated him for it. Loved him for it. But she needed something for her. While it made me uncomfortable as a kid, no one, to my knowledge, gave her any grief about it.

And, here's the deal, if you looked like she did you probably would too. Grandma or not, I call 'em like I see 'em. She was aging like a fine wine. Tall, (somewhere along the way she grew taller than Grandpa) skinny, immaculate teeth, and elegant shoulder-length gray hair that she wore with confidence.

~

"Hello, Norman. Good to see you," she said as Grandpa and I got out of the Galaxy. She hugged him like a best friend.

"Kare-Kare." He smiled affectionately and kissed her on the temple. I told you they were amicable. Not even divorced.

I just stood there. She walked over and hugged me. I hugged her back, but I wasn't effusive with my affection and still hadn't spoken.

"How was your trip, Arthur?"

"Fine."

"He's a little cranky," Grandpa said.

"What's wrong, hun?"

"Nothing," I mumbled.

Then those two exchanged some loaded nonverbal communication.

"I'm sure glad to see you!" she said as she rubbed circles on my back.

"Norman, would you like to stick around for the rest of the day? Maybe meet Rock and say hi to Brenda?" Grandma asked.

"Oh, I'd love to, but I've got a hot date with some alleged Viking runes in Eastern Oklahoma. Give them my best."

When I got to the guest bedroom, I could tell that my grandma was living there. What, I'm sharing? Ugh. This sucks- why are we here? Sounds terrible saying it, but 12-year-old boys don't like to share spaces with their grandmas.

She could tell I wasn't enthused. She came in the room and told me not to worry, that it would be all mine and that she'd sleep on the couch or stay with her boyfriend.

Double gross.

"The house in California is a lot nicer," is all I said as I walked back into the living room, flopped on the couch, and turned on the TV that only had local, antennae-fed channels.

Grandma and Grandpa talked outside for a while before he stepped in to say goodbye. Grandma picked up my legs off the couch, sat down beside me, and started comforting me. I could never be too mad at the lady who raised me. She patted my hair, scratched my back, and told me how good it was to see me. No matter how down or worked up I am, Grandma has always known how to chill me out.

Eventually, she made me open my mouth where she saw all my cavities and told me we needed to make a dentist appointment. Fun.

Then, she got to the tough stuff, explaining that her boyfriend was a serious businessman who needed to travel around a lot, and that she would be gone some days. I didn't really respond. I didn't have it in me to be mouthy about it, but I wasn't encouraging the conversation. It hurt her feelings that I resented her new life, but she was wise enough to know that I wouldn't get it.

She also let me know that I would have to spend time at Brenda's salon when she wasn't around.

SPEAKING OF TIKI MUSIC...

The Retro Cocktail Hour, Hosted by Darrell Brogdon
- Kansas Public Radio

I've lived at this house-turned-studio for various chunks of time over the years. Mikey lets characters like me hang around to give the place atmosphere and foster aesthetic and intellectual cross-pollination. I like to think he took a shine to me when I outdid him on Val Kilmer impersonations. So, I get a place to be creative, and he lets me use the gear if I want to work on music. He's real loose about the rent, but you know in your heart when you're in a funk and taking more than you're giving. So in a rare, unpredictable moment of courageous esteem, I decided to surprise everyone with a feat: mowing the entire two-foot-tall-lawn.

Mike is a workaholic, squeezing productivity out of every minute, always having twenty things he wants to do in a day, but time enough for five. The yard rarely gets to the top of the list, so it can get out of hand.

I did it. Knocked out two-thirds of an acre of tall grass with his old, cool-looking, green and yellow push mower. I gritted through it, inch by torturous inch, going extra slow, tipping it back constantly to avoid locking it up, and only stripping a little with each pass. It took four hours of straight mowing.

By the time I was done, there was barely enough light to put the mower back in the shed.

God, I hadn't used my body in months. Lower back sore, knees creaking, hands and feet covered in blisters. Arms aching so bad from vibration that I could barely make a grip.

I hobbled my fat ass to the bathroom and took a luxurious shower. My dirty old one-gallon plastic bag of hotel soaps and shampoos may be an object of scorn, but I'm never left wanting. Just reach in, grab one, and get surprised by a random fragrance.

In a towel, I was still sweating; it takes a bit for us old slow-metabolism people to quit perspiring after we've had our temperature up for a while. I grabbed an ice-cold Milwaukee out of the refrigerator and proceeded to the den, where the window unit AC had been left on all day.

"The Den," down-two-steps and carpeted, used to be a garage. Now, it's covered in posters and art, a sealed-off place to kill time listening to music or watching TV meant to inspire the rock stars. At the moment, it was the only place of refuge from the heat of the cryptocurrency mining rigs that a neuro trader[5] crashing there set up in the traditional living room. Twenty-four over-clocked graphics processing units turn the place into a sauna, especially in those Oklahoma summer scorchers. Mike loves passive income. "Cashflow is king," he says.

I walked in and flipped on the old Sony radio/tape deck, willing to listen to whatever the previous listener had on. It was the local University of Central Oklahoma classical and jazz station running a tiki music special.[6]

Still in my towel, I did a few stretches before lying down on the floor. Beer in hand, I listened to the swaying, strange sounds of exotic space-age pop, Henry Mancini, Martin Denny, and Les Baxter. I was in endorphin heaven, better than any drug in the world. I lied there on the floor like a baby, naked on my towel, listening to this music cut through the blast of the A.C., imagining myself at a Tiki bar somewhere in time and space that resembled the South Pacific before I drifted off into a deep, exhausted sleep.

5. Mike takes in creatives, thinkers, and tinkerers of all stripes out of the principle of helping others, facilitating innovation for the world, and in hopes of finding unique synergy between various disciplines.

6. I searched for a year and a half trying to figure out what I was listening to. The show is *The Retro Cocktail Hour* hosted by Darrell Brogdon, produced by Kansas Public Radio. For a while I thought one of the best moments of my life had been lost in time like tears in the rain.

BORED ALREADY

There were several days where I was left at Brenda's salon atop Log-Town Hill, overlooking the mildly historic downtown Van Buren and the Arkansas River. I couldn't stand her salon. I hated it. I mean, hated it. I couldn't stand the smell of perms. I couldn't stand the gossip she made with the clients. I couldn't stand the soap operas on her little TV. I couldn't stand the accumulation of old tabloids and housekeeping magazines. I couldn't stand how she held a cigarette in one hand and shears in the other.

So, for a brief reprieve of the misery, I'd cross the street and go to Sherman's Grocery to look at the comic books. Sherman's, now demolished, was a classic All-American grocery store. Family owned. Simple. Humble. Meat on yellow Styrofoam covered in saran wrap. Everything you need, but nothing fancy or distinguishing. Just groceries and a few extras, not a mega one-stop-shop, fifty-acre plaza.

The comics were in the corner alcove by the birthday party supplies and cheap Chinese action pistols and squirt guns. The high fluorescent lights beamed down from the open rafters as I looked through the standard Marvel and DC titles. None of my bread-and-butter hidden gems from local indie presses. Hell, I was getting so bored I was reading through the Archie comics.

On the second day, I saw an Asian kid about my age reading through their only gaming magazine, GamePro. I said, "Hey." He just ignored me and awkwardly kept his face in the magazine while I waited for him to respond. Whatever, man.

Maybe because I looked like a dingus, a goobatron-5000 in my blond flat top I'd spike up with green Jell-O-like L.A. Looks hair gel?

I wouldn't go so far as to say the rejection stuck in my craw.

Two days later, I was in the same predicament, stuck at the salon with nothing to do. So, I went back to Sherman's and there he was again. He looked over and immediately turned back to his gaming magazine. This time I upped my game. "Nintendo huh? I've got one of those back home."

"Do you have a Sega?" he retorted with a hint of venom as he flipped through and pointed to a Sega Genesis ad.

"No. I don't have a Sega, yet."

"When are you going to get it?" he asked.

Shit. "Good question," I said as he lost interest and turned his head.

"I can talk my grandma into buying one whenever, I bet," I said. He considered it and looked at me, unsure of how to proceed. I changed the subject, "You want some ice cream?"

"No. I'm about to leave."

"Okay," I said, "maybe next time." He just went back to his magazine. Frustrated, I mirrored him and glanced through my *Uncanny X-Men* #266[7] before realizing I was supposed to be getting ice cream and walked off, still friendless.

The next morning I was waiting on Brenda, leaning down against the hood of her light-brown 1980 Ford Fiesta. Kicking the tires in boredom, I lifted my head up as a car drove by, guess who I saw! The kid from the store in the passenger seat of a little weird red pickup. Huh! How 'bout that. He lives in this park.

7. I remember this specifically because the issue, now a sought-after comic, is the first appearance of the famously cool Gambit, the suave, dangerous, gambling, New Orleans Cajun.

HANGIN' WITH ROCK

"You Make My Dreams" and "Sarah Smile" - Hall and Oates

Friendless, my summer of pain was to continue its downward trajectory; it was time for my big day out with Grandma and her boyfriend, Rick "Rock" Young. Lunch then the dentist.

I slept all morning on the couch and woke up to catch some Price is Right. Grandma came out of her room with her silver fox vibe maxed out. Even then, I could tell she was dressed to kill. Her silver silk blouse matched her hair perfectly, the room enlivened by her perfume. She was glowing and vibrant in a way that I'd never seen. Ugh . . . What the fuck . . . my grandmother being sexy.

I'll give it to her; she was looking good, better than women half her age. It's amazing she stuck it out with dorky ol' Grandpa as long as she did.

Rock pulled up right on time in a light blue 1989 Cadillac Brougham, the nicest Caddy you could've bought that year.

Stepping out of his car, he looked like Burt Reynolds. Tight jeans over his ostrich skin cowboy boots, a tucked-in maroon button-up with the top button left open for a light coif of hair to poke out, and his cowboy belt buckle was surprisingly tasteful. He had Just a hint of belly poking against the tight shirt. He was healthy and vibrant for a 60-year-old, and his walk let you know that he knew it too. Hair was thinning but it wasn't too bad.

"Good morning, young man!" He put his hand out like a man's man. "Rock Young."

I gripped his hand like a total wimp and looked to the side as I said, "Hey." He knew it was awkward for me, so he tried not to make it worse. Who wants to meet their fling's grandkids?

To Grandma and me both, he said, "You kids get saddled up, we've got some Mexican to eat."

His car had the nicest interior I'd ever been in. He also had a black, zip-up case sitting in the back just for holding his cassette tapes. Caressing the zipper, I wanted desperately to see what he had in his collection. But I didn't want to talk. Through the rear-view mirror he saw me ogling it. "Go ahead, take a look," he said, "And hand me the Hall and Oates tape while you're at it."

I appraised his tape collection, lots of country and Steely Dan, some Motown, some Bee Gees. I found the Hall and Oates *Rock and Soul Vol 1.* and handed it to him. "This one?"

He reached his hand back over his shoulder, I put it in his hand, he looked, "You bet, bud." He slid it in the tape deck. Didn't rewind. We got lucky; "She's Gone."

I wasn't into Hall and Oates at the time, didn't want to be with my grandma and her boyfriend at the time, but the songs were chilling me out.

Which reminds me...

I heard a lecture from prolific songwriter Ralph Murray once, and he said—I'm condensing and paraphrasing—that writing songs and getting people to dig them when you're playing at a bar on Friday night is one thing. They're drinking after a long week, looking to have some fun; you can speak and convey a little personality, show a little charm. They'll clap and congratulate you after the show, maybe buy a CD that they'll barely listen to. Now imagine a lady with a car full of kids on a rainy Monday morning who pops a flat. If your song is on the radio when she gets back into the car and it lightens her mood and she sings along, then you've got a hit.

That's where the gods dwell. That's Hall and Oates level.

TACO RIO

For lunch we went down the road to Taco Rio, an awesome little hometown mom-and-pop order-at-the-counter Mexican restaurant. Even then, it was a little out of date, but in a beautiful way. The décor was 70s faded brown. The food was wrapped in yellow paper and put in brown baskets on orange trays. The ingredients were higher quality than they are today. Ground beef. Grated-that-day cheese. Mostly fresh lettuce.

While their cheese dip and chips weren't world class, they were simple— sufficient in their own cheap way. As you can tell I'm a connoisseur of the cheese arts. Quesoteria maybe?

Rock went behind the counter to talk to the owner. He was a go-getter like that. Something Grandpa wouldn't do in a million years. It was just me and Grandma waiting for the order. I asked her if we could get a Sega Genesis. After explaining to her what it was and why I wanted one, she told me that if someone would only be my friend if I had a video game, then they probably weren't meant to be my friend. Nah.

"Good seeing ya, Terry," Rock said to whomever was in the office. "Good seeing you," he said with a different inflection on the good, which always struck me as a weird mannerism.

Our tray was ready right as he was walking by, so he grabbed it and brought it to the table. "What were y'all arguing about?"

"Nothing," I said.

"He wants me to buy him a video game to impress a local kid he met," she said, embarrassing me, turning my face beet red.

"It's a video game system," I corrected her with a stiff lower jaw.

"She's doing you a favor, kid. That stuff will rot your brain. Summer is for baseball and baling hay." Puke.

I was a little intimidated by Rock; he wasn't the type of guy I was used to, and I didn't have it in me to pout and make a scene in front of a grown man.

Grandma ate like a bird, but Rock and I were scarfing down our food. Rock—dude was in his sixties and still ate like a teenager. Even bragged that he didn't take any medications and hadn't been to the doctor in years.

Lunch was over and it was time to cross the bridge and head into the sprawling metropolis that is Fort Smith, Arkansas.

~

Semi-industrial with an army base nearby, Fort Smith was probably peaking around 1990. In a certain way it feels like a Rust Belt town dropped in the mid-south. Along the Arkansas River on the Oklahoma border, at one time it was the last civilized stop before Indian territory and home to Judge Parker's Courthouse, the place at which wild-west outlaws were hanged. The average American wouldn't be too impressed with Fort Smith, but it has a certain charm. It's a decent place to raise a family. Mostly safe, a little of everything, but with its own peculiar slightly low-brow spin on things.

And the spot we were headed to, one of Rock's businesses, wasn't exactly the trendy spot of town. The far north side, touching the river. All the growth, the new residential and commercial properties, was happening to the south of town. But right across the old bridge, the first one between Van Buren and Fort Smith, stood Rock's Shangri-La.

RAD RANDY'S

Oh man, where to start? Rock owned a place called Rad Randy's. To protect it from flooding, it was on a raised eight foot mound of dirt with stone steps up to the entrance and two sets of double glass doors outlined in off-gold, which felt like some kind of low-budget art deco precursor to mid-century design. It was a big building, must have been a department store built in the 40s or something.

I said something dumb as we walked in, "Your name's not Randy."

Rock, matter-of-factly, goes, "I bought it off Randy." He opened the door. "Run around and look at anything you like."

I wasn't expecting to be impressed, but...

I was stunned. Amazed. Electrified. Emboldened. Enraptured.

An emporium of esoterica! There's a lot to unpack here. I'll do it methodically.

1) In the center was the head shop. All kinds of "tobacco" smoking pipes. All shapes and sizes. From Sherlock Holmes, to corncob, to Moroccan hookahs, to 6-foot-tall purple water bongs. They gave you a package of tobacco with every purchase to legally reinforce their intended purpose.

2) The back wall was fringe literature. The books, front facing, were behind a counter on shelves. There were books on homosexuality, making drugs, the end times, aliens, UFOs, government conspiracy, the Illuminati, left and right wing radical politics, you name it, all the stuff you couldn't find at your local Waldenbooks.

3) To the right were posters, including a black-light alcove blocked off by a black blanket. It had all the traditional hippie posters you'd expect like little gnomes smoking hookahs under a giant mushroom, space galleons floating in a grand cosmos, Jimmy Hendrix, tarot cards, the Grim Reaper, glow-in-the-dark astrology-based sexual position chart, the silhouettes of naked African funk princesses with huge fros, butterflies. Their non-black light posters were mostly cloth and music related, including Ozzy, Iron Maiden, Cinderella, Judas Priest, and a really cool and rare black Metallica *...And Justice for All* banner.

4) The center spaces of the store were filled in with t-shirts on hangers. To include: Confederate flags with some kind of saying on them like "the South's gonna do it again," marijuana themes, smiley face t-shirts, "I'm with stupid." Dragons. Fairies. Motorcycle themed. Old anti-Reagan and pro-Reagan shirts. Combinations of the aforementioned like Confederate flags with big marijuana leaves in the middle.

5) Beside the banned books section was the Star-Trek area. It had life-size stand-ups of Spock and Kirk, and any toys and knick-knacks the store could get its hands on, to include some of the nascent TNG stuff. There were also

some random Hot Wheels thrown in there on the side.

6) To the east of the head shop center was the zodiac and incense area. Tarot, pagan, Wiccan, tapestries, incense holders, calendars, Indian-themed elephants, Buddhas, and fairy/elves/dragon statues. The description may seem disparate, but a certain feminine aesthetic unified the space.

The building had a symmetry such that each side of the building had large separate sections to the east and west that had their own entry ways.

East side: a sex shop. Multiple curtains guarded the entry so that no one could sneak a peek. Huge signs with multiple reiterations that "you must be 18 to enter." You had to ring a bell so that the clerk would come out and check your ID. They were really making sure the "i"s were dotted and "t"s were crossed with the law.

West side: the Cryptic Cavern. It was closed this day. The guy in charge of that section no-showed. This will come back into play.

~

I lost track of time looking around, making several passes, getting stuck on a new detail on each trip before Rock and Grandma came out telling me it was time to go.

While we're at it, I should mention that the store had an awesome radio jingle: "Radical! Radical! Radiiicaaaal RAA Uu UH RAAAA AAANNNDeeees!" Think 80's masculine cartoon, or the jingle to their local access TV show in the movie Wayne's World.

Who would I have been had I not walked into this remarkable place at such an impressionable age? Maybe I'd be in a cubicle filing the day's last paperwork, rushing home to meet my lovely, stolid wife. Maybe I wouldn't be caught in a neurotic, vaporous web of aesthetic impulses?

Next, the dentist. Who wants to hear about that? But, they did have a neat paper mache/plaster of Paris oak tree at the edge of the waiting room that was set-up to look like an entrance to an enchanted forest. That's the interesting part, once on the other side, it's just a Disney movie playing and a floor full of those doctor office toys that are a collection of bent wires you move beads across.

Walking out with a numb frown and a mouth full of fillings, I had enough political cache, feel-sorry-for-me-points to stop at the comic store across the block. The owner, who looked like Harold Ramis, smiled and made a quip about how most of his business comes from post-dental-work-pick-me-ups. That place smelled very particular. Half traditional comic store scent of old comic books plus a unique mister. I could pick it out of ten thousand aromas. Funny how our olfactory memory is like that.

LE CASA DE ROCK

We were going to spend the night at Rock's place, which they thought I'd appreciate. He had multiple spare rooms and much more entertainment. A decent-sized lot southeast of Fort Smith. Tall, thin pines looming over a few acres. His house wasn't crazy unique, but it wasn't a cookie-cutter McMansion either. One cool feature that sticks out was his second story master bedroom that had its own private deck looking over the property. Perfect spot to step out for a smoke and observe your spread.

He had a nice in-ground pool with a diving board. They assumed I'd want to go swimming as soon as we got there. You can tell by looking at me that I probably wasn't a diving board kinda kid, and my mouth still hurt, but I was still gonna get in the water. Rock opened up a Tupperware container full of trunks of various sizes for guys who showed up unprepared.

"Just go in your underwear if you don't like any of them," he said, dropping the box before walking back inside, not interested in my response. I guess I was around too many ultra-nice, overly accommodating people because he struck me as being a little too curt, but I dig his style now. You either want the trunks or you don't; no use going back and forth about it.

As I lurched around the pool, taking in the scenery, I could hear my grandma laughing. They had cracked open a bottle of red wine and put on some Earth, Wind & Fire.

Arms spread out wide down the edge of the pool, looking out into the sparse spread of pines, I thought about the kid I had met in the grocery store. He had something interesting about him. Despite his stubborn reticence, there was some magnetism. I wanted to make him a close friend.

Eventually the sun went down, and I went in to try out Rock's TV. He had mentioned he had satellite, and I wasn't sure what he meant. Cable was all I'd ever known. But once I saw the military grade radar dish in his yard . . . oh yeah . . .

When I walked in they stopped their dancing, and Rock taught me how to use the TV, showing me how to change which satellite the dish points at. This was pretty neat. I damn near wore out the gear box on it that night.

They continued their high school sweetheart shenanigans. You could hear them giggling and cutting up in the kitchen all night. I had to turn up the TV to drown out their music and laughter. Rock was even singing; he could hit some surprisingly high notes. Sarah Smi-i-i-i-llesss

Man, what a charmer. I wish I were doing that now. He had the time, money, energy, and taste to wine and dine thirsty divorcées, getting their confidence back with fun and adventure. A public service.

Viagra came out in '87 . . . ugh .

I fell asleep watching Lost Boys on HBO. They woke me up and dropped me off at the salon in the morning.

In the car she informed me that she and Rock were going to Shreveport for two days, coming back, then going to Branson, looking at estate and liquidation sales for the businesses. It's really fun, she told me. I thought that sounded lame as hell, but now I would think a four-day regional estate sale run would be an absolute blast.

SUMMER AFTERNOON ON THE TOWN

Rock and Grandma took me to the salon around 9:45. Brenda's first appointment, her 10 a.m., an older lady, was already there. Brenda wasn't. Grandma entertained her with small talk until Brenda showed up at 10:15. They said goodbye as Brenda rushed around and got the day going.

I looked through the magazines again, Home and Garden, People, and a well-worn Enquirer about Dolly Parton's love problems. Brenda said I could watch TV, but to keep it down low. The Price is Right was interesting on the little old TV with rabbit ears poking out, but when *As the World Turns* began I told her I was crossing the street to Sherman's again. She waved me off with a nod as she was clipping and talking.

I was there flipping through comic books. Then he walked by, not acknowledging me, and went to the gaming magazines. All from instinct and the pain of boredom I walked up to him, mouth opening to talk before I had anything to say. Drawing a blank. What could sell this recluse? I was wired for having a friend, always have been. Gotta have someone to listen to me talk.

"C'mon dude, let's hang out. I saw you drive by. You live in that trailer park like me. I don't have anything cool. I'm stuck at my great-aunt's salon. You know where they get perms?"

"What's a perm?" he asked.

"Dude I'm desperate. I got nothing. I'm from California." Like that was supposed to mean something. Sorry, I was young. "I am not used to this Arkansas thing. I've got nobody or nothing. I just need someone to hang out with."

He just stared.

"I tell you what. Walk across the street and you'll see you gotta rescue me." I cranked up the melodrama.

I started walking toward the exit. I didn't look back until I got to the door. I was worried he didn't follow, but he was right behind me. We crossed the high-traffic two lane road to the five-shop strip mall where Brenda had her salon.

We poked our heads in. There's a lady waiting, a lady with her hair under the big bowl, and a lady getting her hair cut. Brenda stayed busy once she got moving.

Brenda was talking up a storm when I barged in. As I walked toward her, she just looked at me funny and finished her thought about whomever they were gossiping on.

"This is my niece's son, Karen's grandson." Brenda says to the girls. "He's staying with me."

All I said was, "This is . . ." I drew a blank. "He lives beside you. I'm going to hang out with him all day. I'll get home however he's getting home. His parents are coming to get him."

"Oh all right I guess," she said. Perfect. To my new friend: "What's your name, kid?"

Just barely in the door, he coughed and hesitated for a second, "Loo Dang."

"Let's go," I said, excited my big gambit was working. He's stuck with me now. I closed the door to the salon behind us. "Where to now, boss?"

"Let's go to the IGA." He took off walking. I was right behind him.

At a brisk pace, I followed him across town about a mile, weaving and crisscrossing through the hills and dead-ends in the organic, unplanned splattering of houses that is Van Buren's oldest residential zone until we reached the other major thoroughfare, the more important part of town, the side with a Wal-Mart, McDonald's, Taco Bell, Movie Town, a Chevrolet dealership, and a host of barbershops, banks, and florists.

I can't remember what all I said as we walked, mostly young gibberish small talk; Loo was pushing the tempo.

CV'S- GROCERY STORE #2

There were off-brand soda machines outside, so I said hold up. I was thirsty. That was a long walk by my standards. I pulled out some change and bought us both cans of ice cold Sunkist. Clothes soaked in sweat from the river valley humidity, it may have been the best soda I've ever had.

He went straight to the magazines and comics. I bought us both some Snickers bars. I got there and he already had a Gamepro Magazine open to show me an article about *Phantasy Star II*, the greatest game ever—there was no doubt in his mind—only available on Sega Genesis. It definitely looked cool in the article. I assured him it would be the first game we got once I got us a Sega.

Whoever bought the comics for this IGA place had a little spunk about him or her. They had several obscure, deep-cut, titles that jump out at me to this day like *Zot!* from Eclipse Comics and *Terminator: the Burning Earth* from Now Comics.

Trust me, I'd like to put together a dream list of obscure cyberpunk, martial arts, and yacht rock comics from that summer, maybe even a group of comics that foreshadowed or portended what was to come. But that motif wouldn't run far before you realized I'm completely bullshitting a dreamworld that never happened.

FOOD 4 LESS

He led me across the street through a large parking lot to yet another grocery store. I think this would put us at three of four for the day.

We went in through the automatic sliding doors, past the cart section, and took a hard right down the inescapable, 20 yard tube of sales that everyone was funneled through before being allowed to freely roam the store . But, after the first corner the magazines and comics were right there. This time, he went straight for Electronic Gamer Monthly, scanning through it to show me another article about *Phantasy Star II* before he proceeded to show me every Sega advert in the magazine.

Man, this kid is serious about his Sega. I'd heard of it and I was mildly curious; I wouldn't mind someone buying one for me, but my interest level wasn't in the same stratosphere as his. He was obsessed. But interest levels are like gravity, if someone you like cares enough about something they'll pull you down with them.

Of course I glanced at Food For Less's comic selection. Their selection was Marvel heavy, including Excalibur and Wolverine.

I took a tour of the store. I've always appreciated the stimuli that comes from large stores, grocery or department. The choices. The possibility. The new lives you could create. If you had a person pick their favorite item from each section, the one they covet the most, would the carts tend to look the same, or would they be as individual as a fingerprint?

Halfway through the store, at the long waist-high section with things that need to be kept cool, not frozen, I had a good idea, so I finished up my exploration and headed back to the magazines. Thirty feet away, catching the attention of everyone in the store with my obnoxiousness, I yelled "Where are the arcade games?"

"Wal-Mart" he said.

"Let's go," I said.

"I don't have any money."

"I do." I had the 20 dollars that was supposed to last me an entire week. I was to budget accordingly, teach me some financial management.[8]

WAL-MART

About five stores down in this lake of pavement was Wal-Mart, the original kind, not the Supercenters that have groceries too.

In that front space that runs the length of the store, about 10-15' wide, I'm not sure what you call that area, but it has the games and vending machines. We walked in and started scoping them out, *Cyber Police E-Swat, Chase HQ* (a racing game), a claw machine, and a huge stack of the square gumball machines that had evolved to taking multiple quarters and offering all kinds of junk in addition to gum and hard candy, a pyramid of options, gummy hands, slap bracelets, jewelry, stickers, fortunes, plastic eyelashes, vampire teeth, you name it; if we weren't at the pinnacle of gumball machines, we were close to it. It was an arms race trying to squeeze more and more money out of this ubiquitous yet niche market. A beautiful synthesis of commerce and creativity. I'd love to know what type of businessmen are sitting around talking about which junk toys to go with. Reminds me of the pog craze that was a few years away.

Anyway, I thought more soda and candy for us was appropriate, a necessity really. I went through the express lane, bought us several packs of Starburst and two Mountain Dews and turned the rest into change, close to 14 dollars' worth.

I pumped some money into *E-Swat* and we were off. I knew immediately he was better than me. Talent recognizes talent. The better you are at something, the more quickly you identify when someone is better than you, and I had been raised on video games.

8. Money was given to me in small amounts the rest of the time with Grandma.

We got a couple levels in before we died, and I lost interest for a moment and pumped some money into the gumball machines for a slap bracelet and some hard, sour candy to compliment the chewy Starbursts we had strewn out across the arcade machine.

I jumped back in for a few rounds but chose to just watch. I wasn't helping anyway.

The store was busier than the small town would suggest. I guess people from all over the county were making their once-a-week grocery run.

Maybe it was my imagination, but I thought everyone was checking us out. The two of us looked like a pair. A rare Asian and the California Kid, I was in my acid jeans and "hot lava" pink shirt, my Andre Agassi-esque uniform of the summer, don't think that fad had made it to Arkansas. To some ten-year-old from the country forced to hold on to his mom's cart, we were some far-out cool dudes. Especially once they say how adept and commanding Loo was with the controls, switching at light speed from delicate to aggressive.

I'd watched *The Wizard* ten times since it came out six months prior, so my imagination was running wild with the idea of being his coach and manager, taking him across the country playing our way back to California before unleashing him on the Starcade in Pasadena. Later, I would tell him about my big fantasy, and he just looked at me like I was crazy. He didn't share my love for indulgent, grandiose daydreaming.

~

I never thought I was great at video games, still don't really, but I challenged some modern video game gurus who have spent years of their life on computer games, and I absolutely smoked their asses in classic *Street Fighter II*.

~

A few kids gathered around to watch him beat *E-Swat*. I doubt they had ever witnessed anyone get past the first stage. That brought a smile to my face. It wasn't a true one-shot domination; I had pumped a few quarters in for him, but impressive nonetheless.

We moved over to the racing game, *Chase HQ*, but we were worn out. It was time to call it quits.

He and his dad didn't organize how to get home, so we had to pound some ground. If there wasn't an interstate in the way, it would be a simple mile-long walk, but we were forced to cut an oblique angle through a stretch of woods and around a concrete production yard to get to the train tracks that led under the interstate. Following them for a little while, we were able to get on some back roads that lead to the trailer park. It was a pretty fun adventure. Not an epic one, but adventure enough for me. I was having a good day. It reminded me of something out of Stand By Me, harkening back to the old days when kids ran around the outskirts of town, powered by imagination, fighting Nazis or exploring the Amazon.

I was getting a decent little education about the heart of America.

~

We made it back to the trailer park, and as we approached Brenda's I asked if we could go to his house. He hesitated, but he said okay. His home, with brown skirt and trim, was about four trailers down, the last on the row, bordering a wood line.

Before we walked in he told me the place was a lot messier than usual since his mom was in San Jose for the summer visiting family.

HIS HOUSE

The first thing I saw when I walked in was a small, circular kitchen table across from the front door that was covered in football magazines like Street & Smith and various handicapper's guides.

"Whoa. I didn't know Asian people liked football," I said, picking up a magazine for a glance.

"I hate football," he said.

"Why?"

"All the yelling and screaming. Throwing stuff at the TV. It's so annoying."

The kitchen was to the right. And true to form, as I'll find out, a fish head soup was on the stove.

To the left against the wall was a yellow couch looking at an impressive Magnavox big screen TV, presumably for all the football watching. Past the living room was a hallway with three bedrooms and a bathroom. The layout was much more family oriented than Brenda's master bedroom dominated floorplan.

Loo's room was in the back-left corner. Wooden bunk bed and a little 13" RCA TV in the corner off his dresser. Cords impeding the path across the room. He would slip under them while coming and going. Opposite the bed, was a window with 1/144 scale Gundam models on the sill that he painted himself. Below the window, a toy box full of younger kids' stuff. His little brother was with his mom in San Jose. At the far edge of the bed was an end table covered with gaming magazines; the well-worn Gamepro special on *Phantasy Star II*, of course, was on top. And like most rooms in the 80s, it had a semi-functional Atari in the corner.

I thought the Gundams were really cool, some kind of mech warriors, but don't recall the brands. I didn't really ever watch anime. The ol' noggin doesn't store some stuff as well as others. Obviously, I could rattle off any CDs or records he may have had kicking around.

Which reminds me that there was nothing musical in the Dang house. No CDs, records, tapes, musical instruments, nothing. And I wouldn't mention that out-of-the-blue like some of my musical fart-sniffing compatriots might. I'm just making a point out of it based on what's to come. What does it mean? No idea. But someone smarter than me might be able to figure out its implications, but it definitely didn't hinder Loo.

You know how it turned out for Loo, right?

You don't, huh? Didn't expect that, this changes things. Oh boy . . . I'll hold on to that nugget 'til the end.

~

We played *Journey to Silius*[9] on his Nintendo for an hour before I walked back to Brenda's and crashed after the exciting day.

Without an invite, I was back at Loo's in the morning.

9. Great soundtrack

SEGA

Console Wars - Blake Harris

I'm almost tempted to make you suffer through an hour of me talking about Nintendo and its long, storied, culturally impactful, one-hundred-year-plus history, beginning with their origins as a 19th century playing card manufacturer. But we're just getting started, don't want you turning into a pumpkin before midnight.

And yeah, I could give you an equally long but more specific spiel about the groundbreaking impact they had on kids across the globe in the 80s, the nostalgia of that beautiful red-striped gray box. But you probably already have deep-seated feelings about it, your own world of sentiment, staying up all night with your siblings when you got it for Christmas, or sitting around killing time with your buddies, taking turns to see who could get further.

If you don't have any affection toward Nintendo by now, it wasn't meant to be. I'm sitting here trying to think of an analog for other generations like Red Ryder BB guns, or cell phones, but I'm almost going to say no device dominated both the toy and entertainment landscape as thoroughly as the NES did. Nintendo was relentless, meticulous, and unwavering. Hell, at one time it accounted for 10% of all of Wal-Mart's profits, who wouldn't even carry another console in their stores for fear of upsetting their best supplier. And, in 1990 Nintendo controlled 90% of the twenty-billion-dollar gaming industry, and they had no plans of taking their foot off the throttle.

But, for every action there is an equal and opposite reaction. High quality as it was, the mass-appeal Disney-esque aspect of Nintendo—un-controversial, agreeable, safe for the entire family—left many wanting more. By the sheer nature of the bell curve of distribution, there will be some on the fringe. The right side of that curve was dominated by people like Loo who wanted something edgier, riskier, more daring.

Sega, founded in the 60s under the name Service Games of Japan, was a relatively obscure company who had traditionally focused on arcade games. And they were going to try their hand at in-home console gaming. But how could they ever hope to compete? They wanted to—nay, had to— swing for the fences. And there was only one way to do it, one of the most powerful, yet elusive forces in the human condition: Narrative, the only stone capable of bringing down Nintendo in Sega's David vs. Goliath suicide mission. So, they searched far and wide looking for the perfect CEO capable of designing a new reality, ending up in America making an impassioned plea to Tom Kalinske, a former Hasbro exec who made a name for himself crafting stories for Barbie, Hot Wheels, and Masters of the Universe.

And their one shot was convincing all the teenagers that Sega was a little more mature. A little more exotic. A little bolder, a little edgier, a little rougher around the edges. For the daring, for the risky, for people looking to leave the soft space of Nintendo.

Kalinski was in tune. My generation heading into our teens in the 1990s ushered in that sensibility. Grunge was coming; don't-give-a-fuck plaids and torn jeans were about to push the clean optimism of the 80s aside. He saw it coming. Media and the aesthetic zeitgeist didn't move as fast as they do now. Going viral wasn't a thing yet.

Loo and I were right there at the beginning of the swell, before the tidal wave of landmark games like *Sonic the Hedgehog* and *Mortal Kombat*, that brief but glorious moment in the sun when they surpassed Nintendo in market share.

THE DOG DAYS OF NINTENDO

The boring days are like anti-matter of the narrative. They are not seen but they make up 80% of the universe, pressurizing and molding the other 20%. Without the presence of tremendous boredom, we don't feel the squeeze to adventure, to grow.

Eventually it became a matter of fact that Loo and I would hang out. His house was my default. No blood brothers. No secret clubs. No affection. Just two kids killing time in the same room. A subtle bond that I forced on him.

For the three Arkansas weeks, any specific day that doesn't make its way in the story was spent in this way:

Sitting around at his house while he played video games, I'd look through comics, magazines (both his gaming magazines and his dad's betting magazines), catalogs, whatever I could get my hands on for some visual stimulation. Here and there I would play *Life Force* or *Ninja Turtles.*

Nintendo did most things better than everyone else, but a lot of times the games didn't work. If you were there for real, you remember the struggle. Every household/gaming clique had its own proprietary method of getting them to work, other than blowing on the cartridge, which is a given. Loo was a carpet rubber. I showed him my q-tip trick, essentially just cleaning it out. Together we pushed the bounds of game maintenance research and started coating the connection points, on the cartridge and in the console, with light dabs of rubbing alcohol.

When we couldn't handle the TV any longer, we'd flip through JCPenney and Service Merchandise catalogs, picking out which girl, toy, or consumer electronic we liked the most on each page.

During this time, I would get occasional reminders that I had guaranteed him I could procure a Sega Genesis. So, I avoided mentioning our boredom since complaining had an inherent subtext to the effect of, "If we had a Sega, we wouldn't have this problem."

We ate mostly ice cream sandwiches. His dad was addicted, gormandizing a box a day, but dude never added an ounce of fat. 140lbs, tops. Must be nice.

If we weren't eating ice cream sandwiches, it was instant noodles. They bought specific ones in an orange package from the Vietnamese market in Fort Smith. They dismissed any noodles packaged in English. The usually-empty refrigerator had several different fish/oyster sauces to mix the flavorings. Sadly, I never utilized them; now, I really covet a good fish sauce. There's much variance between them, so I've always wondered what those would have tasted like.

The Best Choice Supreme Blend coffee Loo's dad would make every morning would sit on the carafe until Loo turned it off midway through the day, adding to the complex aroma of the house, which was dominated by fish head soup and cigarettes. Forgive me for my childish sins, but fish head soup grossed me out. The smell and the look.

I don't have too much to say about Loo's dad. He was always nice. He cared. Not a yeller. Skinny guy. I don't want to over extrapolate, but he didn't seem too ambitious. Responsible as he had to be, but he liked a good time. Reliable, dependable, worked his 40-50 hours a week on the assembly line at Whirlpool making dishwashers, and came home ready to play cards and watch some football. American as apple pie.

I checked in with Brenda about once a day. She'd always apologize for not having much in the way of food. I don't think she ate much. Vodka and diet pills provided all her caloric needs. On evenings when she was stuck at home, she'd sit out on her porch under the bug zapper smoking cigarettes and reading gossip rags. On the green steel-mesh table her .38 revolver was always within reach, just behind her coffee can ashtray.

THE BAMBOO

*"It Feels So Right" – Bogdonovich *Busted* Casey*

The bamboo over there grew from just a wee stalk bought at the good ol' Alligator Avenue.[10] Norm, one of the guys who went to buy it, surprised everyone when he used a Macho Man Randy Savage impersonation to ask the shop keep, "You got any . . . bamboo?" That phrase has since become a studio forever-meme.

Similar to the relationship between the Celts of Gaul and large oak trees, the studio has bamboo from which the artists gather strength and serenity.

The bamboo was planted and blessed with blood on their "Vietnam weekend," their yearly, full-day Saturday imbibing in everything Vietnam, trying to coax from the universe the perfect Vietnam music. They'll get a projector and play Apocalypse Now while they jam with their shirts off and faces painted camouflage. Eat steak and drink Budweiser (a Forest Gump play) or go with noodles and Heineken. Listen to The Doors, CCR, and "Paint It Black." Sing the *Mickey Mouse Clubhouse* song. From my understanding, they push it. Trying to take it sixty clicks past the Do Lung bridge if you know what I mean. I applaud their effort and vision. The world needs a psychedelic, post-rock/spoken word Vietnam War concept album.

~

When the Doritos are down to the last of the bag, when the party is over, when it's time to cue "A Whiter Shade of Pale," I'll pour the chips out around the bamboo for crows to eat. They love cool ranch Doritos. They'll pick the entire area clean in the morning. If you're stealthy, you can look at them from inside a window. Don't try to go outside; they'll fly off.

10. Totally awesome reptile store in Oklahoma City. It's a little building surrounded by 40ft tall bamboo, and you walk through a twisting and turning jungle path to get to the building.

SCAR

Scar's music- no music is that badass.

I had just died on my turn of *Ikari Warriors*, so I handed off the controller and got up to go to the bathroom. I thought we were the only people there, but as I put my hand on the handle, the door opened to the inside without my help, my momentum sending me into the scariest, toughest looking man I had ever seen.

Half of his face was disfigured. A crude two/thirds of a circle had been blown off his right side (missing his lips) and quickly sewn back up. Both of his eyes seemed to work, but the skin over his right eye wasn't correct. The lid did funny things.

He stared down at me for what seemed like an eternity. Then he just grunted and walked off.

He was large and muscular. Roughly six-foot-tall, broad shoulders. He wore cut-off, faded maroon corduroy shorts that went past the knee, flip flops, and a soft mustard-colored shirt with the texture of a bathing towel. As he walked his calves fanned out like king cobras ready to strike.

Being from L.A., I thought I'd seen all the kinds of people, but Scar was different. The face cuts. The look in his eye. This was a motherfucker, a man who had seen and done shit. I mean a fuckin' goddamned son of a bitch. The kind of person we pretended to be while playing video games.

I stumbled back into Loo's bedroom.

"Who the heck was that guy?" I asked, not noticing he was deep into a game.

"Who?" he asked.

"The guy with the face."

"Oh, that's Uncle Sao, my dad's friend from Vietnam.[11] He's not

11. Sao is Vietnamese for Scar. I'm going to go ahead and just call him "Scar" from here on out. I like the ring of it.

my real uncle. He and my dad grew up together. He saved my dad and got him to America."

"Really? That's neat." Over my head—I didn't know anything about immigration or the South Vietnamese experience.

"They were best friends as kids. Scar left to fight the Viet Cong. My dad stayed in their hometown near Saigon to run his parents' garage." In the most deadpan delivery: "Yeah, my dad was sick and was just going to stay when the Americans left and the Viet Cong were coming. Scar threw dad on a motorcycle and drove to the coast, got them a boat, then past pirates to the refugee camp."

"Whoa, pirates!"

"My family wouldn't be here if it weren't for Sao. Dad helps him out. He's not legal. He jumped the fence."

"Jumped the fence?"

"At Fort Chaffee, here in Arkansas, where my dad and Scar came."

"Ah."

"My mom and dad met here at the camp. They didn't know each other before." He played *Ikari Warriors* effortlessly and flawlessly, maneuvering his shirtless, head-bandanaed mercenary through the jungle on a rescue mission. "Sao won't get a real job. Just watches football and trains ga choi. Smokes and drinks. Mom hates him."

"Ga choi?" I asked.

"Fighting chickens".

"Fighting chickens? This dude is crazy. What happened to his face?"

"A trip-wire explosion someone else in his squad set-off. They sewed up his face in the jungle without a doctor."

"Hardcore."

"Yeah. He's killed people. And was some kind of gangster."

"Whoa! For real?" I had never met anyone who had killed anyone.

"I'm pretty sure he's the reason my mom stays in California so much. She can't stand him."

I didn't know what to say about that.

"My dad helped the Americans so he would have gone to a reeducation camp and never would have met my mother." He said without any inflection or excitement.

If you can't tell, no one would have used the words baroque, flamboyant, or loquacious to describe Loo's speaking style. But his sentences had a no-nonsense left-brain perfection to them. Curious, considering how artistic he turned out to be.

~

I couldn't get Scar out of my mind as we sat there and played video games.

SKATING RINK

"END OF LIFE ENTERTAINMENT SCENARIO #1"

- Oneohtrix Point Never

It was another cloudy day. Rock asked if me and "the little Chinaman"[12] wanted to go to a business partner's granddaughter's birthday party. I guess. 11 am? Who parties at 11 am? He reluctantly gave us five dollars. Thankfully we got to spend it all on video games since the party hosts provided the food, drink, and skate rentals. Otherwise, Loo and I would have economized and cut out the skating.

I didn't know anyone there. If Loo did, he didn't mention it. Outsiders, we were mostly ignored by the hosts. But the mom had some southern hospitality and made sure we had plenty of cake and pizza, my first taste of the aforementioned Pizza Parlour.

To Loo, I whispered commentary on the birthday girl's presents. "Psshh Canadian Barbie? Lounge Singer Barbie is better and newer." Sue me; I looked at every page of every catalog.

Toward the end, I wound up getting into a fight, a limited skirmish rather, when an older kid, 14 or so, the local skateboard bully, cut in front of me for my turn at the Main Event four player wrestling arcade game. There was a long line and kids were getting nasty, temperatures were rising, and he shoved his way in front of me so I pushed him and he pushed me back harder, knocking me into the other kids. Not really a big deal, just embarrassing enough for me to walk out in a huff as everyone gawked. Loo and I walked around outside for an hour. Loo didn't mention it, but he stood around with me in solidarity. It was an off-and-on-again rainy day. Cloudy and overcast, occasional drizzles.

Eventually the blue Caddy swung around and we got in.

12. It wasn't completely a better world back then. But he said it with a smile on his face as lighthearted as if he would have said "your silly goose friend." Obviously that kind of thing isn't acceptable, but Rock considered himself a friendly guy with a cheeky streak. Please don't hate him for this.

"What are you doing out here by yourself?" Rock asked as his window rolled down.

"I got into a fight," I said, relishing feeling tough and edgy in front of them.

"Oh yeah, John Wayne?"

"He cut in front of me and pushed me, so I pushed him back," I said.

"Not with the granddaughter, right?" Rock asked, hoping it wasn't bad politically.

"A snaggle toothed skater." I said.

"Oh, well fuck that guy," he said. Loo and I laughed. We got in. He turned up the Steely Dan as the rain started coming on stronger.

"We're stopping by Randy's."

"Awesome," I said and turn to Loo, "You're going to love this place."

We get there and start walking around. He was mildly impressed at best.

What's this? The section to the west that was closed last time, The Cryptic Cavern, was now open. I ran over there to check it out.

My life would never be the same . . .

THE CRYPTIC CAVERN

"Lord of the Rings" - Blind Guardian

My trot to the door ended abruptly, hitting a wall of awesome. Entering the Cryptic Cavern for the first time was mesmerizing; it may have had the highest concentration of cool the universe has ever known.

To my right was a thirty-foot-long, waist-high glass case full of hand-held weaponry: cheap knives with every imaginable wild embellishment, spiked brass knuckles, shurikens, throwing stars, nun-chucks, sais, ball and chains, maces, you name it. Asian, medieval, modern, and every possible combination thereof, including a Christian cross with switchblades at all four ends. The last third of the glass counter was full of pewter dragons and skulls with green plastic gems for eyes. Behind the counter on the back wall were Century brand karate gis, Kung Fu outfits, made-in-Pakistan samurai swords (mostly three sword sets), wooden swords, and a three-foot-tall wizard sculpture for $200.

The whole room was, I'm guessing, forty by forty feet, eh, let's say half a basketball court, absolutely full of interesting stuff, hardly any real estate was wasted.

As I turned the corner from the case to the outside wall, I passed the tinted glass door that leads to the gravel parking lot. Outside, a bellied man with a slicked-back skullet smoked a cigarette, leaning an elbow on the bed of an old brown Datsun with an orange and tan strip down the side. I looked at him for a moment as he stared toward the cloudy sky, taking long drags off his cigarette.

Half of the big open area was several rows of head-high, wooden bookshelves, the kind meant for displaying the front of books. Over the course of my time in Arkansas, I spent hours going through these role-playing books so I can recall the titles:

Mechanoid Invasion, Valley of the Pharaohs, and *Robotech,* the *Palladium* shelf. *RuneQuest, Star Frontiers, Rolemaster,* and *Cyberpunk* were some other notables. There were two shelves of official Dungeons and Dragons, one for 2nd edition with all the classic wizards and dragons covers you know and love, the other was the newish-at-the-time *Greyhawk Adventures* and *Forgotten Realms* campaign modules and literature with the cool Larry Elmore artwork. Admittedly, telling you this stuff, I'm either speaking Russian or you get a little sentimental surge of "Oh! I remember those," a little bond between us. Nostalgic allusions are either homeruns or strikeouts. Excuse me. Rather, I should say either a 1 or a 20.

The back half of the floor was dedicated to miniature warfare. *Warhammer 40k* and *Battletech* each had their own elaborate, well-painted landscape table, 4'x8' or so, the opposing factions carefully staged on each side, awaiting next Saturday's big game. There were also Civil War, WWII, and classic, high fantasy tables. Rule books the size of the *Yellow Pages,* those games are not for amateurs.

Loo found his way to the *BattleTech* table the moment he walked in.

Along the walls were supplies and un-painted figures for all these miniature games. The top of this area was lined with cool comic book and fantasy posters in varying levels of uniqueness. There was one, though, man, it was awesome. Two elven archers atop a crenelated watchtower, ready to fight to the death as an epic army of ogres marched toward them. It had that 60s-70s Daw Science fiction oil paint cover art feel. The best art in the history of the planet. The stuff we should send to aliens to let them know we deserve respect in the galactic art scene.

As I stared up at the posters, taking them all in, I heard the door chimes jangle.

Daryl Rudisill.

Maybe the craziest, raddest fucker of them all was walking up to me. Tallish, 6'1" or so, with a potbelly attached to an otherwise decent body for a man who looked to be in his fifties. He was wearing karate practice pants that were essentially sweatpants without elastic at the ankle. The waistband was six inches tall with a big emblem that read "Macho." That's the brand name of the pants, not a deliberate self-description. His shoes were the black generic ones with two Velcro straps.

"Konichiwa, Aiya, Nuqneh, Good evening gentlemen!"

"Huh?" was all I could muster. My brain was overloaded.

"Japanese, Elven, Klingon, and the King's English."

A dumbfounded beat.

Then, elocuted like he was teaching a Shakespeare class, "Peruse the grandeur, explore the cosmos, search for the great hidden truths of imagination, or..." he looked us both in the eye, making sure he had our attention, "live in a world of self-challenge, the only opponent: stagnation."

I was instantly compelled to start seriously looking at the books and supplemental adventures. I went to the nearest book, Palladium Rifts.

"Ah, excellent choice, young Musashi. I'm running a campaign in it now." Then he looked at us ominously, eyes wide in a way that's an obvious affectation, creating a scene. "You two remind me of characters in my *Rifts* campaign. Otsu and Ketsu, homeless boys, one from the ancient desert planet Imtikar, the other from 23rd century Tokyo, both selected by the time traveling Kung Fu master, Toshiko Tomi, to be one of The Seven, his team of master martial artists using rifts to travel space and time, searching for understanding and arbitrating justice."

"Sweet fantasy," I said.

"It's not fantasy," he says with a conspiratorial gleam in his eyes before turning back to the counter, "at least not all of it."

As he sat down, I went up to the counter and started looking at all the martial arts stuff again, hoping he'd tell me more.

"Do you do karate or just sell the stuff?" I asked. He made an amused, condescending snort as he pulled a Pepsi and gas station pack of peanuts from a brown paper bag.

He smirked with all the confidence in the world. "There is a secret strain of Ninjitsu, passed down secretly from generation to generation. The chosen ones."

Breathless counter punch: "How do you become a chosen one?"

He gives me a coy shoulder shrug and a wink. "Here, they call me Daryl. Some places I'm known as Master Yamaguchi."

I stared at him in amazement before he continued.

"I may or may not have learned from the late Master Miyamoto. He only trained five people. And he taught each one a different part of the art. Every year we meet up for a day somewhere in the world and teach each other parts of what Master Miyamoto taught us. I will do the same. Teach five and send them into the wind to learn, discover, put the art into practice, marry the lessons of the Earth with the lessons of Ninjitsu, earning true wisdom that he can pass on to his brothers in arms."

"Whoa. Are all your five slots filled?"

"I have two vacancies." He winks again, starting to put the peanuts in the Pepsi. Gross.

"Dang, only if I weren't from California." I pointed to Loo. "He lives here." Loo was too shy to talk, but his eyes and posture said it all: this guy's a lunatic.

"It's a life of humble dedication to the craft. Working common jobs in plain sight, while training religiously in the shadows. Constantly growing, sharpening the blades of the mind, body, and soul to the finest edges."

"Then what? Fight bad guys?" I ask.

"Enforcement is sometimes necessary. Championing honor, defending the helpless, restoring balance. But remember, while we prepare for war, we, Shinobi, always pray for peace."

I nod.

"*Shinobi* is a Sega game," Loo adds.

"There are no award ceremonies and parades. It is for those with the purest of hearts and intentions. Those who take pride in the craft and understand that personal growth is its own reward."

He was losing me with the philosophy. "What kind of neat tricks do you learn?"

"Put me in any kitchen in the world, and I'll be able to construct all the toys a Shinobi needs."

"Like what?" I was enthralled.

"Well, first and foremost, the most important tool: a sound amplifier so you can hear several rooms over when you're sneaking around."

Ah of course.

"Then you'll need silk floss for loud hinges and pesky locks."

To this day, I still haven't figured out how a piece of floss keeps a door hinge from squeaking.

"Food for dogs," he continued, "improvised caltrops[13] for your escape, and tangerine juice for writing secret messages."

"Secret messages!" Oh man, I was excited.

"I've already said too much. The rest are sworn secrets. Only given to the most exemplary students, not even our own children are taught the best stuff like making explosives with common items."

"Ah man."

"The good stuff that separates a true ninja from a dilettante or a mere enthusiast is the little details. The little details that are only transmitted verbally from a master to his students."

He never even tried to sell us anything. Good on him. But the performance was wearing him out. He started packing his Pyramid Brand cigarettes and said he needed to step outside for a minute. We left while he was gone.

13. Metal spikes you drop on the ground.

When we were walking back to the Caddy with Rock, I sang Daryl's praises. Rock just snorted and rolled his eyes. I could tell Rock thought he was a goober, maybe even holding something back like, "You know he lives with his mom, right?" But the uneven smile said he appreciated Daryl's salesmanship and enthusiasm. Rock definitely didn't give a damn about nerdy shit, but for some reason, somehow, he gifted us, or at least didn't hinder, this beautiful, singular manifestation.

Daryl Rudisil . . . man o' man. He and his shop—not what you'd expect to be Arkansas's hidden treasure.

If he put on a performance like this for every kid who came in. . . . Thank you. What a necessary but underappreciated field of endeavor. Anyone who has shit to say about Daryl can go fuck themselves.

Let's take a pee break and refill our drinks. The essence of Daryl needs to sink into your soul and ruminate for a little while.

PHOENIX VILLAGE MALL

It was pouring when we left Rad Randy's. Speaking up over the sound of the rain, Rock asked, "Y'all wanna go to the movies? My treat. I've gotta stop by one of my bars. I saw that Karate Turtles movie is playing."

"Ninja Turtles," I corrected before looking to Loo, who gave me no indication either way. "Sure," I said. Rock nodded and turned up his *Reelin' in the Years: The Very Best of Steely Dan* tape.

I dig Rock's type of work, just bouncing around putting out fires and overseeing, making sure everything is running smoothly. It's its own brand of stress and uncertainty, but hardly ever tedious or repetitive.

For some reason, I'm not sure why exactly, but I get the impression— or maybe my imagination— that the holy rollers of Fort Smith, of which there are many in the River Valley, thought Rock was a sleaze ball, an unmarried, childless womanizer who dealt in the business of sin. But he definitely showed Grandma a good time. I wish someone gave me so much attention on a Saturday night.

~

After a few minutes of driving in a torrential downpour, he pulled up in front of the mall. He handed me three dollars.

"This isn't enough," I said, "Movie tickets are five bucks."

"Not here. Trust me," he said. I hesitated as the rain dumped on the car; I would have argued with anyone else.

We jumped out and made our way through the rain.

"I'll be right here in two hours," Rock yelled.

Man, Arkansas malls are shitty. This place was a ghost mall twenty years before it was a thing. Just a few lonely people walking around.

Soaking wet, we trampled around looking for the theater. He was right. The tickets were only a dollar. It was a cheap theater. The catch—in addition to the fact that it was old, small, and rundown—was that the reels were worn since the movie had been out for six months and were hand-me-downs from the bigger theater, creating a degraded picture quality, an issue from the old analog days.

During the previews, *Dick Tracy* or *Robocop 2,* Loo confided that he hadn't seen the movie yet. I assumed it was every red-blooded American male's birthright and moral obligation to see the Turtles live action movie. "What!" Unfortunately, in classic Arthur Regulski style, I had a running commentary throughout the movie. At least there was hardly anyone there on that rainy day. Which, by the way, created a memorable effect: occasional thunder and lightning cracks against a constant drum of rain against the roof.

I'm sure you've seen this classic, the highest grossing indie film of all time up to that point. I won't waste your time going through the details.

Rock was right where he said he'd be when we got out. We just got in the car. The Steely Dan turned up, Rock didn't have much to say, which made me a little uncomfortable; Loo was right at home. We headed back across the bridge to Van Buren, the part of town with Wal-Mart.

"Let's get a bite to eat before we pick up your grandma," Rock said as he pulled us into Long John Silver's. He was a decision-making kind of guy. He circled the brown-roped sides of the restaurant and started ordering two kid's meals for us, fish not chicken, stopping halfway to ask if that's all right. We didn't respond quickly enough. Without an instant objection, he picked up from the one-second pause and continued with the order. He got us all root beers. The kid's meal included water-squeeze balls with the faces of pirates on them.

As we sat across from him at the table, he decided he better try to talk to us. "So you got in a fight, huh?" I repeated the story again. Unamused, he said, "You can't make getting pushed around a habit."

He was finished pretty quick. We weren't done but he told us to hurry up. On the way out he told us we could move some firewood at his house to pay for the meal. Huh? Do what? He was only half joking.

We went back to the park and picked up Grandma. She was all gussied up. The three of us were going to stay the night at Rock's.

We had to stop at one of his bars. Grandma waited in the car with us. It was time to ask about the Sega again. I had to show Loo I was putting in effort on his dream, show him I was for real.

"I'm sorry, Sweetie. I just can't right now," she said.

"We'll get Grandpa to pay for it. He can come back for a day or send you the money." I said.

"No, no. We can't be bothering him over that."

"Why not? He'll be fine."

"That's not right."

"We've got to have it!" I moaned right as Rock got back in the car.

"What's all this about?" he asked. I didn't say anything, wasn't any of his business.

"Oh, they're trying to get me to buy them a new video game system," Grandma said.

He scoffed. "Don't do it. They get more than they should already. You're not doing them a favor when you buy them something they didn't have to work for."

Thanks, Rock.

I looked at Loo. His face was turned out the window like he wasn't even listening to the conversation.

He continued, "Besides, y'all don't need to be sitting in front of a damn dumb-dumb box to have fun. Summer is for fishing and chasing snakes around old rock fences."

Yeah yeah yeah, you said the same shit last time. I stayed quiet. I needed to keep Rock out of this.

We got to his house. The downpour had stopped, but it was still overcast.

"You know where the swim trunks are. We've got five acres here. Feel free to run around. Start a mud fight."

Hmm maybe—probably not.

We did go swimming though. There was a hint of disappointment for both of us over the Sega; the mood matched the overcast weather. But it wasn't all that bad. We went back and forth between the pool and the satellite TV before passing out on the couch after a long day.

I know... the swords and ninjas, but we aren't even to Florida yet.

SCAR'S HOUSE

One day, sitting there bored, trailer warming up from the summer heat, I talked Loo into beating the greatest game of all time, *Mario Brothers 3*. I could only make it to the third world and really wanted to see what it was like in the later worlds. Despite it being a little passe for him, he indulged me.

That ate up the first part of the afternoon, then we were back on the dregs, the dog days of summer. He asked me about the Sega again. I couldn't spin any positive news. Grandma was stonewalling me. He just snorted when I told him I'd find a way.

We were rubbing on each other's nerves; it was getting a little claustrophobic. But why dwell on that? Maybe one of life's mercies is that we tend to forget the piddly, banal bad stuff.

We tried going outside, but it was hot and he had no lawn toys; no one in the trailer park really did, but it's not like we would have played basketball even if there was a court.

We were so bored we were going back to *Deadly Towers* and *Cobra Triangle* (the worst games he had) in thoughtless hope for some stimulation, some dopamine. Kind of like when you keep walking to the kitchen and compulsively open the refrigerator in a weird hope that something has magically become appealing.

Then we heard the door open; finally, someone to take us to rent some fresh games.[14] Loo went out to see who it was, then I heard him speaking Vietnamese. I instantly could tell his interlocuter was Scar.

Loo came back in and said Scar would take us to Star Video if we helped feed and water the chickens. The thought of spending time with Scar made me nervous. He intimidated the hell out of me.

14. You'd think I'd tell you we rode bikes all over town, but we didn't. You'd think the families would encourage the exercise, but Van Buren was too geographically sprawled out with lots of interstate and four lane roads, and few sidewalks. It was dangerous. We were in a ride catching paradigm.

From the living room he yelled, "Feed chicken, water. Get out house, boys." His English wasn't the best, but Scar must have sensed the boredom on us.

Scar had a faded red Suburu Brat, the unique, infamous cross between a light-weight pick up and El Camino, known for having seats in the bed facing the tailgate. I was both excited and hesitant. You're not supposed to have seats in the bed. I couldn't help but notice there was a badass looking knife tucked between the driver's seat and the center console, handle poking out for rapid access. It was half bowie, half kukri, a big belly widening toward the tip.

Behind his seat he kept an SKS— the cheap, ubiquitous, mass-produced-across the-second-world, semi-automatic carbine.

Heading northwest of town,[15] Loo and I sat in the back watching the landscape pass us by. I had never been into rural Arkansas, so it was kind of neat. Houses got fewer and farther in between until we were driving on a dirt road with thick woods on each side.

The clouds were getting dark as we rolled from one dirt road to the next, each a little smaller and more unkempt than the one before it. We eventually turned off onto a path that was nothing more than tire tracks cutting through thick ivy and vines hanging from large, leafy oaks. After a few hundred yards we got to a little gate at the far-left corner of a one-acre fenced off area that was full of pens for his fighting chickens.

Each gamecock had its own tipped-over 55-gallon drum full of hay to sleep in and about five-by-five feet worth of cage to roam. There were roughly thirty of them.

In the back was a little barn, a 40'x 20' building that looked like a screened-in porch. 7 ft tall, probably 12' at the crown. Tin roof. A cinder block border on the bottom for anchoring the beams that supported the trusses. The floor was dirt. The bottom half of the wall was made of tin with chicken wire on the top half.

15. In my latter-in-life research, I identified that we were near the mouth of Webber creek, a small tributary into Lee Creek, a large tributary to the Arkansas River. There are lots of creeks coming down from the hills of the Ozarks into the Arkansas River Valley.

We went in to get some feed. There was a lot to absorb, but he was rushing us to get the chickens fed before it started raining. The feed sat covered in large, plastic garbage bins. He had old coffee cans to ferry it out to the chickens.

It started to drizzle. We walked through the chickens. I was amazed at how fierce and exotic they were. Bright red crowns, and tail feathers that shone like blue steel. I took the feed out one-coffee-can-at-a time, gingerly dumping a quarter in each cage. The drizzle turned to a sprinkle, and Scar yelled to hurry.

We started flinging handfuls into their cages. You could hear the chickens pecking furiously at their little metal bowls. My heart was racing. I didn't want to let Scar down. My mind spun up a situation that was more dramatic than reality. A race against time to get the chickens fed; God only knows what Scar would do to me if we failed. I was running back and forth between the shed and the cages, picking up and delivering the feed. With a quarter of them left, the rain started coming down.

By the time we had just a few pens left, it was a full-on monsoon. "Done!" I yelled as we finished the last one and I sprinted back to the shed.

Soaking wet, chilly but not cold, I stood there taking in the whole shed. The wind blew through the chicken wire that was the top half of the wall. The inside bottom half was plywood on the inside. You could close the windows with a crank and pulley system that brought up plastic-weave curtains.

To the left there was a cot covered by a mosquito net, a wood burning stove, and a flat of Milwaukee's Best. That's when I realized this was his house. The same wall had several sets of deer antlers nailed up; on one rack hung an olive drab green military field jacket. I wish I knew what type of insignia was on it.

The right side of the house was cordoned off for his cock fighting supplies—feed, caging materials, etc.—but most notably, a row of sharp steel spurs hanging on nails.

In the middle of the shed there were some huge fishing rods. The longest I'd ever seen, not that I was particularly familiar with angling gear. I had never been fishing. But these poles were clearly meant for catching something big. I asked Loo if they took those to the ocean. He laughed. Scar looked at Loo who translated what I said. Scar laughed.

"No, catfish in the river," Loo said.

"Catfish? What's that? Does it look like a cat? That's crazy," I said. Loo laughed at me. And he spoke in Vietnamese to Scar and they shared another laugh.

Loo said, "We're going to take you catfishing."

"Sweet."

We just stood there, quiet, watching rain the come down, listening to it pound the tin roof. Thick lines of water poured from the corrugations in the tin overhang. You couldn't see it, but there was a creek roaring nearby, somewhere down the hill behind the shed.

Scar cracked a beer and stood there looking out through the rain into the dense green foliage, smoking one cigarette after the next.

Looking at him looking out into the woods has developed into one of the more poignant moments in my life, percolating through my mind for decades. Who knows what he was thinking? Who knows what all he had experienced? Your imagination can run wild with back-story possibilities.

Living off the grid, outside the system, without properly in-processing as a citizen, Scar left nearby Fort Chaffee, Arkansas, where they were housing Vietnamese refugees who had come from overcrowded camps in Indonesia. Only some of those broken, beaten, scarred people got to go to the USA. What strings did he pull in that bureaucratic mess to make that happen? Who did he bribe? Who did he coerce? What favor was exchanged for him and his buddy Van— single adult males, the lowest priority— to get the coveted spots? Could be luck. But relying on it after having made it that far? Scar? Nah.

Popular culture, the documentaries and specials, *Apocalypse Now, Platoon, Full Metal Jacket,* and all the other war porn I was raised on center the narrative on the U.S. versus the Viet Cong. But the truth is that the war between the north and south was much nastier than the American experience. For perspective, the death toll: 58 thousand Americans, 250 thousand South Vietnamese soldiers, 1.2 million communist fighters, and roughly 2 million Vietnamese civilians.

Scar made it out.

I am not sure how old he was. I'd wager he was born in the mid to late 1940s. Right at the end of the brutal Japanese occupation. A time when the Vietnamese were starving. But there was no time to relax. Up next was war against the French who reoccupied after World War II. So, whoever Scar's parents were, they lived hard, lived through war, lived through multiple occupations.

The south may have had the U.S. on their side; they may have represented freedom, liberalism, and capitalist democracy, but they were a mess. Constant political machinations, powerplays, infighting, corruption, criminality, attempted coups, crippling nepotism, all while dealing with traitors and spies. They never had a chance against the unwavering communist heart.

Scar was a soldier, but also, probably, a gangster; the line wasn't distinct in South Vietnam. Hell, the Bin Xuyen crime syndicate hated the communists more than the South Vietnamese government did.

It's safe to say that from the time he was a teen or earlier, Scar was in the business of danger and violence. There's no telling how many times he faced life threatening danger, having to be ruthless, cunning, cowardly, whatever it took to stay alive. Trusting his instincts, taking huge gambles. Then again, maybe I'm underestimating him? Maybe I'm sensationalizing him? Maybe he was the clever guy who made it through the war without getting his hands dirty? No. Dandies don't have faces like his.

But let's think about his last days in Vietnam, the only ones I have some clues about. After the Americans left, the north was emboldened. The southern army was in disarray. Without being propped up by the Americans, they had little ammo, little fuel, and little resolve. Thousands were deserting every month.

Endless caravans of scared refugees pushing south.

That was out in the field. Meanwhile, the already-corrupt Saigon was becoming Casablanca on steroids. Everyone looking for a way out while avoiding communist agents. Bribing, killing, stealing, marrying the last few Americans, whatever it took to get out of Vietnam—bag of cash, bullet to the head.

When Que City and Dha Nang fell, there was no doubt. The route was on. Saigon dissolved into chaos and anarchy. ARVN officers were committing suicide. Families were burning photo albums and any other clues that might get them killed for being sympathizers.

Dang Van, Loo's dad, was apparently sick when Scar arrived. Maybe money was involved, maybe honor between the families, or maybe just good 'ol fashion friendship, whatever the reason, Sao showed back up to his hometown, and forced his lifeless buddy on the back of his motorcycle. Communist rule meaning reeducation camp or execution, they raced through mayhem.

Once out of Saigon, they would have had to make their way through the Mekong delta to find passage across the sea, walking on the razor's edge, death on each side, absolutely no room for error or weakness. Decisive action at every turn, whether it be violence, hiding, running, disguising, whatever means necessary to escape the invaders. Thousands died trying. Scar made it while carrying a sick person on his back, literally and figuratively. No telling how he acquired the boat.

But the boat was assuredly not meant for the open water, not the 300 miles between Vietnam and the refugee camps in Indonesia, not the open sea full of Thailander pirates preying on the desperate boat people. Two or three weeks is a long time for a fishing boat to operate in constant use without breaking down. Maybe it was smooth, easy, unmolested sailing. Maybe they had to kill some pirates and float adrift barely getting to land before starvation. Nevertheless, they made it to Indonesia, processed through the refugee camps, and found their way to Arkansas, USA.

If we could only find the guy now and get the story out of him. But I think he's long gone, and the truth will never be known, but, God, it would make a great book—not a doubt in my mind.

Maybe after his hard life, he now looks over the garden walls into paradise. Out of all the ways things could go for a Vietnamese man born in the mid-1940s, he wound up in a chicken fighting shed hidden in the woods near the Arkansas River with little L.A. Art Regulski.

My guardian angel.

~

Oh, and I'm painfully aware that any of my visions of Vietnam and the life of Vietnamese people around and after the fall of Saigon are probably inaccurate, romanticized, oversimplified. I need no reminding that I am a fat American hedonist with only an amateur understanding of history. But like they say, "You go to war with the army you got, not the army you want." Well, I think, dream, and imagine with the brain I got, not the brain you and I wish I had. For whatever chaotic, crazy circumstances of life, you're listening to me. Is it fair? I don't know. What's fair?

Anyway it was a moment that means a lot to me. A connection to the big passion plays that shape our lives. A joining of the intensely personal sensations and the incredibly impersonal movement of history.

~

I was sweating it, but after the rain let up, he held to his word. Riding back to town in our wet chairs in the bed, we stopped at

Star Video. I rented *Predator* even though Loo was against it. That movie was the most intense, hardcore thing in the world to me at the time. He re-rented *Journey to Silius.*

It was still raining; you could hear it hitting the roof of the trailer. We had just had our little heavy time out in the woods. I felt it was the perfect moment to watch *Predator,* which was why I gambled and forced it on them.

I was right.

Loo was too cool to mention being scared, but you could tell the tension was getting to him. He was scrunched up into a ball on the corner of the couch. Even Scar came in halfway through, noticed it, and smoked a few cigarettes watching. I would have killed to know what he thought about the movie, but he gave zero commentary, verbal or nonverbal. Wouldn't know if he was enthralled or thought it was corny. I'm not sure how well he could keep up with the English though. Either way, he left before the end.

VAPORWAVE

Lethargic lilacs, calm corals, and tranquilizing turquoise. Stone busts, palm trees, and old Macintosh computers. Hypnagogia, the tweener state separating awake and asleep. A genre that, when at its best, evokes nostalgia with the precision of a surgical knife.

It's not a bunch of quick-hitting bangers. It's intentionally ambient background music, atmosphere. When you're working on one thing it takes the other part of your brain, relaxes it, gets it out of the way, gently escorts it to a comfortable alternate universe.

The speed at which definitions and authoritative explanations of vaporwave run from you is proportional to your proximity. The closer you get the faster they slip away.

"The memories from a past we never had" is an expression in a comment section that I like, similarly the word "anemoia," invented by writer John Koenig, is defined as nostalgia for a time you've never known.

Maybe all art and history are that? Repackaging impressions so that they're more aesthetically pleasing and memetic.

Shit—I don't know. All kinds of big-brained prognosticators with the pedantic, just-for-YouTube cadence are making stabs at this nowadays. Fuck it. I'm too drunk and probably wouldn't have what it takes anyway.

I'll get on with the big show, we've got those Yakuza to talk about, but know there's a little vaporwave in this story, aesthetic overlap, if that's not obvious.

You can't look too hard for it; it finds you. The best songs come on as you're falling asleep, never to be heard or experienced again. The universe gives it to you just when you need it. That's why a curated vapor playlist for this adventure kept slipping through my fingers, but here are some albums to use as a starting point.

Vcr-classique – Floridacatalogue

Luxury Elite - Cruise

猫 シ Corp. - NEWS AT 11

desert sand feels warm at night : 濃霧

Windows96 - Enchanted Instrumentals and Whispers

Mydreamyadventure

16-Bit ELEVATOR

骨架的 : Reflections\

Holograms.zip

Phoenix #2772 : You Are Already Dead.

FISHING TRIP

I was at Loo's house bright and early to go fishing. We sat there and played video games again all day, at least Loo did; I watched *Predator* again.

Scar never came.

I was a little disappointed, but also slightly relieved. Being around Scar is intense. Everything about him is intimidating, the facial scarring simultaneously repulsive and magnetic.

By the next day I had completely forgotten about it. I moseyed down there around noon, and I hadn't watched Loo play for 30 minutes when I heard the door open and Scar barked, "Fish Time!" across the house in his guttural, staccato way.

Loo flipped off the Nintendo and grabbed the Predator tape. We hopped in the Brat and were on our way. After returning the VHS, we headed north into the country again.

We sat in the back with three cane poles, a coffee can full of worms, and two five-gallon buckets. I wasn't sure what was going on, I guess we weren't going fishing with the big poles, whatever they were meant to catch. I felt a little disappointed.

I was right, kind of. Somewhere along the dirt road that led to his cockfighting hideout, we pulled over at a seemingly random place, trees on both sides. Scar and Loo grabbed the poles and buckets and climbed through the barbed wire fence lining the road.

Loo explained to me what was going on. We were going to catch perch which would be used as bait for the catfish.

Walking through the briers and brambles was a mess. We had to cross two different barbed wire fences. I totally sucked at that. Too clumsy. Loo had to work me through one leg at a time, holding the lower-middle strand of wire down with his foot and pulling the upper-middle strand up so I could squeeze between, unhooking me when my shirt inevitably got hung up. He was a natural, just floating through the wire.

We ended up fighting through the underbrush for about a hundred yards before we arrived at a little pond surrounded by cedar trees and circled by knee-high green grass in and out of the water. I asked Loo whose property this was. He just shrugged his shoulders. Trespassing . . . nice.

I was confused, excited, feeling adventurous.

Scar and Loo made quick work of getting started, untwisting the lines from the poles. They didn't put entire worms on the little hook; they broke off little pieces of them. That made me squeamish. As soon as their worms hit the water, a perch bit it. A feeding frenzy. Loo and Scar were putting two perch in the bucket per minute. It took me about five perch before I got the hang of getting them off the hook. I was excited. I was catching fish. No one else seemed to think it was a big deal, just part of the process.

Once we had about fifty in the bucket, we headed out, ten minutes back to Scar's place.

He dumped the leftover worms into a 55-gallon drum; I didn't realize he had a worm farm too. His ecosystem got more interesting every trip. We fed the chickens and loaded up the catfishing poles. They faced the front of the truck, sticking six feet up into the air like antennae.

Then we headed back through Van Buren and turned east once we reached the river bottoms and followed the road along the levy until we reached Lock and Dam 13, part of the Corps of Engineers' elaborate process to make the Arkansas river deeper, more navigable. But for our purpose, it created a place for fish to congregate.

First, he got me and Loo set-up. Watching Scar pull a perch out and run a huge hook through its stomach was tough for a city boy like me. It looked painful. There was a big lead weight about two-foot above the hook. Scar walked over a few feet to the right, reared back with his 8-foot river pole and let it rip, sending the weight and the perch forty-fifty yards, kerplunking into the river. He handed the rod to Loo, and did the same with mine. Then, Loo explained to me how it worked: we sit there with our hands on the poles, waiting, feeling for something to take the bait, at which time we jerk the pole and start reeling it in.

I was constantly asking him if I had something. The movement of the perch and the flow of the river made it hard to tell.

~

A note about the Arkansas River:

The land around the Arkansas River is pure, swampy jungle, full of mosquitos and water moccasins. The water is deep, muddy, and swift. To wit: dangerous. There are stories of kids jumping off the bridges and being anally impaled by tree limbs below the surface. The general, non-sensational guideline is that you don't get in the river because the undercurrents will suck you to the bottom. Not to mention, it's just nasty. Tulsa and other municipalities from Kansas through Oklahoma pump their sewage into it. The real gem of Arkansas River cautionary tales, though, is the story of catfish the size of Volkswagens. Legend has it that some Frogmen—Navy Seal, Police divers, private recovery contractors, the story varies—went down to the bottom by the dam to look for a body, shined a light, and saw something that sent them on an ear-popping scramble to the surface, refusing to ever get back in the river.

Bear this in mind. The Arkansas River might come back into play.

~

While we sat and waited for action, Scar was getting after it. He was snagging. Right under noodling in the hierarchy of badass fishing skills, snagging isn't for the soft or weak; it is an active sport. His line was just weight and a big nasty treble hook. He would cast it as far as he could, sixty yards or so, let it sink to the bottom, then yank and rip ferociously, looking to hook a paddlefish or catfish in the stomach along the bottom. Then, he would reel in the slack he created and try it again.

Only the leanest, meanest fisherman try this. It's taxing on the body, testing both strength and endurance. Scar had a cigarette hanging from his lip the entire time and a six pack of Milwaukee within reach.

Watching him transfixed us for a bit, but eventually we got bored. I resorted to small talk, talking about the only thing that would get him going, Sega. I asked him again why he wanted to play Phantasy Star. So as we sat there, he repeated his spiel about, and I am paraphrasing, how it was the most ambitious, grandiose game that's ever come out, bigger, bolder, more complex. He didn't mention how the world is quasi-Greek mythology set in the constellation Perseus beset with *Dune*-esque political and economic intrigue.

He didn't have to talk too long; Scar snagged something! Feet fighting for purchase, he was in a dog fight, pole bent over like it was about to snap. He dug his heels into the red clay. I jumped up and ran over to him. Loo had enough wherewithal to stay by our poles.

The fight was awesome. A war of attrition, the tension never left, first to give up loses. Slowly, a few inches at a time, Scar's violent backward jerks created little moments where he could take in some slack. The fight felt like it lasted hours; it wore me out just watching. Realistically it was only about twenty minutes. Once he got it closer, I sat on the edge of the bank waiting to see the monster he was fighting. It made huge waves. In my imagination I thought he was about to pull out a shark. It turned out to be meaner. A brown, ugly 50lb flathead catfish. Scratched and scarred from a life in the dark underworld, this 20-year-old predator of the deep had met his match. Live by the sword, die by the sword.

Scar handed me the pole and walked into the water to pick it up. He hoisted the vanquished beast over his head by the gills before carrying him onto shore. With no delicacy, he ripped out the thoroughly engorged treble hook and carried the catfish to the back of the Suburu.

I guess Scar was worn out. He sat down behind us to smoke. Loo and I hadn't had any luck. Eventually Scar took control, reeled-in our lines, re-baited them, and cast them back out. That must have done the trick; Loo's pole doubled over. Scar started giving instructions in Vietnamese. Loo brought in a nice 8-pound blue cat. Soon after that, Scar got out a pole and started fishing traditionally like us. He ended up catching several 3-5lb cats. Loo even caught another.

After about two hours of cooking in the sun, my face and legs were as red as lobsters. I thought I must have been doing it wrong; nothing was happening, but all of a sudden, out of nowhere, my pole instantly bent over forward. I screamed. They yelled at me not to drop it. Once I gained my composure over the excitement and rush, I began to reel him in. The fight, which would be repeated and embellished to anyone who would listen for the next month, was epic. The biggest tussle of my life. With their coaching, I was able to get the 8lb channel cat up on the bank.

I was so excited that even Scar smiled. We ended the adventure on that note.

All the catfish rode in the back with us. They took forever to die. The big one that Scar snagged oozed blood from its stomach the whole time, creating a pool galoshing against our feet. The big channel cat I caught became like my animal brother. In some vague I've-watched-Red Dawn-too-much kind of way I felt a kinship to him.

It was such a long day. I was fuckin' plum wore out, as a good ol' Arkansas fisherman might say. The excitement and sunburn had me yawning. I thought we were done, but the adventure had another chapter. It was time to clean. I stood there like a dumbass as Scar pulled them out of the truck and nailed their tails to the oak tree in the backyard. He and Loo skinned several without me getting involved, but Scar handed me the pliers when they got to the fish I caught. I was being dainty with the pliers when he showed me where to grip and rip. "Pull. Pull. Pull," he grunted, so I gritted my teeth and ripped the skin off. Satisfied with myself, I handed him back the pliers and watched him cut the meat off for filets.

Loo's dad came home from work with some groceries, including two 12-packs of Heinekens and a carton of Pall Malls. He and Scar worked on dinner. Loo and I sat on their yellow couch, watching some Gilligan's Island reruns as they cooked. The loud, splashy sizzle of filets hitting the hot grease was the only thing keeping me awake.

I dozed off I guess, and then a guttural, "Bữa tối" from Scar woke me up. I looked at Loo, confused. "Bữa tối," he said, "Dinner."

Don't have to tell me twice.

I was at the table in no time. Scar sat an ice cold can of Pepsi down in front of me. Check. They made fried catfish and hushpuppies. At first I was a little unsure. I had never had fried catfish before. But, I hadn't eaten all day, so I dug in. And man, I loved it. So good, one of the best meals I've ever had in my life.

I ate more than my fair share, kept reaching for more and more. It was so good; I couldn't stop myself. The batter had the perfect amount of salt and spice. They looked at me and laughed, pretty sure they were calling me a fat American, but oh well, it felt endearing. They seemed proud to have cooked something so delicious.

As soon as I was done, I went on to their couch and fell asleep. If it offended them that my clothes were covered in mud and fish juice, they didn't say anything about it.

Sometime while I dozed, two other Vietnamese guys showed up. The four adults played cards, talked shit, drank beer, and smoked cigarettes all night, screaming in ecstasy and anger after the flop. They'd wake me just long enough for me to move my face out of a drool pool and find a fresh section of couch pillow.

THE BEAST

If this were a horror story, I'd make Milwaukee's Best mandatory since it sponsored TNT's Saturday night *Monstervison* hosted by Joe Bob Riggs. Combine that with the fact that I remember Scar drinking it, and I assumed it would be my beer of choice, but when I first started going to parties I remember asking an older guy, a veteran of the local adolescent drinking scene, about getting some Milwaukee's Best, and with an expression like it was the most important thing he was ever going to tell me he looked deep into my eyes and said "Stay away from The Beast!"

So I took his word and stayed away from the Beast. I wasn't surprised to learn that Scar's beer of choice was tough to handle. I didn't like beer too much to begin with anyway. Easy advice to follow.

Then one day, something like a decade later, broke and thirsty, before I tried to leave California for good, I rounded up crinkled one-dollar bills and change from the couch cushions and went to the nearest gas station to buy some beer. Down in the dumps, feeling like I deserved more pain, I grabbed a dusty sixer of The Beast from the top right corner of the reach-in.

Out in the parking lot I took one big gulp, expecting the worst. It wasn't too bad, better than Bud Light. Pleasant surprise. Salvaged my week.

Nowadays, I consider it the best of the cheapies. The old, off brand gas station down the road is the only place that sells it around here. Cool place, co-owned by an old thick-jowled, red faced man who always wears a cowboy hat and will talk the hind leg off a donkey. His partner is a nervous Arabic man who refers to everyone as "My friend." Odd pair.

~

I was kidding on the phone when I told you I picked up aluminum cans along the highway on Christmas. But, allusions to waking up half-naked next to an empty plastic bottle of whiskey on a cheap linoleum floor, well, they're not far fetched.

LET'S GO TO FLORIDA

How did we get to Florida? A bag of chips.

Brenda had had the same old yellow bag of generic potato chips since before I got there. Every time I told her we needed more snacks she told me just to eat the chips in the yellow bag, despite me repeatedly refusing and saying they were gross and stale.

I was at Brenda's for the night, giving Loo a break, no special reason, just figured I'd eat at my own house for a change. She told me to eat the old off brand chips again. "No way," I said. An hour or two later, she needed to make a run to the gas station to pick up some cigarettes, so I talked her into buying a new bag of Cool Ranch Doritos.

That was nice. I sat on her worn-out white floral couch and ate over half the bag while watching her taped-off *Can't Buy Me Love*, afterwards falling asleep to some *M.A.S.H* on TV.

I woke up the next day, watched a little Price is Right and went to Loo's for a while. I got hungry while he played some *Mega Man 2*, so I decided to walk home and grab the Doritos from last night.

The whole time, in case I haven't been building up the tension as well as I should, but daily, almost hourly, Loo had been asking me when I was going to get a Sega, and I racked my brain trying to find a way.

Well, all right, actually, the truth is that he had quit mentioning it earlier on, which hurt the most. Loo had written me off as being a bullshitter. Me obtaining a Sega for him barely crossed his mind as a viable option. He didn't take me seriously. Yeah, we'll see. I'll show you. The thought dominated my psyche.

Anyway, I walk in Brenda's trailer. She was at work. The Doritos were rolled down at the top with a big orange, made-specifically-for-bags-of-chips, clip on them. Good Job, Brend.

Well, I opened them up, took a big handful and closed my eyes in anticipation of that beautiful cool ranch zing, zest, and tang. Well-rehearsed in the chip-eating arts, my jaw was synchronized with my hand, instantaneously compacting the chips as they hit my mouth.

It took less than a second to realize what I was eating and started puking all over the kitchen floor. She had combined the old yellow bag chips with the Doritos.

Thin saliva is rising to the top of my throat just thinking about it.

The first splash of vomit covered the linoleum. Without hesitation a second hurl followed. During a momentary break in the action, I tried to crawl to the trash can, getting barf on my hands, legs, and feet in the process.

I was going to puke more anyway but once I stuck my face in the nearly full trashcan and met some old rotten, rancid popcorn that had hung out in Brenda's room for a week before hand, I doubled down, blowing out as much as I could as fast as I could to end the misery. I went deep into my bowels, pulling out every drop of acidic bile from my stomach, plus ten dry heaves for good measure.

Finally, I leaned up against the refrigerator to take in that relaxing post-puke endorphin rush, simultaneously traumatized.

A picture shook loose from its magnet and fell on me, and it all happened. It clicked. Long blond hair lifted in a breeze, surfboard in his armpit, smiling ear to ear, there was a 15-year-old picture of my uncle Kenny as a teenager. My man! I had a plan. Arkansas, it's been real, but we're off to bigger and better things.

~

I stormed in, flinging open the bedroom door exaggeratedly like Kramer on *Seinfeld*. Loo was running his fingers over his gundams in the window. He turned his head around nonchalantly.

"Pack your bags. It's Sega time!" I announced.

"When are we leaving?" Loo, that crazy fuck, was on board, no questions asked.

"As soon as possible. We're going to stay with my uncle who will get us a Sega," I concluded with a slow and theatrical, "...No doubt."

~

Walking back to Brenda's trailer with excitement, it was now time to make it happen. The first call would be to Kenny.

FIRST CALL

"Hello?"

"It's your nephew, Arthur." I said with hopeful, nervous excitement.

"Arty! My man, what's up? Are you all right?"

Reading his tone, that he was both worried about me and proud I thought to call him when in trouble, I instantly adjusted tack. I work hard not to be disingenuous, but my childish instinct on this issue was "by any means necessary." "I'm staying with Brenda and Grandma's boyfriend, and it sucks. Mom left with her dumb boyfriend on her dumb tour."

"But you're okay, right? No one is hurting you?"

"Not exactly. Well I just ate some gross chips that Brenda had and I threw up."

"Well that's no good." He was having a hard time figuring this out, "What can I do to help?"

"I want to stay with you for a little while. Me and my buddy Loo."

All this had him by surprise, but his good nature took over. "Yeah, sure man. If it's all right with everyone else. Your mom. Mom and dad."

Tripping all over myself, I said, "I'll get my mom to say it's ok. We're going to get a Sega Genesis while we're there and play it. It's like Loo's biggest quest in the world, and I am helping him get it."

"Sega Genesis? That's a new video game console, right?"

"Yeah. And you need to see your Dad too," I said.

After a slight hesitation, he said "Probably do. You're right." He didn't know what to say to that.

"I'm gonna get with grandpa to call you and work on the details."

"All right, bud."

"Bye bye—THANKS!" I said as I hung up the phone.

My mom would be hard to get a hold of, but if I could that'd be perfect. Despite her constant dependence upon my grandparents, she had the ultimate say about what I did. She called once every few days to check on me. She said I rarely answered, which may be true because I wasn't home, but I didn't deliberately dodge her. And Brenda didn't have an answering machine. Hopefully, I would catch her and make sure I got her on my side early. There was a hierarchy of who made decisions about me. Mom at the top, then slightly under were the grandparents. Mom and one of the grandparents and I was in. Mom versus both grandparents would be a slugfest. It would depend on my mom's willpower. She definitely knew how to dig her heels into the ground, but she's too preoccupied to die on just any ol' hill. Kenny could be a tiebreaker in a stalemate.

Then again, Grandpa was needed for driving, but if push came to shove, I'd threaten to get on a bus. I called Grandpa on his cell phone, but the reception was terrible, don't think he ever had a clear conversation on it. It was a glorified pager. He called back twenty minutes later, and I told him about my big idea, embellishing Kenny's enthusiasm and emphasizing that he, Kenneth's father, needed to go see how he's doing. That got his wheels turning. I sensed, even though no one explicitly said, that Kenny was being aloof and uncommunicative with the rest of the family.

But ultimately, there were lots of "We'll see," "maybe," "I doubt your grandma will go for this." He didn't say no, but he was circumspect.

We'll call that a tie. The final boss, Grandma, was up next. And, I knew she would try to put the kibosh on it. I waited awhile before asking her, in fact I hung around at Loo's the rest of the day, pumping him up for the big trip and making sure he was committed. We got his dad on board easily. I told him all about my grandpa and uncle, and he said sure. He probably was more interested in a two-three week break from parenting than he was convinced by my nervous salesmanship about my family.

This helped. It would be part of my pitch to Grandma. "But Loo's dad already said it was okay." And I worked on that pitch constantly in my mind as I waited for her to come home from Rock's. But I didn't get the initiative in the conversation. I was sitting on the bed in our shared room catching an afternoon nap and she opened the door.

"I don't think it's a good idea, hun."

Though still half-asleep, I came up swinging, "Everyone else does. My mom, your son, your husband, your grandchild." Not exactly sure why I put it that way, just came to me in the heat of the moment.

"No, no, I don't think that's a good idea." She knew in her gut; her wise, hard-earned grandmotherly wisdom could tell this wasn't smart. She was right, but she didn't elucidate a strong rational argument.

"Aren't you worried about him? Someone needs to see him." I said, "He could be in trouble."

"If he's in trouble, you don't need to get involved," she said. Good point, my bad.

"I mean lonely. He might need to see his family." I adjusted.

She stood there thinking for a second. "He'll be too busy to look after you. He's working hard on his business."

"He said it was fine and it's okay for me to stay at home by myself," I said, now wide awake and getting up off the bed. She cocked her head down and an eye toward me, her look she gave me when she knew I was bullshitting. I followed up, "Besides, Loo is already ready to go. His dad said it was okay."

"Maybe you should have waited. Maybe you'll learn a lesson about assuming too much," she said.

"Maybe, but my mom can still say I can," I said.

"She might also say you can't."

"We'll see. But I'm going to get out of this place one way or another," I said. Yikes on the childish melodrama.

She's smart. She sensed where this could go if I kept pushing: a referendum on her relationship with Rock, everyone hearing me shout out details, spun to make it sound like it really made me uncomfortable. I didn't want to do that.

She tapped her nail on the edge of the door and puckered her lips in difficult thought. She knew staying with Brenda wasn't the best hosting situation either. I would be a morale problem if she didn't let me go. And Kenny needed some attachment to the family.

"If your mom and uncle say it's okay, and your grandfather will take you, I guess I can't really stop you. "

A Bada Bing, A Bada Boom. Mom called soon and loved the idea. She loved her older brother and thought spending time with him would be great for me. We were on our way.

~

Things weren't that bad in Arkansas, honestly; it was a good way to spend a summer, but it wasn't enough at the time. Life be like that sometimes. Various forces, patterns, waves, whatevers, all come together at the right moment to make something crazy happen. I went with it. When I get an adventure on the brain it's hard to let it go.

~

Relax, young Takezo, "the Sword of Shoguns" awaits.

WAYMIRE PART II

After the war Tokyo was chaos, both administratively and culturally. Japan was destroyed. Its people were broken, beaten, scarred, and starving. The homeless numbered in the millions. People were living in bombed-out shanty towns, scrap houses made of cardboard and chicken wire. Previously well-to-do families were walking to the country to trade precious heirlooms for vegetables.

The large U.S. administrative team was full of bored, energetic soldiers with nothing to do. MacArthur didn't want a cruel occupation; no barbarism was to be tolerated, so the U.S. used mostly young soldiers who hadn't seen combat, boys out on their first big adventure.

It was a perfect storm of debauchery, a giant playground of corruption. The Yakuza, Japanese organized crime, took over in their illegal, but proud way, reorganizing the construction, stevedore, and trash collection industries, as well as providing all the entertainment the American servicemen needed, including the largest brothel in the world.

Long story short, the Japanese have a different relationship to organized crime than Americans do, and with the fear of communism in China and Russia, the U.S. was willing to play fast and loose with criminal and civic ideology as long as Japan recovered and played for the right team. "We'll help you rebuild if you become democratic capitalists." Hell, Eisenhower even met with a Yakuza boss who offered to put down left-wing student protests with baseball bats.

Big Charles didn't have anything to do with the contraband or any other of the business of sin, but he was ambitious. He was a man with a plan, big dreams, a vision. As it was told to me, you conjure a lot of those in the military though, especially during the most boring days. All the time to think sends your head in some crazy places. But, most soldier dreams get forgotten when confronted with reality.

But not Big Charles; he focused all of his energy on creating a life for him, Rosalinde, and their families. First, he had to rebuild her family's estate then start saving so he could buy a nice farm back in Nebraska for them to raise kids on.

For money, he was even willing to do a little wrestling, the Japanese pastime. They'd pay him good money to be the heel. Just like the WWF, they were all about the narrative and the theatrics. His name was "Woo Pig Sooie," the big, dumb, pig farming oaf from the USA. They framed it like he was a proud star in the USA. Then, for what would be the modern equivalent of a few hundred dollars, he'd take a semi-choreographed ass whipping from a Japanese wrestler as the crowd cheered on, releasing their embarrassment over the loss in the war. Charles even fought the great Rikidozan, the most famous Japanese wrestler of all time.

But, he still wasn't making nearly as much money as the other soldiers who were stealing and selling army supplies and nearly all of them were making extra bucks by shipping Japanese souvenirs home, most notably cheap imitation samurai swords.

I guess Big Charles was tired of being the good boy. His body was hurting from all the wrestling, and these young bozos who didn't even see combat were getting filthy rich. So, one day when he saw a pile of confiscated samurai swords in an office, he grabbed one and put it in his locker. He didn't think it was a big deal; he'd seen hundreds sent home.

Well only a few days before there was an ostentatious sword turn-in, a symbolic gesture of obedience. All of the aristocratic families had to turn in their swords, emblems of their martial heritage, a ceremonial castration, a humiliation. An intense match the night before, Big Charles was too tired to notice.

A few days of business-as-usual, then one morning the entire post is alive with the buzz that an ancient samurai sword is missing. The Honjo Masamune. Nearly 700 years old, it was crafted by the greatest swordsmith who ever lived. It was turned in by descendants of the first Shogun, Tokugawa. 300 years after his death he's still the most famous warrior/conqueror/unifier in Japanese history. It's hard to find a cultural equivalent. Imagine if the British Royal Family actually had Excalibur.

Extreme punishments were mentioned. Court Martial. Rumors of rewards. With phrases like "diplomatic crisis" in the air, Big Charles was sweating bullets. He wasn't comfortable with it to begin with. Authorities searched the HQ up and down, and made several passes through the barracks. Since no one suspected big, honest Charles of having it, his mattress didn't get examined.

He caught a ride to the Philippines the first chance he could. Practically running to the plane, he was nervous as hell on his way to Manila. But no one thought a soldier carrying a samurai sword was uncommon. The Japanese had recently started mass producing cheap replicas.

He landed in Manila and walked through the struggling country to Rosalinde's hamlet. He greeted his in-laws. Looked at them. Looked at the sword. Thought about what all they'd been through. And he realized he had no idea what he was doing. The best course of action was to get rid of it.

He thought about doing the easy thing, the safe thing, and just throwing it into the ocean, but he couldn't allow himself to do it. Ruining something so grandiose didn't feel right. There was no way he could get away with selling it. Where would he start? Who would he talk to?

His only option? Hide it and never mention it again, leave it there forever or until he came up with something better. Maybe send someone an anonymous letter once all his in-laws had moved to the states. He wrapped it in cloth, found a long ammo can, and in the middle of the night he marched several hundred twisting-and-turning yards through thick jungle before he buried it five feet deep.

Not long after, he and Rosaline married in a Catholic Mission near her home, and when it was time, when the occupation of Tokyo was winding down, they moved to Northern California where he worked as a logger to earn a few more bucks before buying a farm back home in Nebraska, eventually having kids and living the American dream they had earned.

For over 40 years, he never told a soul.

LEAVING ARKANSAS

The big day came. All my stuff in a duffel bag, we were ready for him. Loo had a plastic "Thank You" grocery bag with some underwear, another pair of shorts, and another t-shirt. He wore his yellow cotton shirt, gray cotton shorts that only went about half-way down to the knee, and black generic shoes with the two Velcro straps, just like Daryl's. Clothes, packing, wardrobe—just weren't his thing. But, it all came together. The ultimate bang-for-your-buck aesthetic.

I, of course, was wearing my best for the big day: stretch waisted black pants and a blue Bugle Boy t-shirt with neon green and pink geometric sharks on it.

We sat on Brenda's porch. We were way too early. Grandpa wasn't going to be there until 9 a.m. or so. We were antsy. I would get up, walk around the front of the trailer, kick around on the wooden porch that wasn't exactly dilapidated yet. I played with her windchimes and garden frogs. And, I don't mean I got in the zone exploring their inherent wabi-sabi.[16] I just walked from one to the next, touching them with my foot. Loo was better at being bored than me; self-contained, he sat on the porch.

Eventually the Galaxy pulled-up along the street. Loo and I jumped up, and I began to take control, opening the back door to the camper portion. By the time Grandpa got out of the truck, Loo was tossing his sacks into the back. True to form, Grandpa had his khaki boonie hat on.

~

"Whoa what's going on here? A stowaway?" Grandpa says.

"Loo is coming with us," I say, without stopping my loading, for some reason feeling that nonchalance was the key to getting

16. Wabi Sabi, in this case, in my words, is the appreciation for ephemeral, ego-less manifestations, blessed accidents that are beautiful in the eye of the beholder, a charming crack in porcelain or a gnarly bend in a tree. Not art in the traditional sense with a strong-willed, vision-driven creator, but an art-like moment in time. Mundane. Personal. Fleeting, idiosyncratic, and unsymbolic.

this to work. "Grandpa meet Loo Dang. Loo Dang, Grandpa."

Loo is too awkward to even look at Grandpa. Grandpa reaches down to force a handshake, "Nice to meet you, Mr. Dang."

Loo replies, without looking him in the eye, "Hey."

"He's coming with us to Florida," I say.

"Looks like it," Grandpa says.

"Hop in, Loo," I say.

"Now buddy, do you have permission from your parents?" Grandpa asks.

Loo nods his head in the affirmative before saying, "My dad said it was okay."

"Yeah, he did. I heard him," I say to Grandpa as I push Loo to hurry up and get in. Grandpa slowly climbs up and gets comfortable. We wait in silence to see if the gambit is going to pay off; I never mentioned bringing a friend.

He looks at us for a moment and says, "Not that I don't trust you, but I want to talk to your parents myself. I'm not interested in any interstate kidnapping manhunts, getting the FBI involved. I'm not cut out for doing hard time in Leavenworth, turning big rocks into little rocks." He was trying to be funny, but it went right over our heads. We weren't in the mood.

"We can't leave him," I blurt out in fear. "His mom is gone and his dad is working."

"Oh now, we're not going to leave him." He thinks about it for a moment, does the math, "We'll just have to find your dad. Running off with a kid before you've talked to his parents isn't right."

"Then we'll have to wait until he gets off work then," I say.

"He's at the cockfights," Loo says.

Grandpa looks at him, "Do you know how to get to the cockfights?"

"Kind of. They're in Oklahoma." He points an arm west, paralleling the nearby interstate 40.

"That's not a lot of help, boys."

"I bet Brenda knows," I said.

"She might."

"I'll go ask," I say as I hop out of the camper. I run up to the door and just barge in the trailer. Brenda isn't out of her bedroom yet. I knock on her door. "Hey Aunt Brenda, do you know where the chicken fights are?" I ask with way too much energy for the morning. I only hear a moan. I knock and ask again. The door opens just enough for her to get her face out. Brenda looks like she's had a rough night.

"What are you asking, hun?" she asks with her finger and thumb on her forehead.

"We need to go to the chicken fights. Where are they? You're the only person who would know."

She closes the door in my face. I stand there dumbfounded before she opens it and walks out in a floral robe with her cigarettes and lighter stacked on top of one another in her hand.

"I think they're in Muldrow," she says, brushing past me on the way to the kitchen. She opens up the fridge and pours the last of a bottle of orange juice in a glass before reaching for the handle of cheap vodka on the Formica countertop.

There's a knock on the screen door. Grandpa comes in. "Hello, Brenda."

"Norman, good morning," she doesn't waste any time, "When you get to the Muldrow exit, go north on the main road. You'll see it. Just ask for more directions when you get to a gas station."

"Great!" I say.

"Thanks," Grandpa says.

"Taking up cockfighting now, Norm?" she asks.

I answer for him like it's the most important mission in the world. "We've gotta find Loo's dad to make sure he can go to Florida with us."

"Taking the little Asian boy, huh?" she asks.

"They've got some big plans cooked up," Grandpa says, "think Kenny is going to spoil them, let them eat junk food and play arcade games all day."

"He probably will," Brenda says. "Tell him I said hi."

"Will do."

THE COCKFIGHTS

"Gallo Del Cielo"- Jason Boland and the Stragglers

We pulled off the interstate in Muldrow, Oklahoma, stopped at the first gas station, and Grandpa got directions from the clerk. Cockfighting, back then, wasn't a clandestine, secret-password thing like it is nowadays. Grandpa even mentioned they used to fight them all over the place in California when he was a kid like it was no big deal, like going to hobbyist RC car races.

The directions were easy to follow. We pulled onto a nicer gravel road, and quickly thereafter we saw grass parking areas on both sides with probably 60-70 cars. The atmosphere was reminiscent of a hyped-up high school baseball game.

"What's your dad's name?"

"Van," Loo says.

"Dang Van," Grandpa says.

"Van Dang," I say like he's a dumbass.

"In Vietnam the surname is first," he says.

"Really?" I asked Loo with a whip of the head.

"Yeah, but in America we do it like Americans," he says.

You learn something new every day.

We get out of the Galaxy and walk through trampled, dusty tall-grass, heading toward a circle of bleachers covered by a tin roof.

Grandpa led the way with his slightly belabored gait, knees and hips tight from driving all day. His faded red Hawaiian shirt Grandma probably bought for him in the fifties was only partially tucked into his khaki shorts; he missed a spot in the back.

"Go find your dad, bud," He said to Loo.

Loo took off running, excited and nervous, a weird clash of worlds for him.

The bleachers surrounded several circular cinder block pits in the ground. The cinder blocks were stacked three high with poles stuck in to hold up eight feet of chicken wire that folded in at the top to nearly form a dome.

Two small, portable sheds stood outside the arena about 10 ft apart, one a concession stand full of candy bars, chips, hot dogs, and canned soda, the other for placing bets.

We walk up into the bleachers filled with people from all over Western Arkansas and Eastern Oklahoma, but distinctly either rednecks or Vietnamese. We were getting funny looks.

Loo spotted his dad and ran up to him, speaking in Vietnamese. Grandpa and I slowly made our way up to him. Scar sat nearby clad in shorts and flip-flops, sunglasses on, smoking a cigarette, relaxed, feet propped up on the row in front and his arms extended along the bleacher behind him.

"Any luck?" was the first thing Grandpa said to him.

Van stood up and nodded affirmatively. "Yes, good day. Thank you."

"It's been a while since I've been to a cockfight. They haven't changed much in 50 years," Grandpa says. Van doesn't know what to say about that so he shakes his head and smiles.

"Mr. Dang, your son here wants to accompany my grandson and me to my son's house for a couple weeks. They want to play a new video game system or something. They said it was all right with you. But I thought I should hear it myself." Grandpa said. Chickens erupted into squawking, and the spectators started screaming. Despite the cacophony, I was focused on my embarrassment that he used the word "accompany."

"Fine. Fine," Van said as he peeked at the action of two game cocks fighting to the death, simultaneously ashamed to have broken focus with Grandpa. Van, fighting to get his attention back to Grandpa, overcompensated and acted super nice about it. "He need to get out travel the world during summer. Good for him."

"Nothing wrong with that," Grandpa said.

"Don't be afraid to spank if needed," Van said.

"Oh he seems like a good kid. Shouldn't be necessary."

"Yes. Yes." Van looked at his Loo proudly, "I gave him some money."

"All right, I guess we'll let you boys get back to it. See you in a few weeks. I'll make sure he calls and tells you how he's doing."

"Yes. Bye bye," Van said.

I asked Grandpa if he would like to stay and watch some, and he said, "I thought you wanted to get to Florida?"

"Yeah, you're right." I said, oblivious to the fact that he probably didn't think this was an appropriate environment for kids. I've always wished we would have stuck around to see a good fight from start to finish.

We start to walk off. Scar, who had been casually watching the entire conversation, whistled at Loo, who came back over to him. Scar handed him some money. "We have good day." Loo took it without saying anything and ran to catch up with us.

ON THE ROAD AGAIN

We raced ahead and got in the truck. "You boys ready to get on the road? Continue the big adventure?" Grandpa asked as he opened his door.

"Heck yeah," I said as he grabbed the handle and pulled himself up and in.

Once we were on the road, it was pretty much smooth sailing. Sun overhead but still in our faces, we remained perked up with excitement and expectation. But by the time we reached Clarkesville (about an hour east of Fort Smith) we were bored. I looked through the ol' Rand McNally and got rankled about how many more states we would have to cross.

Grandpa's company-provided Motorola bag phone was quite the novelty at the time. We burnt through a good 45 minutes playing with that, testing the reception and trying to call people.

After a long quiet period, Grandpa said to Loo, "First generation American, huh? You're more American than me. I was born in Poland."[17]

"What?" I exclaimed, "I didn't know that."

"Yes, sir. I was a baby in my mother's arms when she came here," he said. I just sat and thought about that for a while. It changed my conception of my family. I had never really considered their arrival to the U.S.

It felt like it took forever to get to Little Rock in the slow-ass Galaxy, but once we were there we stopped at a Rally's Burger. It was an old-fashioned place, just a small drive-around building, no lobby, a few picnic tables in the front.

To stretch our legs and get some air, we ate at the picnic tables. I had my burger with meat and cheese only. Grandpa would breathe hard in discomfort at the mentioning of an altered order.

17. The only time I can think of that Grandpa fibbed a little bit. He was actually born just as his mom made it to California, but I'll tell you about that later.

Loo and Grandpa were adults; they ordered without any modifications. No one raised in the depression would get anything special at a fast-food joint, but G didn't have it in him to say no. We had milkshakes for dessert, vanilla for me, chocolate for Loo. The most memorable part of the experience is the fries though. I still have salivating daydreams about the seasoning on the fries that day. Who knew these southerners had mastered the art of seasoning a French fry?

It was a pleasant, breezy summer evening with only the sucking sounds of empty milkshake cups. "Well boys, it's time to get back on the road," Grandpa said.

We drove another hour or so to Cane Creek State Park south of Little Rock, camping by the water. Grandpa put out some Tiki torches and sprayed us with bug repellent. Mosquitoes are bad in the Delta. The water was full of lily pads, snake heaven in our imaginations, so we were disinclined to do any swimming. Loo and I ran around, checked things out. It was neat, but we were soon bored, no classic all-American mud fights or tree climbing.

Grandpa set up his lawn chair and perused through the regional radio stations as he looked out over the swampy lake. Loo and I sat there with him and listened to peculiar talk shows that have since disappeared, rantings too small and insignificant to be committed to memory much less recorded. We toughed that out, not saying much before we found our way to the camper where we laid down to sleep, just able to hear mumbling through the walls. Again, Grandpa stayed up listening. If he was secretly drinking, he was a master at hiding it. I know I wouldn't be able to listen to the radio all night without catching a buzz.

No breakfast. Lunch at Burger King in Hattiesburg, Mississippi where I talked the G-man into getting me and Loo the Burger King Kid's Club special edition, collect-all-four, Ninja Turtles VHS. We both got *The Great Boldini*, a Rat King episode. That was exciting.

The south seemed to whizz by at a snail's pace. I had my head out the window staring into the pines. Loo sat in the middle with his head between his knees, a weird way of sleeping. He really hated riding. Grandpa had to wake him up to shift. Most of the talking we did was pretty dumb, rehashing how cool it was going to be to get to play the Sega. I leaned on that because it was the only thing that excited Loo.

At one point I asked Grandpa if what he did in the army was the Vietnam war and told him about Scar and Loo's dad before he could answer. He listened and explained he served in the conflict on the Korean peninsula where it was much colder than Indochina. Then, I told him about *Predator* and *Commando, Full Metal Jacket, Apocalypse Now* (yeah, I watched all those at an early age), and he explained that he didn't do any of the fighting. He was just the guy who fixed all of those guys' radios, toughing through his exasperation at my overly macho and misconstrued sense of history and the fact that I'd found ways to watch all that stuff that wasn't fit for me.

Florida finally! After we crossed the state line, Grandpa let us know that Florida was connected to Africa before the Paleozoic area when the Atlantic opened up.

Grandpa could tell we were getting worn out so we called it a night early in Panama City Beach. He splurged on a hotel to get us out of the camper for a little while. It was getting kind of sweaty in there. Despite all his travels and book learning, Grandpa didn't realize PCB is a party town.

We stayed at an old, blue four-story motel. We ordered some Pizza Hut delivery. Grandpa toughed out one slice, before he pulled out his crank radio and sat out on the balcony. It wasn't a private balcony, just a long, straight concrete walkway that gave ocean-facing access to all the rooms. Out there you could faintly hear all kinds of loud drunk talk and hollering in the distance. He sat out there on the lawn chair[18] he brought, the kind made of thin, white and blue plastic thread, as he looked out over the gray, waning crescent moon.

Loo and I were inside flipping through channels looking for something interesting, mostly getting nightly news and commercials. Then we started to hear some commotion from girls coming

18. Not dissimilar to the one you're sitting in now.

down the long balcony, escalating to an uproarious racket of laughter. Loo and I scrambled over to peek through the old floral curtains. Their giggling intensified as they approached Grandpa. Until finally they stopped in front of him, one girl yelling "do it!" before several pulled down their bikini's and jiggled their boobs in front of Grandpa and ran off in drunken laughter, supremely amused with themselves.

Loo and I, wide eyed as could be, both doubled over, falling on the floor laughing in astonishment at what we just witnessed. Grandpa just shook his head. It took thirty minutes before we settled down enough to even look at the TV. Because it was funny and outrageous, not because we were little perverts; we were still a year away from waking up every morning so hard a cat couldn't scratch it.

We stayed up watching TV, but would periodically both break out laughing thinking about that.

Grandpa rolled us out of the rack at 9:30. We had a McDonald's breakfast. I've never been a breakfast guy, but he let Loo have as many pancakes as he wanted.

With the sun on our flank, we headed down the peninsula full of excitement. Our big day was here. Occasionally throughout the drive, whenever I would make eye contact with Loo I would move my hands up to my chest and pantomime big bouncing breasts. He would laugh pretty hard every time. I was proud of myself. Grandpa acted like he didn't know what was going on, which made it even funnier to us.

UNCLE KENNY

"Holy Sunset" - Horii Katsumi Project

So, Uncle Kenny. I guess it's about time for a rundown on him. No ifs, ands, or buts, the coolest motherfucker that's ever lived. Offering the gift of easy acceptance, he wasn't particularly judgmental, but he's still the imaginary friend I'm trying to impress.

The first thing you'd notice about Kenny is his long, thick, wavy blond hair. He quit the rock n' roll life, but he didn't let the look go. He was proud of his hair. You'd have to find a picture of him when he was in elementary school to see him with it short.

Kenny spent over a decade trying to be a rock star in Southern California, before moving to the Keys to start over.

His main band, his big shot, Martyrs of Cool, was a mixture of classic California surfer fun-in-the-sun, with a little punk, a little reggae, and a heavy dose of 70s arena rock. They would kind of remind you of a less-talented, less sexually suggestive Def Leppard. Actually, I would say they would most remind you of the fictitious band, The Wyld Stalynns from *Bill and Ted's Excellent Adventure.*

Let's just say The MOC got mocked every once in a while. Kenny's California music scene wasn't the midwestern, indie twee scene of the oughts where it was cute to have a little band, and all your friends would show up and support you regardless of how pleasurable or moving the performance would be. From what I understand, Kenny's band could come off as dorks. And if you didn't have the stuff in that scene, the raucous crowds of young people could be ruthless. Not that the band was terrible, they got gigs and made some money. But, they never got the big record deal. They were never the "it" band. They never had their faces on even local magazines.

Good, but not good enough. The entertainment business is brutal.

Kenny was the go-getter, the bulldog of the band. The one who cared the most. The one who wanted it more. The one who would always do a little extra to increase the band's chances of success.

But time takes its toll on bands. Energy and motivation wanes, and it creates backward momentum, a negative feedback loop. You lose confidence and it shows in the live performance, further lowering morale. Members start to leave and you're forced to replace them with players that are less motivated or less talented.

They did cut a demo with their own money, but those days were different; using analog gear you only got a few tries on your parts. Tape was expensive. So if you wanted to spend a lot of time to get everything right and make it sound polished or extravagant, a rich person had to believe in you enough to front the money for a serious recording session with a good producer. Nowadays, any Tim, Dick, or Betty Sue can labor behind a computer until they get it right. He didn't push the demo real hard, so I don't think he was too proud of how it turned out.

As he struggled, giving it his all, foregoing college and anything that resembled an orthodox career plan, he watched band after band from the area tear it up and go huge— resentful of Van Halen, Metallica, Megadeth, Mötley Crüe, and, more recently, Guns N' Roses, those young California success stories.

A cold-blooded thinker doing the life success calculus could have concluded the Martyrs of Cool's chances were limited when after the first year they barely had any more fans than when they started with.

He did have the advantage of a tech at home. Grandpa didn't care a lick for the music, not that he'd ever go out of his way to antagonize anyone by saying so, but Grandpa always tested the vacuum tubes in Kenny's amp before big gigs. It takes a lot more technical prowess and attention to keep a rock band going than most people appreciate. Having good tech support won't make you great, but it will keep you in the game longer. No telling how many bands have had their gear break down at the most inopportune moments, altering their fate.

A bitter pill for Kenny to swallow, no one pontificates about success like the nearly successful. It's much harder to be special than most people imagine. A lot of things must go right to make it to the top 1% of an artistic endeavor, the ones who are appreciated by the general public, and subsequently rewarded with fame, fortune, and possible immortality. Talent, work ethic, precise execution, personal consistency, interpersonal cohesion, unity of vision, and the timing of being exactly what the public is consciously and subconsciously looking for at the moment. All these crucial facets must align and be peaking at the right time, and the chances are slim. Not to mention, it takes an army of producers, engineers, and organizers to get great music and performances to the masses. The performers are just the tip of the spear.

For the last few years the band and his sense of self slowly spiraled downward toward rock bottom, that phase in life when you hear famous peoples' birth years and quickly do the math, hoping their accomplishments happened at an age older than yours. When you realize another birthday is coming up and you get a sinking feeling in your stomach knowing you're one year closer to death without anything to show for it. I'm guessing and projecting all this; he didn't exactly tell his nephew all his problems.

I remember walking in on him crying with a bottle of whiskey watching *Lonesome Dove*. I feel ya, Uncle Kenny. Been there, brother, been there.

But no matter how rocky his music career or personal life may have been, he was always good to me, always met me with a smile and encouragement. He was too proud and responsible to show an ounce of negativity around me. He would never be that selfish.

Apparently it's a genetic, evolutionary thing that men are particularly protective of their sister's (from the same mother) children, sometimes even more so than their own kids, because men instinctively know that those kids carry their genetic material. There's no guarantee if the children are related to you on the semen side of the equation; infidelity comes into play. Just a little concept to nibble on, doesn't mean too much.

What? I have a lot of time to listen to podcasts these days.

Anyway, his band had done a little summer circuit around the Gulf of Mexico a few years before, and he fell in love with Key Largo. A former surfer and pretty natural in the water, it was time to get back to it. He planned on owning a few boats he would rent out and for various purposes, saving money, and investing in the burgeoning Florida Keys real estate market. He even mentioned maybe captaining yachts and sailing rich people around in the world. Which, by the way, is a pretty good deal. When the owners aren't in a boating mood, the crew hangs out in Miami on the clock doing their own thing until they get called on short notice for a pick-up on along the Eastern Seaboard.

He had mentioned it once or twice without much demand for attention, and no one really took the idea seriously. Then one day he sold a bunch of his stuff and loaded up his purple Nissan and headed across the country for a fresh start. No one can ever say he didn't have gumption.

WE MADE IT

Hammerhead Ranch Motel - Tim Dorsey

Skin Tight - Carl Hiassen

Traveling the length of Florida takes longer than a kid would expect. After leaving PCB, I thought we'd be there any minute, all the long hours through Arkansas and Mississippi would finally pay off. Nope. Our journey was only halfway done. Ugh. Intolerable pain and suffering.

Once we got to the Everglades west of Miami I knew we were close. Driving down 997 has a southern, tropical, swampy uniqueness, but I was too young and preoccupied to appreciate life's little treasures like that.

Finally, Key Largo. As we drove through, I started to realize it was strikingly blander than I imagined. There seemed to be none of my suburban sprawl amenities, namely pizza and video games. It was almost rural, lots of trees with the occasional mom and pop souvenir shop with kitschy anthropomorphized sharks and alligators.

I had just spent three weeks in Arkansas. This L.A. kid wanted to be back to normal. I deserved it. Who knew Kenny was living in some tropical wasteland? But I held off judgment, assuming the good stuff was nearby, further south.

Grandpa had written out directions on paper to Kenny's place. There really wasn't too much to it, just a matter of when to turn off Highway One.

We pulled through a couple of small gravel roads, and there was Kenny's little house tucked away with only a bit of yard that was surrounded by mossy, thick trees. In the driveway: his slightly lifted, dark purple '87 Nissan Hardbody truck with off-road tires and neon blue splash art down the side.

The house was a small, white, two-bedroom-one-bath simple affair with a screened-in porch in the front where Kenny kept his Soloflex workout system.

I jumped out of the Galaxy quick as I could and ran up through the screen door, as Kenny came out. I was so excited and unsure how to show my affection that I hit him in the stomach. He grunted before picking me up in the air over his shoulder. "What's up, you little punk?" he asked as he rubbed the top of my head in a light noogie kind of way.

Grandpa had made it to about the wood steps. "Nice place you got here."

"You all come inside. I haven't sprayed for mosquitoes recently," Kenny says.

Grandpa started on a little diatribe, "You know the reason Florida isn't more settled than it is? Pesticide. Before DDT you had to make it all the way to Key West before the mosquitoes wouldn't eat you alive. Well that and air conditioning."

Kenny and G-pa didn't hug, just said hi. They're like that. We're all like that, except for Mom. She makes it a point, maybe an obligation, to be a little more touchy-feely.

Kenny just said "What's up, bud?" to Loo. He could tell Loo was shy, so Kenny didn't torture him with introductions and small talk.

A guy I didn't recognize was on the couch watching baseball. He just nodded, said, "What's up?" and kept to himself, probably evaluating his new little roommates.

"That's Chad. He lives here." Kenny said.

The brown appliances from the previous decades clashed against the all-white walls. I was a little disappointed that his house didn't look like his room back at my grandparents' house. When he lived there, Kenny would constantly paint and put pictures and posters on the wall; it was a wicked, ever-changing collage.

I scoped out Kenny's TV, a wood paneled 1984 Zenith that sat on the floor like a huge butcher block. My grandparents' old one. It would suffice.

Grandpa said, "They kept talking about this damn Sieko Exodus, Leviticus."

Irritated, I over emphasized the pronunciation, "Sega Genesis."

"Yeah, well, we're going to have to get one, so they have something to do when you're gone."

"Let's all go get something to eat, and we'll go to K-Mart and pick one up," Kenny said.

"You'll have to go to Miami," Chad chimed in.

"Hop in the Galaxy. Looks like the only vehicle we can all fit in and you haven't seen it yet have you, Kenneth?" Grandpa said. The four of us proceeded to pile in. All scrunched up on top of each other, Kenny guided us down the road to a nice little Cuban-influenced roadside bakery between the north and south versions of Highway 1. I was skeptical; Cuban didn't sound like something I'd like. But it turned out to be pretty good. I had some donuts, ham and cheese empanadas, fruit juice, and finished it off with cheesecake. I remember Kenny being real proud of the coffee. Grandpa probably got their cheapest sandwich. He wasted money on his kids, but the man wouldn't spend a cent more than he had to on food, regardless of occasion. I didn't inherit that gene.

Loo and I sat there eating our food as the adults gingerly played catch-up, Kenny explaining where he was at developing his water business, trying to convince Grandpa of the commercial potential of the Keys, hoping he was selling himself well enough for Grandpa not to worry about him.

After that we headed back up the brand-new K-mart, our best shot at a Sega Genesis. Even with what the guy on the couch said about having to go to Miami looming large, we still couldn't help ourselves from getting excited.

As soon as we got parked, I led the charge across the parking lot and into the store. We sprinted around the store like we were at a track meet, found the electronics and saw only Nintendo. In thoughtless, childish desperation we ran around checking every section of the store.

You're thinking "Wait you weren't the one into Sega." And you're right. But by this time, I had completely started living through his desire. "Vicariously" wouldn't be the right word. I had synchronized with him. Admittedly there was probably a sense of redemption after my early fails at connection. And it's just fun to be on a journey. I'm gonna go so far as to say that being committed to a quest is one of life's great pleasures.

The adults didn't mind. They were doing a leisurely stroll, probably talking about my mom and grandma, feeling each other out, looking for clues and subtext about how things were really going.

Loo and I came running back up to them. I was putting on a performance of being flummoxed, jaw dropped, arms stretched wide in indignation.

"They don't have it," I said like I was the forward scout looking for an oasis while my caravan died of thirst.

"I guess we will have to go to Miami," Kenny said.

I was stomping around and pouting like a brat. Loo was displeased, but he'd rather be dead than emote in front of another family.

"You all, lighten up. We'll go to Miami tomorrow. Toys R' Us definitely has them. We'll have a fun trip. I promise," Kenny said.

We were disappointed, but oh well. Getting closer. Our great, Joseph Campbell-esque quest wasn't over. The Knights of Sega must trek on.

Next, G-Diddy supported a little nutritional procurement mission. Kenny was prideful and didn't add much to the cart as we systematically went down every aisle. Meanwhile I loaded up all the goodies. Cereal, candy, popsicles, ice cream, frozen pizza, and about five boxes of Shark Bites. Loo was hesitant. Some old guy buying him stuff didn't feel right. But, I made sure Loo was taken care of. When we were in the grains section I asked him if he wanted some ramen noodles and he said he didn't. He wouldn't eat Americanized noodles.

We got back to Kenny's and unloaded the groceries. Tuckered out, Loo and I sat on the couch and started working on our candy stash. Someone had left the TV on—*The Beastmaster*, USA network.

Kenny and the G sat out on the screened in porch having a father-son talk.

Finally, Grandpa knocked on the door and told me to come say goodbye. He gave me $200 in twenties, told me to give half of it to Loo and that we needed to be responsible with our food money.

"You be good. I'll be back in three weeks or so. I'll be traveling around. You know my cell phone number by heart, right?"

"And it's on a sticky note by the phone," Kenny added.

I had to say it: "Did you give Kenny money for the Sega?"

"Oh darn. That's right. How much is it?"

"One eighty-nine, ninety-nine," I said.

His jaw dropped.

Kenny laughed and added, "And they'll need money for games that cost 50 dollars apiece."

"Good God!" Grandpa blurted. He shook his head all the way back to the Galaxy. You could hear him banging around getting to his little money chest he had hidden away. He came back with crisp bills, snorted, and shook his head. "I played with a nickel's worth of marbles." He handed Kenny the money. "Take em first chance you can. Otherwise, you'll have mutiny on your hands. I've overheard Arty make many promises to his buddy that his uncle would save the day."

We were quiet for a moment and then he said, "You guys take it easy, 'bout time I got out of your hair." He started walking back to the camper as Kenny and I said goodbye.

OH FLORIDA, MY CAPTAIN — OH FLORIDA, MY PRINCE

My ode to the land with the highest rates of insurance fraud and crystal ball ownership

Land of the lazy
Home of the dreamers
Land of the crazy
Home for the schemers

~

Born to want more
Born with an itch
The poorest of the poor
The richest of the rich

~

Home of the chill
No pace too slow
Home of the shrill
No time to grow

~

A trip for the newly wed
A dream for the nearly dead

CHAD

Chad, who had the vehicle that could take us all, was just now waking up, or coming out of his room, at least. "You ready?" Kenny asked.

"Yeah, yeah," he says as he walks into the bathroom. We're waiting on him, resentful, Kenny can feel it on us.

Kenny hollers, "These dudes are gonna kill your ass if you don't hurry."

"I could kill a thousand 10-year-olds," he said as we heard the shower turn on.

"Twelve!" I yell like a dork.

~

You'll get to know Chad plenty, but I'll give you a first impression, a general aura.

From afar, judging by appearances in this day and age, he might be hard to like, his personality a little out of vogue. Hell, his name is a meme. But he wasn't like that kind of Chad. Dude would never put up with football or the military, or exercise even.

If you blended the older brother from the *Wonder Years* with Kenny Powers from *East Bound and Down*, you'd end up with Chad. Or, imagine a younger version of the bad-boy golfer from the 90s, John Daly, who, accoutered with parachute pants and a mullet, lived off whiskey, cigarettes, and popcorn.

You would never use the words "demure" or "understated" to describe Chad's wardrobe. He always wore shorts, mostly jean or jersey, with cut-off-sleeved shirts, ranging in style from Ric Flair and Macho Man Randy Savage wrestling shirts to Rat Rod-esque, you know the kind with a crazy monster guy sticking a long neon tongue out between gnarly teeth, riding a hot-rod racer with exaggerated pipes coming out the back. That is unless he was in one of his many Jose Canseco baseball jerseys.

His ever-present arms and shoulders were smooth slabs of sunburnt beef, not all fat, not all muscle. He was probably about six foot, 230 pounds. He had a dirty-blonde pseudo mullet to match his white-framed Oakley Blades sunglasses showcasing the new ultra-rad orange and blue reflective lenses.

He was ornery, but not a bully. He talked trash, but with a gleam in his eyes. Yeah, if he had a little brother, he'd slug him on the arm and call him squirt, but he was just a dude looking for a good time. His voice had a perpetual tone that he was slightly trying to fuck with you, creating an atmosphere of rascality in any room he entered.

Loo instinctively didn't like Chad. I imagine he reminded Loo of some of the rednecks in Arkansas who were probably prone to using some of the racial epithets they picked up from Vietnam war movies. Loo was thinking, "Man this Sega better be worth it." Chad could tell, but he took it in stride.

Twenty years old, Chad was a fry cook at the bar and grill Kenny worked at, and I guess it just worked out that Kenny had a room to let. Chad didn't seem to have a long time-horizon. Fun from one minute to the next. He mentioned community college, bitched about it sucking ass.

He and Kenny seemed to click well enough. Kenny was always good with difficult people, knew how to find a way to get along, knew how much distance and leeway to give, when to bow-up and make a stand, considering what's best for all parties.

~

Chad came out of his room, ready-to-go with his green Jose Canseco jersey and his best jorts. Sticking his hands in the air and bellowing a Ric Flair impersonation for all to hear, "It is... WOOOOO Miami Time, Tony Blanchard!"

~

Chad Johnson

MIAMI

Finally, we got in Chad's teal-ish, off-green Suzuki Samurai and headed up Highway 1 to Miami. Top-down, wind in our hair, final leg of the Sega adventure. It felt good; victory would soon be ours. Even too-cool-for-school Loo Dang had a smile shining through his sun-pounded, squinched-up face as we sliced through the mangrove swamps.

The older guys were a little awkward. They were still a few days away from being acclimated to dealing with our young energy levels. We were all getting a feel for each other. I was perfectly comfortable around Kenny back in California, but I hadn't seen him in a while; we'd both been growing. But I've always had a knack for finding my way through new or awkward social situations. Loo was circumspect, alert. Chad was like a high schooler you look up to. Twenty-year-olds seem cool, important, and action-packed to twelve-year-olds.

Once we started getting close to Miami, Chad thought he'd prime us by putting in a mix tape that had been circulating Southern Florida: Vanilla Ice's "Ice Ice Baby." The version that set off the global phenomenon was still a month and half from being released. This was a cruder precursor.

Chad was alive with it. I was digging it; good thing I had on my Gecko brand Hawaiian parachute pants. Loo and Kenny were repulsed.

He blasted it on repeat as we made our way up through the good ol' A1A1, Beach Front Avenue. Chad got us hyped up, telling us this is where all the Lamborghinis and supermodels would be. So, when we finally saw a Ferrari Testarossa we unleashed the pent-up anticipatory excitement in the form of oohs and ahhs.

But after that, the adventure ended with a whimper. I wish I could tell you the cruise was right out of our collective nostalgia of the 80s, but all that is a memory of something that never was.

We didn't see any *Baywatch*-esque babes strolling down the beaches in bikinis. Just a few old Jewish couples walking around getting their daily exercise. Lot of construction. But, it was still neat driving amongst the big condominiums.

Loo and I, of course, just wanted to get to Toys 'R Us first, but Kenny convinced us we had to go there last since there isn't a top on the Samurai and someone could steal the bags out of it.

Our first stop was the Miami mall. I had told Kenny that Loo had never been to a bigtime arcade like the Star Palace in Pasadena. He reckoned that was as good a place as any after looking through the yellow pages. I felt a slight tinge of disappointment that he hadn't kept up with arcades.

The Mall of America! I hear it's pretty much one of those ghost towns of a mall these days, but in 1990 it showed no signs of letting up. If 1990 wasn't peak mall, it was close to it. Nothing about this place was rundown or low-key. The arcade was loud, blinking, and bustling. Sirens and flashing lights cut through the cacophony of yells and laughter.

The two big games were *Aliens* and *Michael Jackson Moonwalker.* The coolest looking, most cutting-edge arcade games to be found anywhere in the world, sans Tokyo. They had several of each to handle the demand. But still there was a frenzy, lines forming, trepidation and anxiety over the integrity of the line order. Those guys must have been making money hand over fist. At least the *Moonwalker* was a four-player. I psyched Loo up while waiting in line, telling him he needed to show these Miami pukes how it's done. Funny thing: he didn't know who Michael Jackson was. When it was finally our turn, he didn't disappoint. People gathered around to watch him as players at the other three slots kept rotating in and out while he kept the game alive. There was a collective groan when he died after about twenty minutes.

We got tired of waiting in lines for the premier games. So, we played the less-attractive ones until we decided to wander around the mall looking for the other two. That was fun. Like a big maze. We ended up finding each other, then we walked around the mall together as long as we could stand it. Four boys together get restless. Everyone had had a few stores in which they had a vague interest, just enough curiosity to check it out, but that's a bigger ask when you've got three guys dragging their feet. Chad forced a Footlocker visit. Barely remember anything else other than Kenny trying on some tight-fit colorful Ralph Lauren Polos that were too expensive for him. Loo might as well have been on a different planet. Consumption and style were not on his radar, but he was a good sport.

Much to Chad's consternation, up next was a record store. The highlight of Kenny's trip. It was a small spot in a strip mall. The store was so barren of personality it was an interesting aesthetic all to itself. Just a room with crates of vinyls.

While the rest of us sauntered around haphazardly, flipping through storage crates trying to catch some cool cover art, Kenny talked to the owner about how much he loved the other stuff he'd bought there before. He and the pedantic employee chatted it up about Japanese Jazz fusion until we were staring at the door. Kenny was a dream customer, consuming everything the store could stock. Apparently, he was one of the few people in the region obsessed with the genre. I don't know how or where his passion took off. Casiopea, Masayoshi Takanaka, Hiroshi Suzuki, Jun Fukamachi, T-Square, he loved them all. That day, I believe, he left with Serenade by Takanaka and Make Up City by Casiopea, which has badass sci-fi cover art.

Chad rolled his eyes the whole time. Kenny didn't care what Chad thought.

~

Japanese Jazz fusion was a different world from the California Rock n' Roll in which Kenny had spent his life. JJF was music that he didn't have any stake in or competition with, just an art form to be appreciated. There was no failure shining in his face.

Hey, it's as good a theory as any as to why he went a completely different direction with his musical taste.

~

Next, at my suggestion, we hit a nearby comic book shop since we were all advocating for our favorite stores. Wasn't a particularly remarkable store. I've since tried to find out its name, but it's harder for me to get people to help me in Miami with little artifacts. Maybe it was so short-lived it never entered the public consciousness, or maybe Miami just isn't a comic book town.

Everyone just kinda looked around. I was excited, pulling up various books, but my perusal wasn't as thorough and all-encompassing as usual since we had a Sega waiting on us. I grabbed a *Captain N: the Game Master.* Kenny, however, bought the *Ninja Turtles RPG* here on a whim.

Last stop before Toys 'R Us. I had told Kenny that Loo only ate a certain brand of noodles, embarrassing Loo. "Accommodating Kenny" didn't mind at all. He was excited for an excuse to go to an Asian market. I was like Loo was at the mall: out of place. I didn't like any of the food, but Kenny went down every aisle with excitement, filling up his cart with weird vegetables and sauces. I laughed as Chad made gagging noises after every selection.

Toys R' Us

We raced to the door of Toys 'R Us, but I was hit with a conundrum. Follow Loo and his momentum to the video game section or perform my normal, most-prized ritual of methodically circling the store, checking out every single toy on every single aisle.

I compromised and just did a full circle, racing around the store as fast as my blue and white British Knights would take me, only stopping to look at a *Betelgeuse* mask and Crocodile Dentist. Loo beat me to the gaming section in the far left corner, the end of my circle. Chad and Kenny had just gotten there.

There it was. Loo had already pulled the box off the shelf.

"Does it come with games?" Kenny asked.

"No." Of course Loo had that scoped out already.

"One game each," Kenny said. Then we each started to viciously scan. There weren't as many games as you'd expect. I remember a soccer game, *Truxton*, and *Super Hang On*. Sega was still on its slow trickle into the U.S. We were the vanguard. Chad got *Tommy Lasorda Baseball* and *Arnold Palmer Golf.*

"Two?" I asked indignantly.

"I'm paying with my own money, doof," he said.

Loo found *Phantasy Star II*. Thank God. Poor kid would have killed himself if they didn't have it.

"*Revenge of Shinobi*! Perfect," Kenny had found his game.

I was down to *Altered Beast* and *Golden Axe*. I went with *Golden Axe* because the cover reminded me of the *Beast Master* movie we just watched.

We were all set to go. Kenny paid, and we were on our way home, the big beautiful Toys 'R Us plastic sack in the back seat with us. I think they deliberately messed with us and took the longest route home through Miami, an evening amongst the palm trees.

FLORIDA

"Partly 曇った" - Dan Mason

Various minutia will be scattered through the episodes; the day-to-day will get covered tangentially when I hit some major points, but here is the gist of our time in Florida: peak life, peak human existence, heaven on Earth.

Late June through mid-July, the old Kenmore window AC unit with a faux-wood face roared and rumbled like a Studebaker as we sat, day-in-day-out, in the living room playing Sega, drinking soda, eating junk food, and watching cartoons. Comfort. Ease. Excitement. The planets aligned for our happiness.

As an adult, three weeks flash by instantly, but that stay felt like a lifetime. It takes up a radically disproportionate part of my consciousness. I have entire years I can vaguely recall, but those three weeks, each day, although not especially individuated, make up the bulk of my memories.

I often wonder how different the world, and my life would be if I didn't force our way down there. And, if given an opportunity to go back in time, would I change it? Would wishing it all away be the right thing? Is it all my fault? Depends on my mood. But damn, I'd hate to lose that memory. I wouldn't even tell you this story if this wasn't the best summer of my life. I'm not a sad story, woe is me, kind of guy. Well I may be, but I do my hurting in private. No use bogging anyone else down with it.

~

I was a little disappointed; I assumed our glorious Pizza Hut lifestyle would continue, but Kenny had moved to uncharted land where family-owned shops and unique fare was the standard. Key Largo is still a little backwards, but back then there wasn't anything about it that resembled my 80's suburban America.

No Red Lobster, no Benihana, no Applebee's, no Blockbuster. It was a little wild west of entrepreneurs, grifters, dead beats, beach bums, retirees, people living the salt life. The rules were loose as the weather was nice.

At the same time, we didn't get out as much as you'd think. Mangrove swamps, snorkeling, scuba diving, fishing, days on the water, everything you'd associate with the Keys, not much of that.

We settled into a routine. Kenny worked nights bartending and assistant managing the Wharf Rat, a wooden, seaside nautical-themed, Jimmy Buffett-wanna-be bar and grill that stayed open late catering to people coming off the water.

By day he was working on his aquatic career, helping Big Al, his business mentor, which was intermittent work.

Chad had a mixed schedule as the fry cook at the same restaurant. He may have had some friends he hung out with here and there, but nothing too time consuming or consistent.

It didn't take long for me and Loo to get comfortable with having the house to ourselves. Loo would get up early to get some "me time" on *Phantasy Star.* Since I stayed up so much later, he'd always get two or three hours to himself. He really loved the long-form escapes. I was more into the bonding and camaraderie of two player games.

He took *Phantasy Star* seriously; it was a hard game. He had a pencil and notebook, taking prodigious notes to keep track of all the dungeons and conversation. It was the largest game ever at the time of its release.

Loo got the early TV time except on Saturdays. Saturday mornings were for cartoons. I would soon grow out of this phase, but I had been a devout follower of the Saturday morning cartoon tradition. The mid to late 80s classics were thoroughly ensconced into my schedule. *DuckTales, Transformers, Gummi Bears, Snorks, Muppet Babies, Flintstones, Scooby Doo, The Real Ghostbusters, Pee Wee's Playhouse.* I mean, I'd make sure someone woke me up back in California. In Florida, we used Kenny's alarm clock.

Loo knew how to set it. We'd get up at 9:50 am, so we could watch *Ninja Turtles*. Garfield and Friends, and Bill and Ted.

My eyesight was failing me, even then, undiagnosed nearsightedness, so I lied on the floor with a pillow under my head and my feet propped up on edge of the windowsill to be closer to the TV and the AC.

In the evenings, if Chad was there, it was baseball or weeknight summer reruns of *Magnum P.I., Murphy Brown, Designing Women, Who's the Boss?, Charles in Charge* or that weird shopping cart show.

If I was choosing? Movies. Here are some I remember: *Killer Clowns from Outer Space* (scariest movie of all time), *Ernest Goes to Camp* (Loo judged when he saw me cry during the sad parts), and *Major League* (A compromise to get Chad to watch a movie, still pretty funny). We also wore out the tape on one of our all-time favorites, *The Goonies.*

We had watched *The Goonies* back at Loo's. Hold up, I've got a thought, and this is me reaching again, but I'm gonna let the alcohol speak from my subconscious and say that *The Goonies* felt better, or feels better in my memory, at Loo's house. It's my favorite Goonies house. Location matters. The lighting and color scheme in their living room augmented the experience perfectly.

One day we built a blanket fort around the TV and the AC, hoarding all entertainment and the cold air. That was our own awesome little ice box gaming center. It lasted an afternoon until Chad came home to a hot house and tore it down around us.

The 4th of July was just another day for me and Loo. It was one of the biggest workdays of the year for the older guys. People were on the water all day and at the bars all night. Kenny put on a little cookout on the 5th of July as a matter of principle, feeling bad that he didn't give us a proper holiday. He may have been new age in many ways, but, to him, kids were supposed to have hamburgers and hot dogs on the 4th and shoot fireworks. So, we set up one of those three-legged mini grills, shot off some blackcats, and tossed a few m-60's.

Speaking of food, we ate well. Fried oysters, clams, shrimp, onions, cheesy Biscuits, and mozzarella sticks. Kenny and Chad would bring back as much fried food as we could eat. Other than the Flintstones push-pops, Doritos, and popsicles, we pretty much lived on food from the Wharf Rat.

I can't help but think Kenny was diet conscious; he was vain about his figure. Kenny made raw carrot or broccoli packs to take with him to work, and would make comments to us about our diet being unsustainable, but he didn't belabor the point. Some things just aren't meant to be. There is no universe where the 12-year-old version of me eats vegetables, and besides junk food is cheap.

Everyone was curious about what the specialty noodles Loo brought back would taste like since we made a big deal out of buying them. Chad said something to the effect of "gross, Ramuchan is way better."[19] Loo hated him for that. Chad wasn't too fazed, amusing himself by giving Loo a hard time. He would say Loo Dang with a dragged-out, deliberately obnoxious sing-songy cadence, "LoOOooOO dAAyAAYYaaaNNGUUH," then laugh when Loo would give him a stink eye. He'd even put Loo in headlocks at random times, not mean ones, but uninvited playful physicality. Chad knew Loo was uncomfortable around him, but he was either going to make Loo come around and like him or torture him for not. It was up to Loo; Chad wasn't going to change or let Loo dictate the vibe. Chad felt like he was doing Loo a favor, trying to get him to lighten up.

And Chad always ragged Loo about his plain clothes. I mean, Loo did only bring two and a half total outfits—two pairs of cotton shorts and three plain color t-shirts, purple, yellow, and blue.

Chad would sit out in his Samurai at night occasionally. One time, I snuck up and scared the hell out of him right when he was putting flame to his crushed aluminum can. You young

19. Ramen noodles with a little oyster sauce. Go with beef or chicken flavor and only use half the packet. It's the perfect food for a back-against-the-wall cyberpunk mood in the middle of a humid night or a Spring afternoon *Magnum P.I.* marathon with the silk trees scraping against the windows.

kids don't get it now, but getting caught with weed used to be a big deal in some states. You were an official druggy, "Drug charges on the record."

FREEZER POPS

"Breeze" - Mitch Murder

Freezer Pops, Pop-Ice, Fla-vor Ice, Otter pops, everyone calls them something different, or just uses the catch-all word for frozen sugar products, Popsicle. The ubiquitous accessory to the American childhood; rich or poor, city or country, you invariably had clear plastic tubes full of colored sugar water in your freezer.

My right incisor and whatever tooth is below it are disproportionately worn out from all the freezer pops I've ripped open.

The different brands are nearly identical, but each has a slightly different taste, even when the colors appear to be the same, but that's not the interesting part.

See, I never liked them right out of the freezer--too cold, hard on the teeth. So, I would let them thaw for various amounts of time depending on my discipline and then smash them up a bit, essentially creating slushies. Get this: they thaw out differently based on color. Greens break down into more solid, large crystal-like chunks of ice, whereas reds and purples will break down into a nice consistent mushiness. I may be imagining it, but I believe that if you just let me tongue the ice to feel for texture (with flavor removed to isolate the variable) I could tell you what color Popsicle it is.

Random, esoteric? I know. Who could confirm or deny? A chemist? A gustatory scientist? If you know someone, get back to me on that.

.....And they make them with alcohol in them now. Watch out. They'll sneak up on you.

REGULSKIPIECE THEATER

That's what Kenny would call Thursday nights, his night off from the Wharf Rat when he would carefully select a film for us all to watch.

During our first trip to Miami, he bought the *Ninja Turtles* role playing game. He wanted all of us to try it. "Dungeons & Dragons" is what most people call tabletop role-playing games. Kenny had always had a nebulous, from-afar interest in them, but never found a chance to play. With us there and my enthusiasm I showed for all the stuff I saw at the Cryptic Cavern, he thought he'd finally found his opportunity to give it a whirl. He picked up the Palladium *Teenage Mutant Ninja Turtles & Other Strangeness* RPG in hopes that using our favorite cartoon might get us more involved. It had a cool look with the Eastman and Laird style artwork, which predated and differed from the familiar aesthetic of the cartoon. It was captivating to just peruse the book. He had our cooperation and interest.

Kenny made big plans for a game night for our first Thursday there. He was really looking forward to it, had plenty of snacks and drinks ready. We got off to a slow start. Despite him doing some homework, it took us forever to get started. My ADHD symptoms wouldn't really let me dig in. There was too much waiting and reading, too much downtime between turns, too much indecision. Loo was too polite to be uncooperative, but he wasn't exactly tipping over the table with excitement. Chad was on the couch watching baseball and calling us gay. Kenny was having a tough time as the dungeon master. He would spend a few minutes every turn going back to the rule book, trying to figure out how to adjudicate a situation. We were yawning here and there, and that was getting into his head. Being a dungeon master takes a lot of practice and experience and he'd never even played before, so it wasn't destined for success. All in all, things weren't going too well. D&D is like anything else in life, you'll get out what you put in. It takes several all-Saturday-long attempts before a group can play fluidly.

Frustrated, tired of rejection, Kenny seemed to be racking his brain for a way to salvage the night. Then he had his eureka moment. He went to his room and brought out a movie for us to watch. We all obliged and assumed our places in the living room.

Kenny gave no introductory commentary or preamble. He just put it in. *Heavy Metal*. From the opening, we sat captivated. The animation. The babes. The nakedness. Enraptured. Enthralled. Enlivened. Invigorated. An impeccable choice for twelve-year-old boys. No one commented on the sex, though. Awkward or perfect? Another life changing moment. We may have sucked at D&D, but we leveled up in cool that night.

He was so proud of himself, he made it a thing. Thursday night movies. Next week was *Blade Runner: Director's Cut*. Hell yes! After that, *Videodrome* by David Cronenburg. Whoa. We had a hard time following them, but the intensity kept us involved. After those, he got a big head from his success and tried to amp up the class and taste with some Kurosawa, *Throne of Blood*. Understandable choice considering the title, but it was just too slow moving, not a good pick for your first Kurosawa. Everyone bailed. You could tell Kenny was toughing through it himself by the way he was looking at his Casio G-Shock and shifting in his seat.

He got the drift that we had our limits, so he brought it back home next week with *Alien*, just the right blend of aesthetic growth and entertainment.

Chad used the opportunity of Regulskipiece theater to talk Kenny into buying him a six pack for the occasion. Chad was interested in starting to drink. Kenny was hesitant to buy Chad alcohol for some reason. Not completely sure why, but my guess is that he didn't want blood on his hands if Chad turned out to be an alcoholic or something, which didn't feel like a stretch, and turned out to be unfortunately prophetic. Anyway, Kenny brought him some Sierra Nevada, one of the few independent breweries operating at the time, back when every town didn't have ten different microbreweries. Chad didn't like it at all. Next time, Kenny brought him Bud Light. If you can't tell already, Kenny always went out of his way trying to foster other people's sense of quality and novelty.

~

If you're thinking *Akira* would have been the perfect movie for Kenny, you're right; it would have been. He was aware of it and even requested it at the VHS store, but for whatever reason, maybe relationship with their distributor, they couldn't get it.

THE DOJO

Kenny was taking me and Loo to his karate class that he'd been raving about, taught by Steve McGuinn, Kenny's idol, a world-traveling, master of multiple martial arts disciplines. You could tell Kenny thought he had it all: skills, respect, cool, success, class, taste, and a sense of humor.

We pulled up to the large, semi-industrial looking, black-trimmed tan building that was McGuinn's internationally reputable Dojo.

The three of us walk in. There's a lot going on, people working the kicking bags in the corner, some people in gis grappling, others stretching. Uniforms were informal, wear what you feel like, which was ultra-modern at the time. Kenny points out McGuinn who carries himself like the obvious leader, dressed in a sweet black gi with a black belt, no undershirt. He waves at us and continues with the block of instruction he's deep into.

I'm gonna say the large sheet metal building was nicer than you're imagining from the words sheet metal. I think it was corrugated tin actually, but do I seem like I've spent a lot of time around construction sites? The bones of it were thick steel I-beams, needed for the weight and impact from the long kicking bags swinging around.

The back wall was lined with tall mirrors. Flags were spaced out about five feet apart above the mirrors. American, Brazilian, Japanese, Thai, and Filipino. There was a ring in the back right, all the punching bags filled in the rest of the space on that side. There was a 20'x20' mat for grappling and a 4'x8'x8" pad for practice falls. The remainder was open area.

The left side of the dojo was a wood-paneled wall that separated the training area from the office and locker rooms. On the wood paneling were pictures of McGuinn with various celebrity martial artists. Kenny had a spiel about each one. Ajern "Chai" Sirisute the godfather of American Muy Thai kickboxing, Dan Inosanto, training partner of Bruce Lee and Jeet Kune Do authority, and Helio Gracie, patriarch of the Gracie fighting dynasty.

But the biggest trophy was a framed copy of McGuinn on the cover of Black Belt Magazine, February 86. "New Kid on the Block: Steve McGuinn brings Filipino fighting arts to the USA."

McGuinn felt like a cross between Jeff Speakman the lead in *Perfect Weapon* and Mark Forrester, the bail bondsman Max Cherry in *Jackie Brown*. If you haven't seen those films, do yourself a favor, ya damn uncultured swine. In the meantime, let's just say he's 6'1" with a lean, agile body for a 44-year-old.

He broke from his small-group instruction and headed toward us. His walk toward us gracefully evolved into an attack trot that crescendoed into a playful, light-contact, barrage of kicks and punches, before bringing me down with an elegant, embellished sweep kick that led his opposite leg to a fluid heel-hook take down of Loo. Before we could even react to being on the ground, he was poking us with a plastic practice knife that he had hidden somewhere.

And then just like that, he popped up, pulling us up with him by the arms, and with a gregarious, infectious laugh he says, "Pleased to meet you fellas!" Then, "Bạn, có chuyện gì vậy?"

Loo is confused for a second. "Xin chào."

"Tuyệt vời," McGuinn responds. Man, he came off as an awesome guy.

He looks at me he says, "Your uncle Kenny tells me you're men on a mission, don't take no for an answer kind of guys."

"Yeah," was all I could come up with.

"You can have anything you want with the right amount of passion and energy."

He then shook hands with Kenny, who had been enjoying the display. "Go get loosened up, do your joint rotations and some jump roping, and I'll get with you here in a bit after I get these guys going."

Kenny bowed.

"Come with me, guys." We followed him to one corner of the dojo.

~

We did some kicks and punches, but he could tell from our lackadaisical and timid demeanors that it just wasn't meant to be. He didn't force the issue. He started stretching and bullshitting with us. Over the sounds of the rafters shaking from people hitting the heavy bags, he told us about how much he loves his stops in Ho Chi Mihn City when he visits Asia for martial arts events.

I asked him what all martial arts he knew.

His pitch and tone for self-promotion was polished. He started in Kempo Goju Ryu Karate, getting a black belt at 18 before joining the air force. For the past twenty years he had been trying to master Filipino Dumog (wrestling) and Escrima Kali (stick and knife fighting) and lately Brazilian Jiu Jitsu.[20]

I asked him why here.

"I'm originally from Wisconsin, Oh yeah, the accent might come out when I drink a little," he said, nailing a thick Wisconsin accent. "I was bouncing around, training, doing seminars, and I kept getting hit-up to work down here. Loved the atmosphere. Loved the lifestyle. Loved the growth potential. So, I set up shop. It was time to put down some roots. Key Largo is cheaper and is in the right spot to give serious once-a-week private lessons to clients from both Miami and Key West, like that guy there." He pointed to the freckled Asian man with a full-leg Polynesian style tattoo. "He's special forces doing a stint as a dive instructor at the Army dive school."

wink

The conversation started to dwindle as he stayed squatted, yet propped up on his toes. He was observing his students. Then

20. BJJ may have been all the rage the past 15 years, but he was way ahead of the curve on this one. Non-martial artists wouldn't have known about this discipline before the Gracies mainstremed it.

a total babe came in, a done-up blond in 90s neon aerobic outfit, looked like she could have cruised to the dojo on roller blades.

McGuinn popped up, "Excuse me, gents." He started walking away, then he turned back to us, "You guys explore. And there's a refrigerator in my office with soda and candy bars. Feel free to help yourself. Mi casa, es su casa."

We quickly found said mini-fridge, full of Pepsi and Snickers. It was a different world back then; even the fitness people indulged in soda. And people weren't as fat either. I'm not sure what the disconnect is. Portion size?

We helped ourselves.

He had a thick, gray steel desk covered in paperwork. He wasn't as tidy as Mr. Miyagi we commented.

Kenny stayed late bullshitting with the guys while Loo and I continued to wander around, getting bored. As cool as McGuinn was, I think the best part about knowing him for Kenny was that the respect was reciprocated. McGuinn treated Kenny like he was a really cool guy. And he deserved that because he was a really cool guy.

I'm gonna go ahead and say that—the beers and the Key Largo Sunset have me loosened up for grand pontifications— that may be the secret of any interpersonal success I've had in my life. If a person can tell you see them and respect who they are and who they want to be, they'll be cool to you.

THE REEF RUNNER

Another episode in Florida I wouldn't trade for anything.

Big Al was a burly guy with a Santa Claus beard and chicken legs. A Vietnam veteran who had been left out in the sun too long, he had cool, low-fi tattoos—skulls and tigers—up and down his right arm. On his left calf, he had a diver flag with a hammerhead shark superimposed over the top. This dude was "salt-life" long before it was a thing. He had those ubiquitous, Wal-Mart blue slip-ons (they were everywhere for a few dollars a pair back then) short, cut-off jean shorts, and a sleeveless western pearl snap that barely contained his pot belly.

He was Kenny's mentor, you could say. He ran Reef Runner, a one-stop-shop for all of a tourist's seafaring needs. Fishing, spearfishing, scuba diving, snorkeling, or just leisurely strolls upon the waves. Not being specialized didn't hurt branding like it would these days, and it kept it more interesting for the proprietors.

His partner, Veronica, a retired New Yorker, would sit in the little shed/shop they had as a storefront, answering calls, keeping the books, and coordinating step-off times, but mostly she read Harlequin romances and watched soap operas on a little TV in the corner.

Kenny thought it imperative to take us out on the water with him at least once, show us his world, who he is and what he wants to be. Loo had never been in the ocean before, so all morning he was a little nervous and shy about it. But Kenny wasn't taking no for an answer. We had to at least go snorkeling.

So, there we were. He introduced us to Big Al and put us on the twin engine catamaran. We didn't get all of their attention; they were working. It was Kenny's job to make sure everyone had fins, a life vest, and goggles that fit. And, he had to get two five-gallon Igloo coolers full of punch ready, one of them augmented with pure grain alcohol.

Clouds rolled over the water, no rain, but combined with wind it gave the day an ominous feel, like a storm was near.

Kenny lathered on the sunscreen, and encouraged us to do the same, talking about skin cancer. Me? Cancer? Ha yeah right. Loo had never worn sunscreen before in his life and didn't start that day.

The catamaran had a sweet sound system. Big Al had several mixtapes he would cycle through to set the mood and get everyone relaxed. I remember there being a lot of Bob Marley and yacht rock. One song though..."Key Largo" by Bertie Higgins. I thought it was gross, but I stumbled across it on youtube as an adult and sobbed.

We got to the reef, and it was finally time to do some snorkeling. I cannonballed in. Loo was scared. He inched into the water. And once he was finally in, he stayed close to the boat. I would swim out a ways then come back and check on him. He was jealous when I told him I saw a big turtle.

Big Al stood at the edge, encouraging him to go out a little further. When Loo got up the guts to adventure he would only go about five or ten feet.

I heard Big Al yell, "Turn around! Turn Around. There it is." I looked over and saw Al point at something for Loo who was kicking around, trying to dive down to see something. Afterward, Loo asked Big Al how many people got to see stingrays. "Not many. Not many at all, kid," he probably lied. Loo was proud.

When we pulled back in, and Kenny started putting the boat up for the night, we moseyed around the docks and parking area. I noticed an old, brown Jeep parked there with a Vietnam service ribbon bumper sticker and a pipe coming through a hole that had been cut through the hood.

Later, I saw Big Al walking to said Jeep. I asked if it was his.

"You bet! My pride and joy," he replied, taking a sip from

his flask.

"What's that sticking up out of the hood?" I asked.

"That's a snorkel."

"A snorkel? You can't take cars in the water."

"Bullshit you can."

"Nu-uh."

"You boys get in the Jeep!" He said as he looked at everyone to indicate Loo and Kenny too.

We got in and started heading down Highway 1. We didn't go a half mile before Big Al saw a snow cone stand.

"What flavors you boys want?"

"Cherry," I said immediately.

Loo, "Grape."

Snow cones in hand, us kids scarfing them down fast as we could—snorkeling will get the blood sugar low—we drove down the highway just a ways and turned off onto some jungle-looking dirt road, more of a trail than an official thoroughfare. We hit a few mud puddles. That was neat. I'd never been properly mudding before. Each puddle was bigger than the next, and mudding's thrill is the unknown; the dirty water could be like quicksand or some other mysterious pit that swallows you whole, cartoon adventures' ubiquitous trope of danger.

"You boys ready for the big one? Hold on tight," Big Al said. We weren't sure what he was talking about then he turned the corner and we were looking at a little swamp that might as well have been the ocean itself. It was a lagoon, nothing that you'd ever think you could take a wheeled vehicle through.

We were scared. He didn't give us any time to complain other than loud whimpers as we stood up and grabbed the roll bars. The jeep hit the lagoon and water started coming in the sides. The Jeep was having a tough time, smoke was coming out the top. The wheels were spinning. The engine roared. Big Al was grunting like he was in a fight. Water to his chest, Kenny was biting his lower lip, scrunching his nose. As we reached the deepest part, the excitement reached a fever pitch. Loo and I screamed and pulled jungle-gym maneuvers to hook our heels on to the roll bars with our ankles.

"Yee Haa," Big Al screamed as the Jeep finally found traction.

That was the end of the trail; we were back on the main road in less than a minute, but our kid hearts raced all the way back to the Reef Runner base.

GUITAR LESSONS

On the days when Kenny didn't have work on the water with Big Al, he would wake up, start a pot of coffee, and read for an hour or two.

Personal suggestion, me to you: try doing that as much as you can. It's a wonderful way to start the day. Wake up whenever you feel like it, make some coffee and stay in bed and read from various interesting books until you feel like getting up and messing around. L.i.v.i.n., brothers and sisters. Especially, especially if it's a rainy day. One of life's absolute pleasures. I cannot recommend it enough.

On his nightstand I remember James Clavill's *Shogun, Fear and Loathing in Las Vegas, Mirror Shades,* and *Neuromancer.*[21] Weird juxtaposition of aesthetics, at home he was "Japanese rainy day," using ancient, stoic Japanese mindsets to contemplate a thrilling, dark, highly technological vision of the future, a smog covered land the color of the static on a blank channel. But his outside life was right out of a Jimmy Buffett song, breezy summer waves under the sun by day and bartending on the beach at night.

Once he was done reading, he would put on one of his Japanese Jazz fusion vinyls while he practiced karate, cooked, cleaned, got ready, or just looked out the window in contemplation.

The rest of us didn't get much of a say in the music choices. He was by most measures a lax, non-controlling guy with little will for the maneuvering and manipulation of others, but he didn't take music suggestions. Kenny felt he was doing us a favor by exposing us to excellence. One of the consolation prizes in the torturous quest for artistic success is heightened appreciation, being good enough to recognize what greatness sounds like.

Chad hated the music. "Retarded ass elevator music," was one of his phrases that stuck with me. Kenny didn't even try to

21. He would have loved Neal Stephenson and Richard K. Morgan. Sorry he missed that.

convince him otherwise. He knew it took a particular, acquired ear to hear the magic.

Sometimes Kenny would hear something he liked on a record and would pick up his guitar and play along. Although he sold most of his rock band gear, he still had a decent two-amp rig that combined both of his worlds, a mix of his California past and his futuristic cyberpunk Japanese vision, represented respectively by his two combo amps, a Mesa/Boogie Mark I and a Roland JC-40. They were ran through a stereo chorus/delay/reverb/ABY splitter Grandpa built that allowed him to combine and switch between the two with varying amounts of delay between them, going from imperceptibly subtle variation all the way to otherworldly, textured width. My favorite tone he would dial in was what I would call "cyber grunge."

But, the highlight, the crème de crème, of his arsenal was his custom, slime green, San Dimas-type guitar, with a Floyd Rose tremolo system bridge, maple neck, and two Seymour Duncan pickups. It was custom built by Charvel when they were just a boutique, custom builder before being bought out by Fender/CBS.

The art on it? Think Trapper Keeper. On the right side, looking at it, toward the neck were 3/4 inch pink squares connected like a semi-translucent glass floor with thin shaded lines of demarcation, break points between tiles. After about six inches, the squares started to separate and fall off. The farther you got to the left, the farther the squares fell. The first few just slightly smaller, recently broken off, by the time the squares got halfway across the guitar, they graduated down to microscopic, looking like they had fallen thousands of feet into a green abyss.

Like I said, Trapper Keeper. I'm proud he was so far ahead on that art. Grandma said there were many iterations of practice for that and that it was just un-sanded wood when he brought it home. Coolest guitar ever. I would stare at it for hours back in California before he left.

~

Cigarette?

~

Every once in a while, I would go pick around on it, but I didn't have the patience to learn. Kenny had already put a lot of effort in trying to teach me back in California, trying to make me his little protégé, his squire, but it just wasn't meant to be. I wasn't a practice routine kind of kid.

But one day Loo quietly asked me if he thought Kenny would mind if he played the guitar. I told him I seriously doubted he would. And for several days he would go back there and pluck on it. Good. I would try to catch some *Denver the Last Dinosaur.*

One day Kenny came back unexpectedly, and Loo didn't hear him coming. Kenny walked into his room and there was Loo sitting on the bed picking around on the guitar. Loo, caught red-handed, looked up like he was in trouble, embarrassed, goose cooked.

Kenny looked down at him for a moment and said, "If you want to be good at guitar, I'll teach you. But, you have to do everything I say." Which seems pretty presumptuous, but Kenny was confident and assumed Loo was interested. Loo just nodded. I was in the doorway watching.

"When I started out, no one showed me how this all worked. I spent years just wanking around like a dumbass. And once I was seventeen and my parents finally got me lessons, the guy just showed me quick and dirty, half-ass ways to do covers. No one ever taught me the fundamentals. How music works. The deep skills that really make a great player."

He took the guitar from Loo. "It will be a lot harder than you think it will be. That goes for everything in life. All the big things from songwriting to kitchen remodels will take twice as long and cost twice as much."

This comment stuck with me and increased my worry for Kenny. Is he actually disappointed with his move to Key Largo?

Are things going to work out for him? But, looking back, it wasn't anything. He had it as good as anybody—hope, and a cool lifestyle.

"First and foremost," he said as he dug out his Boss DB-66 Dr. Beat Metronome, "is rhythm. You've got to have it, and you have to have it deep."

He turned on the metronome. CLICK . . . CLICK . . . CLICK . . . Real slow. 40 beats per minute. God, what an annoying sound. I could never be a serious musician.

"Now tap your foot." Kenny demonstrated and Loo quickly picked up. "Now, clap." Kenny started clapping. Loo followed. "Listen. If you can hear the metronome, you're off. Listen closely and synchronize as best you can."

They did it together. For the most part, Loo picked it up. Kenny ended the training and said, "If you do this for three days straight, five three-minute chunks," Kenny said as he got out a stopwatch for him, "I'll let you move on to the guitar and we'll learn a few notes." Loo nodded. "Just be disciplined, do what I say, and I promise you'll be rewarded. Or you'll quit."

A real gamble on Kenny's part. Most kids wouldn't react to such boring regimentation. But Loo did it. After three days, Kenny, true to his word, taught him something else. He hit an open-string low E and hummed with it. He had Loo try. It was too low for Loo at the time, so they started with the open D string. Through humming and listening, Kenny showed what "in-tune" sounded like. "I was 20 before I figured this out. Add this to your dailies. Ten minutes straight of just listening and humming in tune with this D."

Loo did it. Every day. Longer than the suggested amount, even on Saturdays and Sundays.

Halfway through the lessons, Kenny bought a pawnshop acoustic guitar so they could play together and work on chordal harmony. To a metronome, Kenny would play a triad or 7th chord and have Loo find the chord tones all over the neck. Eventually, Kenny would switch chords every bar for Loo to arpeggiate, trying not to use the same spot twice. Stuff that no beginner, or even intermediate, player is asked to do.

Loo picked up the tonal stuff so quick that by the last few days there they were working on enharmonics, suspended chords and such. It was pushing Kenny's ability to articulate and teach. Kenny went off on a diatribe about how the best musicians in the world are the ones who know how to use dissonance, about how most musicians stay within the bounds, but the top 1%, true masters, add spice and tension to their music by controlling dissonance. Life isn't always perfect; music should reflect that, but the artistry is just adding the right amount of dissonance at the right time. Too much and it's a non musical mess. Just the right amount makes the consonance of the money notes that much sweeter.

Rhythmically, every few days Kenny would add a new note or a new way to subdivide the metronome beat into 8th notes, triplets, 16th notes, culminating in four bar phrases where each bar had a different subdivision.

There was a poignant moment that stuck with me one day about halfway through when Kenny was incorporating fretting hand agility exercise into the metronome work.

Kenny said, "If you do nothing else, always always listen. The more you listen, the more you'll start to hear. Force yourself to hear more even when you don't, then one day, unpredictably, you'll discover more to hear. Listen to see if you're exactly on the note and exactly on the rhythm. You always can be more 'on.' Listen and make sure nothing is sounding that you don't want to sound. The more flaws you find, the more flaws you can correct. No extraneous noises."

Loo nodded.

Kenny followed, "Don't let anything get easy."

A beat, then Kenny had an interesting anecdote:

"Musashi, the greatest samurai who ever lived was staying in an inn one day and a maid brought him a gift from another lodger, a commonplace, indistinguishable rose. Musashi felt the stalk where it had been cut and he knew immediately a master swordsman was near."

He didn't over explain.

After two weeks of diligent practicing by Loo, on a relaxed Saturday, Kenny put on a Casiopea record and told Loo to just play along however he felt like it. Just have fun. Don't overthink. Forget everything I told you. Just play along.

Loo cut loose. It wasn't amazing, but he was having fun, especially when he got synced up with the song.

Afterward Kenny asked him how he liked it and told him, "Doing the fundamentals every day even when you don't feel like it, will make your music life so much better when it's time to have fun and explore. You'll know exactly what you're hearing whether it's in your head or someone else's music."

Then a little later, one day in the truck heading somewhere to get a bite to eat—where? I forget—Kenny reiterated with a random sense of knightly mentorship:

"Have fun, create, dream big. All these tough exercises and fundamentals give you the power to make your dreams and visions into reality when the time comes."

By the end, Loo was already past the major scale and basic triads, working on modalities and chord inversions, singing and playing. Swift learner. Kenny sent him home with an entire practice system as well, a way of evolving the drills as they got easier.

~

My favorite thing to do with guitars and music was get a bunch of Boss guitar pedals and arrange them by color, twist the knobs so that there is a geometric pattern in the line markers, then turn it all on to hear the relationship between the visual and tonal.

JAPANESE JAZZ FUSION

Golden Age of Hidden Gods—Spinners of Infinite Dreams—Harbingers of Happiness—Sultans of Satisfaction—Einstein's of Elegance—Swamis of the Sultry

Few and far between are the people who know much about late 70's/early 80's Japanese Jazz fusion, and it's hard to find any ink spilt on this wonderful era of utterly pristine music. If it weren't for Kenny, I would have, like 99.999% of humanity, never known the genre existed. And I use present tense since the internet has made sure that it will cycle between lost and found, until the singularity when we all experience all music simultaneously.

I've shown up at the offices of both Japanese Jazz experts and Jazz fusion scholars, and they had nothing to say. Maybe if I learn to read Japanese the secrets will be revealed to me. But until then, they only communicate with me twelve tones stacked, ordered, and usually guided by the sounds of a rock drum kit. And boy, do they communicate effectively. Coming through loud and clear.

Rarely any vocals, but tight tight tight musicianship, intricate too. It's just three to seven minutes of the best music they can play. The kind of music that makes you glad to be alive for a little bit.

I guess that's out of vogue with a lot of people, superfluous, maybe even nefarious since they are taking your mind off the things you should be pissed off about and just letting you drift in a bubble of good feelings for a few moments. But let's push this to the absurd. Am I and everyone after me supposed to do without pleasure in our lives until we live in a verified, agreed-on-by-everyone utopia?

Whatever. On with the show. Me, my thoughts, and my feelings will all be gone soon enough. Do with the world what you will.

Sorry, enough philosophizing. But seriously, look up this music. Learn it, live it, love it.

~Masayoshi Takanaka

~Casiopea

~Ryo Kawasai

~Jiro Inagaki

~Katsumi Horii Project

~Jun Fukamachi

~Ryo Fukai

~Akira Ishikawa

KEY WEST

Kenny felt that a drive down Highway 1 was obligatory. Not a bad policy if you ever find yourself hosting in the Keys. It's worth a trip just to watch the cerulean blue skies mingle with the aquamarine, turquoise, and even indigo waters. Coconut palms. Swordfish on the scales. Conches for sale. Salt in the air. 7-Mile Bridge.

However, as interesting as Key Weird can be, there's not much to do there as a 12-year-old. As an adult? Whoa. Those nude clubs...story for a different time.

Chad had lots of gay jokes ready for Key West. No reason to revisit those. I'd risk the ire of a modern sensibility if they were particularly clever, but they weren't. They were middle school tier jokes. However, admittedly, Loo and I thought the new-to-us phrases "pickle smoocher," "skin flute" and "rusty trombone" were hilarious. And I'd be lying if I said they didn't make their way back to Woodrow Wilson Junior High. You live and you learn.

Since real estate is so hard to come by in Key West, there weren't our usual comics and record stores to rummage through. It's all bars, souvenir shops, and boutique hotels.

Chad had recently cleaned up the mullet into something more outrageous. He left a little on top, then a slick #1 fade down the sides except the 8-inch long, rubber-band-tightened, rattail extending from the point where his skull meets his spine.

Kenny hated it, mentioned how embarrassing it was to be seen near it. This made Chad happy.

McGuinn and the special forces guy, Charlie, from the Dojo were going to be hanging out in Key West that night too. Kenny wanted to meet up and have sushi with them. Loo and I weren't upset that we were going to be left at a little New York style pizza place, the kind where you pick out a big slice they toss into the oven with a peel.

I'm pretty sure Kenny encouraged Chad to hang out with us, afraid Chad would embarrass him in front of the guys. And, as you'll find out later, they may have had some important stuff to talk about, but Chad wouldn't be left with the kids.

Kenny gave us some money for the pizza and ice cream afterward; they had a soft-serve machine, and you just paid 25 cents a cone. Kenny told us to keep buying ice cream if he didn't come back soon. He didn't want us getting pushed out into the street for loitering.

Kenny had a sense of duty about culturing people, and, I guess you could say, "optimizing interpersonal deportment." Kenny definitely would have been irritated if Chad was talking more than listening when at a table full of older, wiser men. Very Japanese in ethic. Socially, Chad could be a bull in a china shop.

It's no surprise Kenny wasn't gone long. We had time to walk down to the southern-most point and watch the famed Key West sunset.

I think Kenny wanted us out of there before nightfall. There were hints of "Key Weird" during the day, but I don't think he thought it would be appropriate for 12-year-olds, especially ones that weren't his. It doesn't take too much of an imagination to see how he could end up being cast as the creepy, sexually deviant uncle.

~

Another top-down night cruise on Highway 1. Nothing beats it. If I could bottle that feeling and mass produce it, I'd be rich enough to party with the Clintons.

~

My favorite time in the Keys: the Fall. Fewer people. Lower prices. Not too cold. Not too hot. Shove off into the gulf just in time to hit open water by sundown, turn on some Christopher Cross. Magnifique. Do yourself a favor and book a trip.

MCGUINN'S PARTY

One Saturday, McGuinn invited us to his house for a backyard pool party. You could tell Kenny was excited about it. Funny, it was never mentioned to Chad. Kenny put on his only Polo shirt, a soft-blue one, but he still wore his velcro sandals and cargo shorts. It was weird seeing him without a baseball cap.

I was impressed the moment we pulled through the moss-draped trees. The custom black steel gate was fashioned so that the vertical bars looked like bamboo stalks; steel leaves and vines criss-crossed the gate artfully. It was capped with a metal outline of an Asian style two-story palace.

On a little hill, which are hard to come by in the Keys, sat McGuinn's awesome house. Japanese minimalism meets mid-century modern. I've only ever had the mildest interest in houses, but I know well-done when I see it: multi-leveled, light grey almost white bricks, covered by a dark brown roof, with black accent pieces. The hill was meticulously landscaped and segmented with blocks that matched the house, creating little levels like a rice farm, each section containing an exotic plant or a little koi pond.

Sitting at the top of the inclined driveway was McGuinn's hood scooped 1989 fox body Mustang 5.0. With a fresh coat of turtle wax, the jet-black body and the silver rims glistened in the sun. The whole scene was a thing of beauty, never knew I was a Ford man.

Parking the 4x4 at the bottom, the three of us walked past the car, up a few more steps to the entrance way. Kenny knocked, and we waited a moment. McGuinn opened the door with a huge, pearly smile and brought Kenny in for a hug, proceeding through a fierce shadow boxing routine across me and Loo's faces. Our minds were blown at how close he could come to hitting us without actually doing it. Everyone laughed at his last move, ruffling our hair.

"C'mon in guys. Let me show you around," he said as he stepped back and offered the house with his right arm.

We walked in. It was relatively sparse and uncluttered, adorned with the occasional well-placed bonsai tree.

As we walked past a nice, black wooden coffee table with a thin gold trim piece on the outside and clear glass in the middle we heard the laughter of women out back.

He pointed up the open loft above the living room, "I'll take you boys up to the game room after I introduce you to the ladies." A game room? He was speaking our language.

On the other side of the glass by the pool and the BBQ grill, there were babes. Many of them. I noticed. Loo noticed. And, man, did Kenny notice. There were also a couple of martial arts dudes, including the Filipino guy.

"Ladies, meet Loo, Art, and Kenny," he says to the girls.

"Ah isn't he cute!" one of them says to her friend as they both come up to me and Loo. "The cutest little things," as two toned, bikini clad women lean forward to pinch Loo's embarrassed cheeks. McGuinn smiles ear to ear in his short khakis shorts and blue and white Hawaiian shirt, an extra button left open to show his manicured chest hair. Thomas Magnum would have been proud.

In the parlance of the oughts, you might use the word MILF to describe these women, in the teens: cougars. Toned, tanned, probably getting over a divorce, and living ten-fifteen years younger than their age. Nothing wrong with that.

One of them put a hand on my cheek and complimented my acid bleached pants and neon-blue Gecko Hawaii shirt.

"Yeah, that's my nephew." Kenny said to her, trying to get some attention. She just gave him a requisite, but-not-that-interested smile.

McGuinn put an arm around Kenny's shoulder, "My main

man, Kenny, here, is the future of Key Largo." Kenny blushed.

"Oh nice! Real estate?" she asked.

With no bravado, full of self-consciousness, Kenny said, "No, water activities. Fishing, spearfishing, snorkeling, and scuba diving. Whatever you need. I'm working on my PADI master certification."

"Oh cool. What kind of boat do you have?" she asked, politely trying to maintain the conversation. And by the way, this dark-haired beauty, Tina, I believe is her name, had humongous breasts, and only a little bit of them were covered with cloth.

If Kenny were ever the misogynistic, objectifying type, he outgrew it or kept it hidden. He never said anything lascivious in front of me. He was into women in the deeper way, wanting a girlfriend, someone to do stuff with and share experiences. But those breasts filled Kenny's mouth full of marbles. Anyone with any sense of social cues or, hell, a member of the animal kingdom, could tell that Kenny was intimidated.

Nervous, shy, unsure, Kenny told the truth (ugh), that he didn't actually own a boat and was working with Big Al. The only thing that deflated faster than the conversation was Kenny's confidence. Failed musicians doing odd-jobs and bullshit work trying to get a boat business going don't exactly get the female heart racing, I guess, at least the way Kenny was selling it. As cool as he may have been, Kenny was terrible at self-promotion. So ill at ease.

The performance garnered a slap on the back from McGuinn, "Don't worry, buddy. Talking to women is a skill like anything else. I'll come up with some drills and exercises for ya. With thoughtful repetition we'll turn you into a regular Don Juan in no time."

Dating and projecting the better parts of your personality was tougher back when you couldn't do a little internet check-the-box prescreening to see if you're even in the same ballpark of compatibility.

~

Repeat the conversation verbatim?

Let me think....

Nah, I can only remember how it felt, and I don't have much facility for the nuance of nervous conversation. Any recreation would be exaggerated caricature. Disrespect Kenny like that? For no threat or incentive in this world or the next.

~

I can't help but think these babes factored into the problems that were coming. Kenny, feeling the heat on him, realizing he had a finite amount of time left, that feeling in your early 30s when you start to look at the scoreboard a little more. Seeing all those cars, boats, peoples' second and third vacation homes, it takes a toll on the ego, fanning the flames of desire to make something of yourself and grow in importance and significance. All intertwined with the natural inclination to increase reproductive value.

"Let's check out the game room, guys," McGuinn said to us. Loo and I headed toward the door. Kenny came along too.

The pool table was in the loft overlooking the living room. McGuinn gave us a little rundown about the pool table, but for the life of me I can't remember the specifics. It did look awesome, though— clean, tan felt against dark hardwood rails. The cues were high-class too, dragon in-lays.

Kenny, taking a break from the social pressure, offered to play me and Loo in a game of cutthroat. Loo and I had never mentioned pool to each other before, but we both knew how to play, just like we both knew how to play cards. Kids had more random skills in those days.

McGuinn said to Kenny, "You know who is on his way, so head down in a little bit," before he headed back to the pool.

"Gotcha," Kenny said, looking down his cue, before nailing 14 into the corner pocket. En route to winning, he told us he's good because all the time he killed in bars waiting to play gigs.

Kenny ended up leaving Loo and I to play 8-ball by ourselves.

From the corner of my eye while shooting, I noticed someone pull up in a light gray Mercedes and park right beside the Mustang. I stopped, holding my cue, and watched him as he stepped out of the car. Spaulding Meritacre. About 6 ft tall. Thin, hawkish face, with a nose far out in front of his small chin. Six-inch sandy blond hair parted down the middle.

If you could describe the rest of us at the party, both in accoutrement and temperament, as "sun-bleached, Florida neon," his color scheme was "fold out metal chair on an overcast rust belt day." Desaturated brown polo into off-gray slacks, black shoes.

He looked around, being circumspect, evaluating the house. He noticed me looking at him from the window before pulling out his silver block cellphone to make a call.

~

Loo and I bounced back and forth between the pool and the game room a couple times, dripping wet of course—McGuinn too cool to say anything about it—but, we never bumped into Meritacre.

~

On the ride home, Kenny didn't talk much. I asked him who that guy in the Mercedes was. "Just a friend of Sensei's."

FINAL NIGHT OF SHINOBI

"Drive all Night" - Back to 84

Chad got annoyed when Loo would play *Phantasy Star*; it was just too slow and unstimulating for an observer. Pretty quick it became the routine that Loo would play it when everyone was asleep or doing something else.

Chad's *Tommy Lasorda Baseball* was neat for a little while, but it just didn't stick, lack of replayability, more of a game you'd rent for a night. But out of nowhere, for some inexplicable reason, Chad loved *Revenge of Shinobi*, a game he didn't even pick out. Yet sadly, even at his best, on easy mode, Chad couldn't make it past the second stage.

One day, we watched Chad turn off the game in anger and plop down on the couch. Loo walked up to the Sega, turned it on, and at the start-up screen put the game on hard.

"Oh yeah, Loo Dang? Oh yeah? It's like that, huh? Loo Dang, it's like that, huh?" Chad barked without any serious venom. Loo smirked, proud of himself. With Chad watching intently, Loo proceeded to annihilate the first two stages without even getting hurt.

"Fuck me," Chad says. Loo bent at the waist laughing, as much as I had seen him laugh since the boobs incident in PCB.

Loo had played it before unbeknownst to Chad, so it wasn't as badass as it seemed, but we weren't going to tell him. On that occasion, Loo made it to about level five before hitting a wall and quitting.

The next evening when we were all hanging out, Chad suggested Loo play *Revenge of Shinobi*. Whatever, it was all about the same to Loo. Chad watched closely, coaching, and providing unending commentary about Loo's performance. Chad would pull his hair when he was nervous and get upset and slap the ground when Loo died. For some reason, this game hijacked a weird synthesis of Chad's sports-fan circuitry and the vicarious sense people have while watching an action movie.

Loo lost his last life in the middle of the seventh stage (of eight). Chad fell off the couch onto all fours like his favorite football team dropped a game-winning pass. He was sick. Loo was a little disappointed, not because he took the game seriously, but that it meant so much to Chad.

Keep in mind, *Shinobi* is a hard game. Game builders used to intentionally make games hard so they wouldn't expose the fact that later stages were underdeveloped and full of recycled scenarios and bad guys. *Shinobi* wasn't explicitly guilty of this crime, but unforgiving difficulty was the spirit of the time. To my understanding—I dropped out of the video game community years ago—my people, the Gen X gamers, resent how easy games have become.

Chad stood up and walked around with his hands weaved on the back of his head, thinking, then he whipped around with a big idea, "How 'bout this? When I get off work tomorrow, it's the big night. I'll buy all the snacks, food, and drinks we need." He looks away for a second, thinking about his next statement, "And I tell you what," looking into Loo's eyes, serious as he could be. "You like Chinese food, right?"

Loo nodded, less excited than Chad was hoping.

"I tell you what. I tell you what," a long pause before emphasizing, "I tell you what," he looks down at Loo sitting Indian style in front of the TV. "If you beat the game tomorrow night, I'll take you to the best Chinese buffet in the Keys, my treat, the Golden Sun down in Islamorada, best you've ever had." Chad looked at him like a record executive making the deal of a lifetime, "Guaranteed."

"Okay. Sure," Loo said.

Chad started clapping. "All right. All Right! Let's take this seriously. Get a good night's sleep. Don't stay up all night bumpin' your little pee-pees, watching cartoons. Champions need their rest."

Chad went to bed. We pushed it late into the night as usual. Loo clocked out around 2AM. I always have been and always will be a night owl. I would stay up until the morning, catching shows like *Mr. Wizard's World*, a Canadian science education/entertainment show. Much like *Beakman's World* it has been lost in time; Ol' Bill Nye is the only science entertainer our collective memory can hold.

Despite looking like the kind of dude on whose lawn you'd be afraid to step, Mr. Wizard was both a nice and smart man. It was cool to watch as I fell asleep on the couch with the sun starting to glisten through the window shades.

Nickelodeon wasn't the generation defining goliath it would soon become with shows like *Pete and Pete, Salute Your Shorts, Wild and Crazy Kids,*[22] and *What Would You Do?*

~

The next day, Loo didn't even mention Chad's big plan. I asked him if he was excited for the big night and he just shrugged.

At about nine o'clock we threw in *Child's Play*, then at about ten o'clock Chad walked in with a paper grocery bag full of junk food and six packs of Mountain Dew and Pepsi.

Ding! Ding! Ding! In the red corner we've got the master of disaster! The king of sting! The Vietnamese Voltron! The Asian!..." He loses his flow and confidence and stumbles through with "Alexander...?" Then with full brovado he recovers with the unconnected, "Behold the Sword of eternity!" His antics were always good for a smile.

"Are you ready, Loo Dang? It's game time, little brother, motherfucking game time." We looked at him wide eyed. Cussing was still edgy. It had the power to get our attention.

22. Yours truly was a competitor in an episode of *Wild and Crazy Kids* as well as *Teen Win Lose or Draw*. People always find that fascinating, kinda like the fact that've partied with Pauly Shore on multiple occasions, albeit long past his prime.

Loudly with theater-like affectation, "A champion must emerge," "Some men are born to be kings, others slaves," "there can be only one!" he rattled off random mantras as he could come up with them. "Is that you, John Wayne?" He was trailing off. Then it came to him, the final piece of the puzzle, the Michael Buffer trademark, "For the thousands in attendance and the millions watching around the world, Ladies and Gentlemen, are you reeeeeeeady to ruuummmmblllleee!"

He unloaded his bag, "We've got plenty of candy for pre-level energy. Nerds, Starbursts, Runts, and some grape Hubba Bubba to chew while playing. You need gum like baseball players need dip, it makes you focus."

He pulled out some more stuff. "Easy Cheese and Ritz crackers for some real sustenance between levels. First, to get nice and full, we've got two family size bags of Jeno's pizza rolls. You can't play on an empty stomach. I'll put these in. Let me get showered boys, and we'll start. Loo-egie the Genie, start meditating. The big night is here. Do or die. Pressure makes diamonds. We will fight you on the beaches! We'll fight you on the landing grounds!" He trailed off, mumbling. His bank of motivational quotes had run out.

So, we all sat around waiting for the pizza rolls to heat up while we finished the movie. I distinctly remember chomping down on the pizza rolls and searing the roof of my mouth about the time Chucky is all burned up chasing Andy around the living room.

Once the credits rolled, like a grand wizard heralding the coming of a new age, Chad says, "It is time!"

Nonchalantly, without any regard for Chad's desire for ceremony, Loo fires up the Sega and blows through the first level, perfectly, no loss of life, minimal use of resources.

"Good round. Good round," Chad gets up and claps. "Get some fresh gum," he says, taking a piece for himself before tossing the pack to Loo.

The second level, the waterfall stage was as easy as the first.

Chad sat on the couch behind Loo like a corner man for a boxer. Tips. Advice. Encouragement. Pace management. Loo didn't really need it. Chad was talking to himself.

After the second round we took a Nerds break. Nerds, are anthropomorphic......ah hell you know what Nerds are. Chad told us to open both sides of the container and pour them all in your mouth at once. Like I didn't know that trick.

Level three, in and around a dark industrial airport, Loo had his first death. Chad got nervous, but Loo prevailed. Chad demanded a little mental break, had him go pee then do a little stretch/shakeout while Chad made us all a few Easy Cheese between Ritz crackers sandwiches for sustained-release energy and got some ice-cold cans of Mountain Dew. Phase 2 was beginning.

I'll go Rocky here, a battle montage with ring girls strutting round cards across the ring to let you know time is passing. Snacks after each round. A fresh Mountain Dew after level five, Chad squeezing the lactic acid out of Loo's forearms after six. Chad getting up several times to pace nervously.

About 1:30 in the morning, things were starting to get tense. Leaning forward. Eyes glued. Then Kenny came in. Our focus and excitement caught his attention. He walked in at an angle to see the TV. "What's going on guys?"

"Hey shut up!" Chad yelled. Kenny, wide-eyed, was miffed.

In a subdued tone that suggested to keep it down, I said, "Revenge of Shinobi, level seven."

"Ahh, okay," he said and walked back to his room.

Loo finished level seven; one remained. We took the last big break. Chad pulled out some Laffy Taffy he'd been hiding. Made sure Loo peed and got a fresh drink. Loo switched to Pepsi. Then, Chad gave his final pep talk, something about champions being made in the fourth quarter, separating the men from the boys.

Loo got started and Chad leaned forward off the couch like he was watching his A's in the 9th inning. "Slow down. Focus.

Focus." . . . "There ya go, there ya go. There ya go, baby!"

Kenny came in, towel around his hair, and watched us, amazed at the excitement. "I don't think a ninja could carry that many shurikens."

"No shit, professor! He's trying to fuckin' focus." Chad yelled at him. Kenny didn't know what to say. Bemused, he walked back to his room.

Tension rose and rose; the level was arduous, and the longer it lasted the more suspense it built. The boss would come soon. What would he be like?

The excitement became mania. Loo was feeding off it, playing the best and meanest he'd ever played. Moving forward on the proverbial balls of his feet, aggressively slicing through the bad guys.

It finally came: the fade to black before the end boss. With it, came a collective sigh of relief. "Pause it!" Chad blurted. "Take a moment, relax, grab some candy, but not too long. You can't lose momentum."

A drink from his soda, and Loo was ready to go. He un-paused it. There he was, a rotund wizard with the Shinobi's girlfriend in a cage.

Kenny walked up behind the couch and before he could say anything Chad told him in the sternest, most serious voice I'd ever heard him use, "Don't talk." With wide eyes, Kenny shook his head in bewilderment.

Loo had two lives left, fewer than ideal; the final stage had been hard and took out much of his bank of lives he'd stored up. So, there wasn't much wiggle room. Fighting a boss is how fast you can recognize a pattern and execute an effective counter strategy.

This final boss attacks with spinning hair, an admittedly weak image, but beating him was still difficult.

Loo died toward the end of the fight. UGH. Chad and I

groaned. The pressure was on. “This is bad,” I said.

Chad slapped me and screamed, “Don’t get in his head, dummy.” He looked at Loo, “You got this, buddy.”

Loo went right to the last fight without hesitation or deliberation. And despite the nerves in the room from me and Chad, he executed flawlessly. Whipped the boss’s ass. Chad and I were on the edge of our seats waiting for him to fuck up, but he didn’t. His precision was almost anti-climatic; it took out all the drama.

He won! Fade to black..

Then, A beautiful 16-bit synthesizer chord progression eases in as the Shinobi pulls his girl from the cage. Cut to: the two of them holding each other as a beautiful orange-red sun drifts down through a purple sky over distant hills. We watched every last second in awe.

Then, “You all know that Shinobis, ninjas, probably didn’t have girlfriends, right?” Kenny said.

No one responded. The game reset back to the beginning screen like it never happened. We sat for a moment...

Chad jumps out of his chair, pumping his fist in excitement. Loo doesn’t know what to think. After a moment of personal celebration, Chad peers down at Loo with a crazy look in his eye.

With the swift and fluid motion of a WWF wrestler, he reaches down and picks all 80lbs of Loo up over his head and starts singing, trying to imitate Queen in his own tone-disabled way, “Loo is the champion, Loo is the Champion, no time for losers ‘cause Loo is the champion . . .” Flabby hairy armpits jiggling under his neon blue tank top, Chad starts pumping Loo into the air like he’s doing shoulder presses.

Never-more-than-a-smirk Loo was about to pee his pants from laughing so hard.

I was in on the excitement too. It was contagious. I was jumping up and down pumping my fists, making noises, including the Native-American-homage thing where you make a continuous noise and move your hand on and off your mouth for a tremolo effect.

We started chugging more soda, increasing the pandemonium. But, there wasn't anywhere left to go but down. After the excitement we didn't really know what to do with ourselves. Chad put in his favorite movie, *Major League*, to continue the championship vibe I guess. After about thirty minutes, the sugar and excitement had worn off and we passed out.

What a great night.

~

Revenge of Shinobi is simple and repetitive compared to today's entertainment fair. Don't try recapturing any nostalgia I may have given you. Things can only be the perfect thing at the perfect time once.

THE LAST GOOD NIGHT - "WE HAD IT ALL"

We decided to wait for the weekend for Loo to cash-in his free Chinese dinner and all go together, giving Kenny time enough to get Sunday off. It was going to be a two-movie day.

We stayed up late the night before, slept in, and farted around at a Sunday pace. In the afternoon, we all hopped in the Samurai and headed on down to Islamorada. We'd flipped open the newspaper of the Keys the day before and put together a game plan. They were going to see *Days of Thunder* while we watched *Jetsons the Movie*. Then, we would eat before coming back for *Total Recall* as a group.

Before we left, Chad brought out a surprise, a little green Oakland A's Jose Canseco jersey tee. He tossed it in Loo's face. Loo pulled it off his face and didn't know what to do from there. He held it in his lap and looked forward.

"Put it on, jizz breath," Chad said to break Loo's awkwardness. Loo fought to get in it real quick and never mentioned the shirt or his feelings about it, but for the next few days I bombarded everyone with Raphael's pseudo-Brooklyn, Andrew Dice Clay voice: "What's this, a Jose Canseco bat? Tell me you didn't pay money for this."

We made it down to Islamorada.

I love the aesthetic of The Jetsons, the space rocker heartthrob and the colors. It really reflects the era, but there wasn't too much to say about it as we stood out by the Suzuki waiting for their movie to finish, before realizing we might have time to squeeze in a few games at the arcade.

The ol' Theatre 5 didn't have fresh games. Just two off in the dimly lit corner collecting quarters from kids who would play any game they had. Makes business sense. I think they had *Spy*

Hunter and *Kung Fu Master*, from the early-mid 80s, utter relics to us. Might as well have been from the stone age. Funny, I wouldn't be able to tell the difference between modern games and 2014 games. Age and time perception are non-linear, or something.

Before we could pump too many quarters in, Chad and Kenny came trickling out of the doors with a handful of fellow patrons. "Let's go fuckbags! I'm starving," Chad said with characteristic gusto.

~

We could barely walk out of the restaurant we were so stuffed on egg rolls and cream cheese wontons. Crashing from the gallons of extra-syrupy fountain Mountain Dew, we were drowsy enough to fall asleep right there on the concrete. We hadn't eaten anything but candy up to that point, and that had been awhile. Loo and I finished our Starbursts before the *Back to the Future 3* preview was over. Chad, on three different occasions, God bless him, asked the staff to make more fried wontons. Even Kenny indulged in all the bad stuff, albeit he did leave room for some beef and broccoli.

Kenny, priming us, trying to get us excited about *Total Recall*, gave a loose commentary, barely heard over the sounds of our gormandizing, about Philip K. Dick, ramblings about dystopian futures where the lines between humans, technology, commerce, and power all begin to blur and merge. What is a mind? What is human? What is the truth? What are memories?

The walk out into the parking lot to the Samurai, while still belabored, became beautiful at the same time. Our bodies, tired from overindulgence, moved at the perfectly slow pace for appreciating the magnificent setting sun and the cool salt-water breeze hitting our faces.

There was something unifying about the walk. In our own weird, inverse way, we were like a group of warriors or athletes walking from the fields of strife in a brotherhood.

When it was all said and done, I don't think he would have admitted it, but Loo felt like one of the guys. Like he had friends. His people. His gang. His heterogeneous mixture that was greater than the sum of its parts. I may be projecting my sentimentality on the moment, or just plain wishful thinking, but he was as comfortable as I'd ever seen him.

Fortunately, thank God, I didn't address it. I embraced it. I let it be. His cat-like personality wouldn't allow him to be part of something labeled.

"To name something is to kill it." Nietzsche maybe?

HAWAIIAN SHIRTS

I use the phrase "Hawaiian shirt" generically. Aloha Shirt is the more accurate term, I believe. And to some, they, this 1930s vacation craze that evolved from Hawaiian farmer clothes melding with Japanese garment craftsmanship until they were a worldwide phenomenon in 1950s, are all the same, but they're not.[23] There is an ever-changing hierarchy to Hawaiian shirts with no way to truly demarcate between a great Hawaiian shirt and a mediocre one, but it's like porn, you know it when you see it. Some factors to consider: tone, saturation, texture, fabric quality, and the appeal of the graphic itself. Some just have "it," and you're baffled you ever wore anything else.

Ah, and the day matters as well, confusing things unfortunately. Just the other afternoon I looked through my duffel bag to grab one for the day, and my ol' standby just didn't feel right. Something about the mood, something about the weather, it just wasn't meant to be. It might go back to Wabi-sabi; each moment has its perfect shirt. The look that was perfect last week just doesn't jive today.

Be on the lookout, try out various kinds, and you'll start to develop your own taste. Taking chances with online buys is a necessity, but you can never know if a shirt is the one until you've tried it on and given it a spin out in the sun.

~

Movie style and cultural aesthetics come and go, but the Hawaiian shirt guy or gal is in all movies, across time. Sometimes the criminal, sometimes the hero, but never nervous or high strung, always cool. Somewhere, in spirit, he or she has sand in the toes and the trade winds in the hair.

~

23. Dale Hope has a book on the Aloha shirt. Their history is long and complex with tidal-wave like surges in demand.

Don't even think about buying me one. It would be like buying me a guitar; I know what I want and anything else just won't do.

ASKING TO STAY

"Good Morning America" - 猫シ Corp

On the way back, waning moon above us, we were feeling good with our faces against the cool, saltwater-fresh night air.

I leaned up close to speak over the wind, and asked Kenny if we could stay a few more days. It surprised him. A brief hesitation. I could sense it was a disruption to his plans, but he adjusted and acted enthused. "Sure thing, man! As long as you want. You can live here for all I care."

My eyes opened wide with possibility.

"I'm kidding. They would never go for that. You're lucky you got here at all," he said.

He was right. I wasn't going to push my luck. I looked over at Loo and said we're going to stay a few more days. Didn't seem to bother him a bit.

It was a good night.

The next day I called and begged for a week extension. "Please, please, please." He didn't have the heart to say no. He breathed hard for a second and asked to talk to Kenny to confirm it.

~

I may have messed up Kenny's vibe, his rhythm that summer; I know I wouldn't have liked that when I was 30, but he was conscientious enough to make sure he didn't show it. I think, though, on the whole, he enjoyed us, liked to see himself as a mentor, having people who paid attention to what he had to say.

I might go as far as saying that having me and Loo around gave him some clarity of mission. In a world full of doubts, uncertainties, and ambiguities, giving some kids a good time was a no brainer, work that you could be proud of, work that wouldn't leave you disappointed when looking in the mirror.

Kenny was a hard worker, always trying to do the little things to tip the scales in favor of his success. But "The journey to paradise is paradise." I heard that the other day. I think we had our own little slice.

MONDAY, JULY 17TH

A day that will live in infamy.

It started like any other. Waking up late, seeing what was on TV or playing video games. When I finally wiped the sleep out of my eyes and crawled out of my pallet behind the couch, Loo was already working on his *Phantasy Star* account. So, I got up, cracked open a Pepsi, and poured some Fruity Pebbles. Loo already had some Count Chocula, his brand of the week. Chad was at work.

Surprisingly, Kenny barged in through the front door like he had been up for hours. No music. No coffee. No reading. His routine was totally off and unrelaxed. Acting real weird, antsy, coming in and out of his room. At one point, he went outside and tried to meditate. I hadn't noticed him trying to meditate before.

The next time I looked out the window he was doing some stretching and jogging in place. I checked again and he was gone. Whatever. I flipped through the *Time Masters* #6 I bought in Miami while Loo played the Sega.

I wasn't feeling it. My impulses sent me to Kenny's room, and I grabbed the book stack off his nightstand, brought them into the living room, and settled on *Neuromancer* by William Gibson. It reached out to me every time I saw it. But on each occasion, I'd give up before the first page was over. But I desperately wanted to be into it.

After an hour or so, Kenny comes back covered in sweat. He'd been on a run. He storms through the door. Looking around, inspecting the state of his house, looking at fast food cups and soda cans we'd left on the table, "What the fuck! Why don't you two assholes ever pick up after yourselves?" He starts picking up all the trash to make us feel bad, then he rips off a paper towel to wipe up the milk drops and cereal crumbs.

"Fucking Goddamnit!" He says as he throws the paper towels in the trash. Loo and I didn't know what to do. We were too dumbfounded to help out, didn't want to get in his way as he stomped around talking mean under his breath. "Fucking Chad!" he says as he picks up clothes off the hallway floor. "No pride in his personal domicile."

Loo and I both look at each other like what's his deal? He hadn't had a word of admonishment for either of us all summer.

Then he comes back in and saw his books strewn about haphazardly on the floor at the edge of the couch. "I don't mind you reading my books. I encourage it! But don't disrespect them by leaving them around to get stomped and spilled on." He points a finger at me.

"All right," I mumble as he picks up his books and takes them back into his room before going into the bathroom and slamming the door. Loo and I start to do dishes and clean as the hum of the shower permeates the house. We clean until we can't find anything else to clean.

Loo gets back to his *Phantasy Star* campaign as I sit and watch. Kenny, clean-shaven, wet hair, comes and sits down on the couch. He doesn't say anything. He stares at the TV as Loo plays.

"You wanna watch something?" I ask Kenny.

"Nah," he responds.

Loo senses the awkwardness and gets self-conscious about being the center of attention. He turns off the Sega. I take control of the TV and just flip through the channels, nothing but commercials and unappealing content. Kenny keeps looking at his Casio. He finally gets up, walks out, and drives off.

So, I throw in the *Bill and Ted's Excellent Adventure* tape we rented the day before, glad to finally watch it since Kenny didn't care for it, his California resentment shining through, particularly since it glamourized the California suburban rocker stereotype.

Loo isn't feeling it either. He went to go pluck around on Kenny's guitar.

Eventually, Chad came home and sat down to catch the end of it with me. The air conditioner window unit was running low on freon, so it was a little warmer than usual. The best part of summer was over.

Chad had fallen asleep, snoring with his head tipped back and mouth in the air, when Kenny comes back in and slaps Chad on the shoulder, not hard enough to be mean or painful, but not gentle either. "Hey! Let's talk," he says, before going to the door and staring at Chad until he gets up off the couch.

Chad staggers outside. Kenny closes the door behind him.

I'm curious. But I don't get off the couch, until I hear Chad say, "They're fuckin' like twelve. What are you so worried about?"

I move up to the door, but miss what Kenny says.

"Just tell me what's up. This is weird," Chad says.

"I will later. I'm paying you damn good to just do what I say."

"All right, all right."

"You remember where I hide the gun, right?" Kenny asks.

"Yeah, above the sink," Chad replied.

"All right. Take it easy. I'll see you in the morning. You will be compensated, I promise," Kenny says.

"Yeah, but why the hell did you mention a gun? Is this gonna be cool or what?" Chad asks.

"Yeah, it's cool. Or I wouldn't be doing it," Kenny says.

"Okay, man," Chad says exasperated.

"I'm taking off. I'll be back late in the night," Kenny says, walking off.

"All right, all right. See ya," Chad finishes.

When I hear Chad put his hand on the screen door, I hop back to the couch and pretend I didn't hear anything.

Chad sits down. Running his hand through his hair, it's obvious that Kenny's anxious energy transferred to Chad. He took over the TV and put it on WGN, and we watched the homestretch of the Cubs beating the San Diego Padres. The night's vibe was so weird that Loo watched baseball without showing any signs of discomfort.

I couldn't stand it any longer. I stood up from my spot, leaned up on the couch, and I asked him what's up.

"Your uncle and McGuinn are selling a boat or something. I'm not sure," he said. We both knew that story didn't feel right. He followed up, "Some shady people are involved or something. He's paying me to babysit you." Unusual, there hadn't been any mention of paying or babysitting all summer.

WE INTERRUPT THIS PROGRAM...

Chad is asleep on the off-green floral couch. Sunk deep. I'm there with my feet propped up on the windowsill, head on pillows. I had finished *Bill and Ted* and put in *Adventures in Babysitting*, a movie I had watched dozens of times over the past few years. Most people would write it off as fluff, but I studied it during my brief foray into screenwriting and film theory . . . it really holds up. Hollywood does some things right every once in a while.

It's at the part where Sarah goes down the glass windows on the outside of the skyscraper. Real gutsy, a moment of strength in the time of crisis, moxie when it mattered—as you'll soon see, this synchronicity, this coincidence, this portent, radically affected the course of history.

Loo is up in the kitchen making noodles. He had been plucking at the guitar for a few hours. The atmosphere was as lethargic as could be.

BAM!

The door flies open, rupturing the hinges. Before we could even blink, five UZI-wielding guys in all black storm through the door. Immediately there is a foot side-thrusted into Chad's throat.

Loo takes off running toward Kenny's room, but two of the black-clad goons follow him in. I hear Loo scream. Next, he is being carried over a shoulder, his skinny little legs flapping in the air as he pounds his fists against the guy's back. The goon throws Loo on the couch in between me and Chad. I'll go ahead and reveal they were Yakuza, Japanese organized crime.

I didn't try anything. I sat there wide-eyed and stunned.

The sounds of Kenny's room being trashed by the other guy permeate the house.

One of the black-clads reaches down to Loo, pinches his cheek, and calls him something condescending in Japanese.

The foot is still on Chad's throat.

One goes behind the couch. They all have their UZIs pointed.

The main one, without a gun out, standing by the door asks Chad, "Where sword?"

The one behind the couch reiterates with better English, "Where is the sword?"

Eyes red, cheeks puffy, Chad's scared. "I don't know anything about a sword."

Main guy, "Where sword?" He's the one I think was actually from Japan.

"I don't know," Chad says.

The main guy comes up and slaps Chad, "Where sword?"

"No idea!" Chad screams.

The boss punches him in the face. "Talk!"

"They were going to be back later tonight. Borrowing a boat," Chad says, crying. The Yakuza laugh at him in disgust. The one behind the couch throws a belt around Chad's throat from behind and starts to choke him. After a few moments of this, he releases the belt and pushes Chad to the ground.

Chad's on his knees. Face down. Coughing. Gagging. The main guy looks at Chad. He leans down, holds Chad's head with one hand, and with the other hand rips Chad's rattail off.

SCREAMS OF PAIN.

Blood starts running down from the base of Chad's skull. His arms collapse and his upper body crashes to the floor. Screaming. Wheezing. Crying.

The goon looks at the rattail with contempt and throws it across the room.

The same guy kicks Chad in the ribs twice then nods at the other two to help him. They pull him into the bathroom.

From my spot on the couch I hear thuds against the toilet.

"I'm just a babysitter. They left and haven't come back." Thump. Thump. Crying. They're banging his face against the toilet. They call him names in Japanese, but the word "fat" is included. Then, "Where sword, fatty?"

"Please stop!" he screams, barely intelligible through the snot, blood, and tears.

Then the main one and another one leave the bathroom. The other one grabs me from behind off the couch. The main one looks at me. "Where sword?"

I don't answer. Chad's screams fill my consciousness. This is serious. Then, one of them puts an Uzi to my head. Another one grabs Loo and puts a gun to his head.

Fight or flight.

"Where sword? Where Mickgeen?"

No delay, it just came out:

"It's on its way to Master Yamaguchi in Fort Smith, Arkansas. Where it belongs. In the hands of a true champion. Scum like you shall perish under his blade. Sensei McGuinn has a head start. You might as well quit. You won't be able to catch him."

The main Japanese Yakuza guy looks at me. "Where at?"

I look at him defiantly, chin jutted out with self-assurance. "Rad Randy's Cryptic Cavern. Along the river in Fort Smith, Arkansas."

They look at each other and laugh.

"I'm not joking. Please chase them. I want you to die."

The main one bent down and looked me in the eye. He says something in Japanese to the other one who translates: "If you're lying, kid, your uncle dies."

Gulp. I had no idea where Kenny was or what he was up to, but I had to get them out of there. It was the only thing I knew. I muster all my strength for the bluff.

"Leave Kenny alone. Go take your death from Sensei McGuinn

and Master Yamaguchi."

They don't say anything. They just look at me. Then, one of them starts pulling Chad out of the bathroom. Chad just moans and whimpers as they drag him across the carpet all the way through the living room, before throwing him out the window. His face was bleeding, teeth missing, nose demolished.

The main one grabs me by the throat. "You lie."

Through a constricted airway I scream, "No." He lets go, and reaches over to rip the phone line out of the wall. While another starts tossing the TV around. Loo looks worried that the Sega has been destroyed.

They walk out the door.

As we hear their cars fire up, I look outside just in time to see a Molotov cocktail or incendiary grenade— I didn't stick around long enough to get the fire chief's report— tossed into Chad's Samurai.

After we watch them drive off, we run outside to check on Chad.

IN THE LIGHT OF A BURNING SUZUKI

There Loo and I were, trying to mop up the blood coming from Chad's face as he moaned in pain. The smoke, pitch black from all the plastics, streaked into the sky.

"Go get some more paper towels," I blurt at Loo. He jumps and runs into the house. I ask Chad if he thinks he can walk to the main road so we can hitchhike. He responds unintelligibly in a pouty tone.

Loo comes back with the towels. I tell him one of us has to go to the road and flag down help. I quickly realized that it was going to be me. But, we don't finish the conversation. A roar is coming toward us . . . fast.

I stare at Loo like who the fuck can this be?

We look like deer in the headlights of McGuinn's 5.0 as it thunders up the driveway, gravel rooster-tailing behind the tires. He slams on the brakes at the last second and jumps out of the car.

He's all torn up. His shirt is in shreds. No shoes. His legs and feet are bleeding. Scratches all over his head and face. A once-white, now-blood-red t-shirt is tied around his calf.

He's pissed off, approaching with the overwrought gait of a madman. Breathing hard, he looks at us, looks at Chad. We gape at Mac's beat-up body. His chest rising and falling. His lower jaw jutted out.

"What happened to him?" he asks.

"Some Asian guys in all black came in and beat him up. And trashed the house," I say.

"All black 4x4s?" McGuinn asks.

"Yeah," I say, "And lowriders with the things on the back."

McGuinn runs toward the house. I hesitate for a moment and decide to follow him.

As I get up to the door of the house, for no reason other than instinct, I turn around to look in the front yard, a final look at Loo and Chad. But not until I've swiveled all the way back around to enter the house, does it register that I saw a black-clothed thin man in the shadows at the end of the driveway. I whip around to look and don't see him.

I only think about it for an instant before McGuin snaps my attention, "What did they say to you?"

"They were asking us about a sword. They said your name, I think," I yelled out.

"You didn't know anything, right?" he says.

"No. We didn't know what the fuck they were talking about." Maybe the first instance of using the word fuck in earnest that I can recall.

McGuinn contemplates and walks back into Kenny's room.

"We gotta get Chad to the hospital," I yell to him.

"Did they cut the telephone lines?" he asks.

"Yes!"

"We'll get him help," he says, thinking about it to himself. "Don't worry. Did they say anything else?"

I'm not sure how to break the story to him. I'm nervous. "No," I say without conviction.

"Say where they are going?" He asks.

I hesitate, then say, "No."

McGuinn starts walking around. He goes into the laundry room. A few moments pass. I form the resolve to tell him, "I have an idea where they are going."

"Yeah?" He says while preoccupied with finding some clothes. He'd put on a pair of Kenny's jean shorts. The shirt was off his leg, a small chunk ripped from his calve, a bleeding bullet wound.

"I told him the sword is already on its way to Master

Yamaguchi." I say, trying to be strong.

"Who the fuck is that?" McGuinn scoffs.

"He's a great Sensei living in Arkansas."

"Huh?" He asks as he puts on a plain black t-shirt out of the dryer.

"A trainer of ninja masters," I say. McGuinn looks at me like I'm retarded.

"He had a gun on me, and it was the first thing I thought of to get him out of here. I bluffed them," I throw out. I was so nervous. I'm surprised I didn't start crying.

"So they don't know about Meritacre...." he says to himself, trailing off into contemplation.

"Huh?" I say, "Master Yamaguchi is for real. I know him."

McGuinn doesn't acknowledge my response. He continues looking around the little laundry room as I stand in the hallway staring at him.

On his way across to the bathroom, he brushes past me and asks, "Did they say where they are going?"

"To Arkansas. And they said they'd kill me and Loo and Kenny if I was wrong," I screamed. I finally broke.

"They have your uncle tied up in the back of their truck," he says.

"What?" The air left my upper chest.

"Get in the car. Looks like we're going toward Arkansas. I can't leave you here by yourselves," he says, and then thinks, "You better grab his money if you know where it is."

"All right," I say.

"Get any of your own. It might be a long trip."

I go into Kenny's room. It's been trashed. The guitar was used to destroy the record player and the records before it was broken in half. The nightstand was tipped over on its face. I prop it back up and slide out the drawer. Forty bucks. I take it, turn off the lights and run out. McGuinn starts using masking tape to secure a washcloth around his calf.

"You find any?"

"Forty."

"All right. Get some towels and put them down in the seat. I'll lift him up in there," McGuinn says.

I grab a bunch of towels from the closet in the bathroom, then I walk outside and see Loo patting Chad on the head.

"He's gonna load him up, we're going to Arkansas. You've got like five seconds to grab your money."

Loo hops up and runs into the house. I look at Chad a second before putting all three towels down on the seat.

Loo comes running out with the Phantasy Star cartridge and his guitar practice folder.

I start looking into the trees surrounding the house.

McGuinn comes out of the house and says, "It's about forty miles to the nearest emergency room up 1 in Homestead. We'll get him there in twenty minutes." He walks over to Chad, gets behind him, and hooks his arms up under Chad's pits, and, with no concern for Chad's comfort, drags him to the car.

"I saw a man in black in the trees wallago," I say to McGuinn. He stops for a second, looks, and goes back to his task, writing me off as dumb.

"One, two, three," he grunts before struggling Chad up into the car. "Get in," he says to us, putting his seat up so we can get in the two-door mustang through the driver's side.

We hurry up and get in the back. McGuinn starts it up, rips a tight donut in the yard, and blasts down the driveway.

TO HOMESTEAD

"Overdrive" - Lazerhawk

We pulled out of Kenny's driveway and down the street, pure intensity. McGuinn was a man possessed, breathing hard, eyes squinted, nostrils flared, jaw clenched. A high blood pressure poster boy. Loo and I sat in the back on the red, ribbed upholstery. The moment he goosed the pedal our arms scrambled for seat belts.

We were off to the races as soon as we hit Highway 1. Over 220 screaming Detroit Ponies ripping through the night. I mean, hauling ass. To this day, it's the fastest I've ever ridden in a car. At one point I leaned up to see the speedometer. Eyes wide, I mouthed "125!" to Loo.

We settled into a cruising speed of about 115, I'd guess. Loo and I didn't say a word. McGuinn was so pissed. Chad would moan and McGuinn wouldn't even look over, much less give him a word of encouragement. It felt mean, but McGuinn just had too much occupying bandwidth to feel sorry for someone.

About ten minutes in, just as soon as we'd started to get used to our situation, Chad starts coughing up blood, splashing it on the dashboard.

"Ah shit," McGuinn blurts, reaching over, looking for something to catch the blood. The car swerves across the road. He stabilizes it real quick.

"Help please," McGuinn says in the dickish way of someone frustrated. He starts to slow down. I nervously climb my upper body through the center and look for anything to wipe up the blood. I can't get the towel Chad's sitting on to reach up to clean. There's not an extra towel. McGuinn looks at me, disappointed. I look at him, exasperated, confused. He turns around and looks in the back; he doesn't see a solution either.

"Go ahead and forget it." McGuinn says, "We'll take care of it after we've dropped him off." I sit back in the seat, heart racing from my little moment in the spotlight. Up until that day, I never really got put on the spot much. I guess that's what sports are good for.

Once we get to Homestead there's some confusion as to where the hospital is, but we pull in. Your basic hospital. The emergency room is further up the parking lot. It's a lonely night. No activity. No security guards in sight.

All within seconds, McGuinn stops right in front of the entrance way. Jumps out. Runs to the other side of the car, opens the door, pulls Chad out and props him up against the brick pillar holding up the awning.

"Sorry bud. It's going to be all right. I promise," McGuinn says.

Loo and I don't even have time to get in the front seat. McGuinn gets back in, pops the clutch and we burn rubber out of the entrance way. I look to see two nurses and a security guard scurrying out the door. The security guard tries to get a read on our license plate. One of the nurses cusses us while the other starts to examine Chad.

After a mile or so, Mac slows down, tells me to climb up front so I can clean. I crawl in between the seats, use the towels to wipe up the dash and the headrest covered in blood from his ripped off rat tail.

We get on highway 27 north toward Lake Okeechobee, over an hour of intense speed. McGuinn's jaw remained clenched. Loo and I sat up straight in our seats, not making a sound, consumed by the roar of the engine both in our ears and our bodies.

TRUCK STOP

About the time I started to drift in and out of consciousness, a weird purgatory—it's hard to sleep in those older cars going fast, but I was tired— we pulled into a smaller, wood-planked 24 hour truck stop. Somewhere between Orlando and Gainesville, it was a vestige of a bygone era. Not the mega, modern truck stops that feel like a high-gloss shopping mall. This one could have been a set on *Smokey and the Bandit* or *The Dukes of Hazzard.*

But I never got to go inside. Without even a glance in our direction, he curtly told us to stay in the car. He was looking for the payphone before the wheels stopped moving.

I was generally obedient, especially to someone like McGuinn, but I had to pee bad. I tell Loo I'm going. He gets out too. A large gray propane tank brushed against a stand of trees. We go behind it to pee. All the excitement must have dehydrated me, not that I drank a lot of water to begin with, because my pee looked and felt like thick orange juice.

As I shake it out, I start to hear McGuinn on the phone. His tone intrigues me. With my dingy still out, I walk over to the side of the building and walk to the edge where I can hear.

"You'll get it. Meet me in Arkansas." "Tomorrow night." "Fort Smith." "Don't worry. I'll do whatever it takes." Are phrases I hear before he slams the payphone into the receiver.

I turn back around and realize I still needed to pull up and zip my pants. A trucker perched high in his Peterbilt guffaws; he'd been watching the whole scene. Whatever, dude. I didn't have a sense of humor about the situation.

Loo and I are coming out from behind the propane tank right as McGuinn walks up to the car with a Styrofoam cup of old, bitter, late-night, gas station carafe coffee. He's trying to sip it but it's too hot. He cusses under his breath. Then he notices we are not inside. He plunges his head through the rolled-down window before jerking out to scan all around the parking lot, finally spotting us.

"Hey! What are you all doing?"

"We had to pee." I retorted.

He makes a harsh, guttural, unintelligible first sound, but quickly transitions to an embarrassed tone. "My bad. I should have thought about that."

We get in the car and we're back off to the races. He alternates his too-hot coffee between left and right hands as he shifts the manual transmission, spilling coffee on his legs.

He hands it over for me to hold it. "They didn't have lids," he says as I take the cup.

Immediately some hot coffee galoshes over the side on to my arms, "Ouch." He reaches over, while still trying to drive the car too fast, and grabs the coffee, spilling some more on both me and him.

"Goddamnit!" he screams as he tosses the coffee out the window. He shakes his head in frustration and annoyance as he leans forward into his angry-driving stance.

So much for the aid of caffeine.

LITTLE CHARLIE

As the sun was coming up somewhere in the Florida panhandle, I woke up to see we were parked at another gas station.

I sit there confused, still half asleep for a minute or so. McGuinn comes back, puts a fresh coffee in the cup-holder and tosses a grocery bag full of goodies to me. Then he steps out into an open area in the parking lot and does some stretching and jumping.

"Help yourselves," he says, nodding to the bag.

I dig in. It's full of Little Debbie stuff—oatmeal cream pies and Star Crunches. Not what I would have picked, but it was still good; I was appreciative. Convenience stores weren't absolutely packed with options like they are today. To drink, he brought two of those little plastic barrels with tinfoil lids filled with Kool-Aid-equivalent purple sugar-water.

I tried to wake Loo up to eat, but he wasn't interested.

I stay awake for a while after we pull out. Heading down the road, McGuinn seems to lighten up. His posture starts to look relaxed. He looks over at me. "You deserve to know what's up," he says. The sun, sugar, and caffeine have taken a hold and chilled him out. "The day you came to the dojo, do you remember seeing a half Filipino military guy?"

I nodded. "I think so."

"He's the one that drives the gray Ford Ranger with red stripes on it. His right leg covered in tribal tattoos."

"Yeah, I remember those tattoos." Leg full sleeves stuck out a lot more back then, "And he was at your party."

"That's Charlie Waymire, pretty good martial artist, and a Green Beret. He's doing a stint as an instructor at the U.S. Army dive school down by Key West. He'd come up to the dojo about once a week to work on his stick and knife fighting. I've been training guys like him for years. Not too big a deal. But he has a hell of a family story, one that got us on this road. See, Charlie is the son of 'Big Charles' Waymire."

BIRTHRIGHT

With the sun at our backs, entering Alabama, he told me the story of Big Charles Waymire, half of which you've already heard.

~

Big Charles knew better than to say a word about the sword. It could stay buried until the end of time for all he cared. But, Rosalinde brought her ailing mother to the states for hospice. And the mother mentioned to teenaged Little Charlie that he should ask his dad about what he buried. Big Charles wouldn't have any of it, which only grew Charlie's curiosity. He would ask several more times over the years, pissing Big Charles off, forcing him to give an evasive answer. Eventually Big begged Little to forget about it.

Seven years ago, when Big Charles was on his deathbed dying of cancer, Charlie, once again, forced the issue. Charles finally acquiesced and made Charlie promise that he wouldn't mess with it. He told him everything. Charlie asked, "Is it beautiful?" Big Charles said, "I couldn't tell a difference."

~

Big Charles was a guy who'd witnessed the unrestrained brutality and disregard for life by the Japanese at their desperate worst. So it's doubtful he was particularly warm and fuzzy about samurai swords, or even enthused about and admiring of Japanese cultural aesthetics. Not to mention the fact that the Japanese were especially hard on prisoners of war who were tall and redheaded, of which Big Charles was both, sticking swords up the asses of redheads and decapitating people over six feet tall.

I'd hate for him to hear the rest of my story, the parts glamorizing, sentimentalizing the Japanese cultural invasion. Maybe he was so cool and wise that he would see cultural cross pollination as inevitable and positive, the intertwining making conflict less likely? Who knows? I love Japanese/American cultural fusion, but I don't know anyone who died at the hands of Genju Shobun (harsh disposal). Let bygones be bygones? The best revenge is to live well.

~

Big Charles eventually died. Little Charlie—young, dumb, and full of cum—knew in his heart from the moment he heard about it that he was going to get that sword. As someone already into martial arts and weaponry, he fantasized incessantly about the glory of having a Masamune. Getting stationed in Okinawa strengthened his sense of destiny.

Once he got settled into his duty station, he studied maps, locating where his family's home place in South Luzon would have been and then trying to follow his dad's directions through the woods to where the sword was buried.

The First of the First[24] has a high op-tempo, but 'work hard, play hard, hooah' (Mac repeated the Army idiom sardonically) so he got plenty of four-day weekends to spend at his discretion, making several dry runs before showing up with his excavation gear. He spent four different weekends scattered across a year digging up wrong spots. A lot can change over fifty-five years in a rapidly developing country.

No telling what the locals thought of him walking around digging, covered in dirt.

Eventually, he found that a small Catholic Church had actually put a cheap cement pad over it for a basketball half-court, believe it or not, and he had to drive to Manila to rent a heavy-duty generator and jackhammer to bust through their concrete and get the sword. Then paying them again, donating to the church, rather, for their silence on the matter.

"It spread like wildfire, no doubt," McGuinn says after a moment of thoughtful silence.

"Just like his father before him, Charlie got it back to Okinawa

24. First Battalion, First Special Forces Group

acting like it was a junk souvenir sword in his luggage. He says he maintained discipline and didn't tell a soul about the significance of the sword in his gear locker, which would make him unlike any soldier I've ever known.

"Again just like his father, holding onto it made him uneasy. But he stuck to the plan and eventually hopped military charter flights all the way from Okinawa to Key West, never allowing anybody to have a chance at it.

"In his new role as a dive instructor in Key West, he was able to lock it up in the vault where they keep weapons. That's about the time he met me, the only Filipino Du Mah expert in the Keys.

"After a few months of getting to know me and getting nervous that someone was after him, he mentioned it.

"I knew just the man to talk to: Spaulding Meritacre."

"That's the stuffy guy from your party, huh?" I asked.

"Yep. I knew him from my time in the Air Force. He was an officer, just doing a quick stint for the appearances and reputation of his high-brow, big-aspirations, New England family. He is a businessman through and through, though, with a particular cross-section of attributes. As I see it, he is great at networking, straddling legality, and aesthetic sense. Combined with his access to capital, he is a perfect fit for the big auction houses and their off-the-books movement of illegal and contentious items. He gets paid well to remain an unattached mercenary, giving the two big ones, Christie's and Sotheby's, plausible deniability.

"So with as little detail as possible, I talked Meritacre into coming down. It didn't take long before he realized we were sitting on a jackpot. A dangerous one, but a fucking jackpot.

"As we were working out a plan, things started to heat up. Charlie felt like he was getting tailed, and I even thought I saw a weird car parked out in front of the dojo one day. When Charlie came back to see his apartment ransacked, we knew it was now or never.

"For the past week, Charlie walked around with butterflies in his stomach. Meritacre pushed hard on the potential buyers. Charlie would just need to enlist a helicopter crew.

"He had to promise the pilots a lot of money to get the bird in the air, 20K. Remember, kid, it's never about money; it's about how much.

"The plan was for Kenny to pilot the boat. Kenny was going to get 50K. Me, 80K. Meritache was going to get 150, and the rest for Charlie."

"Why the helicopter?" I asked

"They probably had people monitoring the gate. Why not take the helicopter straight to Meritacre? A military bird landing anywhere civilian would look funny and raise questions. Besides, I've trained damn nearly every coast guard guy in South Florida at some point or another, so I had that going for me if we got stopped.

"Kenny was to pull the boat in somewhere random they wouldn't expect. We'd give them the slip and take it to Meritacre somewhere secluded north of Miami. He takes the sword, and it's gone with the wind. Kenny was the person with access to a boat that I trusted the most, so I hit him up. I knew he needed the money pretty bad too; he was being hounded by some credit card debt. With this he'd get them paid off and have the capital to buy his own boat. Me? I'll admit the calls for clinics have slowed down, but my bills haven't. There is a lot of ebb and flow in the martial arts instruction business. Disciplines come in and out of vogue. One year it's Karate, the next it's Jeet Kun Do. One Hollywood star or magazine article can send all the customers to a new style.

"And your uncle eats all this stuff up. He's less into the actual fighting than Japanese culture if you haven't noticed.[25] Just seeing the Honjo Masamune was motivation enough in itself. Once he learned that Tokugawa[26] himself had held the sword, there was

25. Very true. He could quickly compartmentalize and access historical and cultural information, and he could read well. In some parallel universe he's somebody's enthusiastic high school history teacher.

26. Tokugawa is like the George Washington of Japan and one of the central characters of the book *Shogun* Kenny was reading.

no keeping him from this adventure.

"We've talked about making a book about the lost Shinobi scrolls with pictures of me doing the techniques, and if that worked out, maybe a collaborative series of esoteric martial art books. I'll make it happen for him when this is over."

After a few minutes staring into the Mississippi countryside he said:

"Listen. I'm not proud of this situation. I don't like it one fucking bit. But I'm not sure what we were doing was even illegal. No reason to get on a high horse about it. Not in a million years would I want to get Kenny in trouble.

"I had no idea they were going to sniff us out so easily. That's my bad. I underestimated things."

AMBUSH

"Powerglove" - Nightforce

McGuinn continued:

"Kenny and I met down in the parking lot of Flamingo's resort, only a few miles from our spot, a hidden alcove that Big Al showed him a while back. Kenny moved the boat there earlier in the day and hid it in the trees, accessible only by 4x4.

We got to the alcove and we had some time to kill; I retold my stories he loves from Pra Phuttabat studying Muay Thai in '84. When the time was right, we fired up the boat and headed west from Key Largo to meet them about 50 miles out to sea.

It went off without a hitch. Kenny's a pretty good navigator. We got to our rendezvous coordinates ahead of time. We had to wait, but we heard the helicopter, threw out a beacon and they came in almost directly on top of us. I saw Charlie open the door of the Huey, we exchanged thumbs up and he dropped it in a plastic, floating container. Kenny pulled us up right beside it, and I reached over and grabbed it.

Couldn't have gone smoother.

We drove for a little while before I pulled it out of the plastic container. What a beautiful sword. It felt perfect. I'm not a mumbo-jumbo kind of guy, but even riding on a boat in the ocean, you could feel an ancient aura of magic. Your hands instinctively know it's a sword that has shed blood and changed the fortunes of kings and empires.

I even took over driving for a while so Kenny could play around with it. He was amazed, said it was the coolest thing he'd ever seen. We were feeling good.

As we got closer to the beach, Kenny guided us in with the lights off to avoid being seen.

We pulled up into the alcove and blinding flood beams came on from jacked up 4x4s. They were waiting for us. Knew right where we were going to be.

No talking. They just started firing. Fight or flight, my instincts sent me overboard into the mangroves. The boat slid up on to the shore.

I hit the nasty ass bushes and kept going. That's how I got all cut up.

They stopped shooting after they saw me get away. They jumped on the boat and pulled Kenny onto shore.

I heard his screams as they beat him.

~

McGuinn sighed and looked at me apologetically after he said that.

~

They started yelling to me in Japanese and shitty English that he dies if they don't get the sword. I just kept swimming.

I called their bluff, though. They threw him in the truck and shined spotlights into the mangroves, but I was already on my way out. I swam all the way to the nearest resort and ran along the beach to my car. Glad I decided to stop by your place and check on you.

Thankfully they didn't kill him. They would have if they would have gotten the sword. I saved his life with that instinct.

Don't worry, kid. I'm going to get him back. You can count on that.

KAWASAKI NINJA

McGuinn's speed fluctuated throughout the trip. He'd get worn out and let off the gas to about 80 mph. Being angry gives you energy, but it's not unlimited. Then his eyes would squinch, jaw would lift, grip tighten, and we'd speed back up. Crisis mode reengaged.

Right outside Yazoo City, Mississippi happened to be one of the more aggressive moments. We were speeding along at about 105 mph. Then . . .

Bam! Blue lights! Sirens!

"Oh shit, boys," McGuinn says. "Fuck. Fuck. Fuck. Fuck. Fuck." It sinks in for a few seconds. Then, "Fuck!" as he slams the bottom of his fist on the steering wheel and begrudgingly starts to slow down and pull over. I was nervous. The speed limit was 60. Don't they take you to jail for driving too far over?

We get to a complete stop. The officer takes his time. McGuinn leans back and takes a resigned breath like it's all over.

A huge, tall and wide, African American sheriff's deputy walks up to the car. The officer lowers his glasses and looks at us in the back. He's not exactly comfortable with the scene. Two obviously unrelated kids and a wired forty something-year-old. The deputy doesn't know what to think. Who would?

He says something, but his accent is so thick I can't understand a word. As he looks at us and we look back, I started hearing something like a bee buzzing. Within five seconds it's a deafening scream, a falsetto fever-pitch roar of an engine.

...a cutting-edge Japanese speed bike, a Kawasaki ZX11 Ninja, all black except the purple splatter font letters. It wouldn't be released to the public for another six months. It was the most aerodynamic motorcycle I'd ever seen, right out of a futuristic anime. 176 mph top speed.

The driver is in all black with a ponytail sticking out the back of his helmet.

Remaining leaned down, he pulls a gun out and shoots the cop car several times as he flies by at over 150 mph.

It all happened so fast. No one could react. The cop stood there staring for ten seconds before he ran to his car and drove off.

We look at each other.

"I don't think that was a coincidence, Sensei," I say.

"Nope," he says, drifting off in thought.

He gives it a minute then we pull out and continue our mission.

~

What's with the incredulous look? Of course I didn't and don't know shit about motorcycles. I researched it later.

HYPNAGOGIA

We were passing through Little Rock, Arkansas. The trip and excitement had worn us out: red-eyed, unholy-living-dead. "Are you two hungry?" McGuinn asks.

"Yes." I was starving.

"Taco Bell okay?"

"Loo doesn't like Mexican," I say before Loo leans up and hits me on the arm.

"Huh?" McGuinn turns and gives Loo an inquisitive look.

"It's fine," Loo says.

"What about pizza?" I say; I was really craving pizza. McGuinn bobs his head back and forth, unsure about pizza.

"I tell you what. We'll stop at Pizza Hut if you let me catch a nap while we wait," he says.

"Deal."

Like usual in 1990, we had to pull in and ask someone where Pizza Hut was. We get there after some trial and error; it's the beautiful comfort you'd expect. Ultra chill, the place was empty at 3:30 p.m. As soon as we sat down, McGuinn told the waitress that we could order whatever we wanted and that he was going to rest a bit. McGuinn went to the other side, across the buffet from us, and slept in a booth.

The pizza was good. A deep-dish pepperoni. The Mountain Dew was cold and they were generous with their syrup to carbonated water ratio, extra thick and sugary, just the way I like it. Loo and I were less nervous and worked-up than we should have been. Everything was surprisingly chill. Stuffed full of pizza, staring ahead, while The Fine Young Cannibal's "She Drives Me Crazy" played over the sound system. Everything was okay. I heard once that the excessive grease and fat in pizza has a similar effect on the brain as smoking marijuana.

We didn't know what to do with McGuinn. Just let him sleep, I guess. I got some change from the waitress with Kenny's money I had in my pocket, and we took turns playing the old *1942* vertical-scroller. After about twelve minutes, McGuinn gets up, eats the last two slices of pizza, and polishes off both of our remaining Mountain Dews.

"You two ready?" he says as he goes to the counter to pay.

On the road again. The sun was past its zenith. Little Rock was at our backs. The last three hours of driving before . . . what?

SODA TEMPERATURE

So I tried to dabble in some food science and articulate the ideal temperature of each brand of soda in each type of container and paired with different foods. I have various personal visions and facts , but when I really try to drill it down and put a bow on it—a unified theory of soda drinkability— it slips out from under me. There are always more variables to untangle. You can account for container, temperature, and food pairing, but there are still just too many factors like humidity, and the drinker's body temperature, hydration level, and typical sugar intake.

You might be thinking, "DUH," but everyone I've thrown this at has their own opinion, and not just a half-assed opinion I cajole out of them, a full-fledged fire and brimstone opinion, like, "You absolutely cannot have Indian buffet without Pepsi, no ifs ands or buts." Test it; everyone has their own soda dogma.

Picking the right soda is an art learned by experience only. But you know in your heart the perfect soda at any given moment.

~

You will disagree with some or most of these, but here is a chart I've put together:

- Pepsi is more drinkable at extreme temperatures, both in a can and plastic bottle. Very flexible drink.
- Canned Mountain Dew can come down a little bit in temperature, but not too far down. It's gross hot. Too cold, and it strikes the throat in a hard, metallic way. There is a Goldilocks zone. A plastic bottle of Mountain Dew? Cold as you can get it.
- Dr Pepper needs to be a little warmer, just slightly. It's a mellower drink.
- Coca-Cola is the AK-47 of soda. Works in any situation

but never perfect.

- Pepsi may be the best pizza soda. Coca-Cola is also a good one. A pizza soda has to have bite, a crispness. A stale pop won't work. The mellowness of Dr Pepper makes it less of a pizza soda.
- Mountain Dew isn't a glass bottle kind of drink.
- Coca-Cola classic is the best glass bottle drink.
- Root beer is a moody wild card, tough to categorize, but it and Dr Pepper are the go-to at classic drive-in, onion ring and chili cheese coney style joints.
- Mexican food: Coca-Cola Classic
- Indian food: Pepsi
- Chinese Buffet: Mountain Dew
- Italian: Coca-Cola Classic

And of course, fountain drinks are a whole new ball of wax. It all depends on the syrup to carbonated water ratio. Some places, particularly fast-food chains, turn down the syrup, increasing the carbonated water flavor and profits. Most small-town places jack up the syrup ratio to get the drinks extra sugary. This is good if there is plenty of ice, but the more carbonated sodas hold up better as the temperature increases.

THE KATA

About twenty miles west of Russellville, Arkansas, McGuinn saw a sign for an upcoming rest stop. We pulled in. It wasn't the kind of rest stop with bathrooms and an information center, just an asphalt loop that will take you up a hill overlooking Lake Dardenelle. It had a few parking spots for cars and a few for big trucks. There was a little area with two picnic tables and trashcans welded to poles cemented in the ground.

The air conditioning in the Mustang worked like a charm, because opening the door to the Arkansas heat and humidity was like getting blasted with a *Spaceballs* sized blow dryer.

"You two run around and stretch your legs. Do whatever. I'm going to meditate a moment," McGuinn says.

Loo and I got out, but didn't go far. McGuinn popped the trunk and went around to the back. Curious, Loo and I watched him. He pulls out a sword. I had never thought to ask about it. It was with us the whole time. I guess that's why the motorcycle guy didn't stop us when he had the chance. He wasn't sure if we had it or not.

We watch McGuinn as he takes it and walks up the grassy little knoll close to the forest to the north. He sits, legs crossed, eyes closed with the sword across his lap, doing some kind of breathing drill. Too boring to hold our attention for long, Loo and I started walking around the parking lot, desperate for something interesting. We settled on the grass, looked at the lake glistening in the sun, and listened to the sound of the interstate. McGuinn was so serious we instinctively knew not to disturb him.

Eventually Loo taps me on the arm and points up the hill.

McGuinn is doing a slow sword kata, a physical meditation. You'd think it was some kind of Tai Chi. It was a thing of beauty, pure focus as he slowly turned. On a dusty Arkansas summer evening, a Miami international playboy martial arts instructor is spinning an ancient samurai sword in a slow, perfectly controlled motion. Loo and I sat and watched, mesmerized. No one can ever accuse me of not having seen interesting things.

He stops, bows, and starts walking toward the car. “Let’s go, boys.” He pops the trunk. “You two can look at it.” He pulled it out of its beat-up black lacquer saya (Japanese for scabbard). The leather wrapping around the top of the scabbard, Sageo, was purple. “It’s bad manners to look at if it’s not completely unsheathed,” he said as he pulled it out.

He pointed toward the base of the sword at a little chip. “This nick here,” he says as he looks at me. I see it and nod, “About 400 years ago, when this sword was 300 years old, it was carried in a famous showdown between two elite samurai: General Honjo Shigenaga and Umanosuke, a swordsman with many high-profile trophy kills on his resume. Umanosuke carried this sword and he hit the general on the head with it several times, damaging the blade and destroying the helmet. The general ended up snatching victory at the last moment, earning the famous blade. But afterward they had to take twenty centimeters off what was once a longsword.”

He made eye contact with us and slowly ran his finger down the blade. Loo was entranced and serious about the lesson, listening and looking closely.

“It takes a lifetime to get good at sword evaluation, it’s a deep art and science, but the reason Musamune is considered the greatest is the Jigane, the quality of the material of the blade. The steel is both stronger and more beautiful. Look, there are no impurities.”

It was darker, closer to a greyish black than the bright silver you’d expect. People have asked me if it was magical, and even used the words “aura-enshrouded soul.” And the thing is, I don’t know. At the time, with McGuinn talking, I felt like it was the most important item in the world. But, if I go back and objectively think about the sword, in a vacuum with no context, you could have told me it was a fake from a Tennessee junk shop and I would have believed you. But I guess that speaks about my knowledge of swords rather than the sword itself. Some people don't like "What a Fool Believes" by the Doobie Brothers.

We got in the car. The sun was setting in the west, shining in our eyes. McGuinn put on his sweet Ray Ban aviators. The sword shared the back seat with Loo.

After the sun set, we rolled down the windows. "You're almost home," I said to Loo. Then, I finally asked McGuinn what was on my mind all day, "Think you can take him?" I didn't even clarify who I was talking about. We had both switched to thinking about the motorcycle guy. I feel bad for such a gauche question. But what kind of 12-year-old wouldn't be thinking about who would win a potential martial arts showdown of galactic proportions?

After a moment's pause, he says, "Hard to say, kid. It would be touch and go." After we all stare into the night for a minute or so, he adds, "I don't know how this will turn out, but I can promise you I won't let your uncle get hurt."

That was good to hear.

DROPPING OFF LOO

"Time for Action" - Megahammer

"All right, where is a place I can drop you two off?" McGuinn says as we approach Van Buren. "I can't have you two getting hurt."

There is a tricky maneuver you have to make to get you from I-40 to Loo's house. We were twelve. Us explaining and guiding him in was a little awkward, particularly as we could tell he was getting aggravated. But we made it.

We flew through the main row of the trailer park, engine roaring; Brenda was sitting on her porch smoking, drinking, and reading a magazine under the light of her neon blue bug zapper. She looks up as we drive by.

We get down to Loo's and start letting him out. Scar's Suburu is in the driveway. I'm held up. I don't want to miss what's coming. With one hand still on the Mustang door, "You don't know how to get to Rad Randy's."

"Can't you tell me?" he asks.

"Not really, but I have an idea of how to get there." I really wanted to see what happens next.

He bobs his head back and forth in uncertainty. "All right. But I'm leaving you somewhere else."

"Okay," I wave goodbye to Loo and hop in the car. He watches as the Mustang whips a donut and speeds out.

When we pass Brenda's, she is out by the chain link gate looking hard to see who is in the car. I wave at her.

Getting him to Rad Randy's proved to be tough. McGuinn ended up getting pissed when I took him across the wrong bridge into Fort Smith, the interstate one, not the old one that leads you right to it. So, we took a frustrated detour driving around the north side of Fort Smith. I was lost, but, pointing toward the west, I knew it was probably in that direction. He deduced that if we stayed by the river we'd get there, and we did.

That's when things got real, 8:45 p.m.; darkness was finally creeping up.

Across from the entrance way to Rad Randy's was a liquor emporium, Four Leaf Clover. McGuinn parked the Mustang at the far end of their parking lot. He told me not to get out of the car, but if I heard anything like gunshots I needed to hide in the liquor store. He left the AC and the radio on for me before he grabbed the sword and started to sneak toward Rad Randy's through the ancient oaks, the kind that can survive an Arkansas River flooding.

I found KISR 93.7. The River Valley's hit station. I wasn't feeling the Bobby Brown and Mariah Carey. After five minutes, I decided to go see what was happening.

~

Personality test: would you have stayed in the car?

SHOWDOWN

"Chinatown" - The Revenge of Shinobi Original Soundtrack

The moment you've been waiting for, the reason you hunted me down, the big hoorah for which you've suffered through my ramblings.

I'll tell it chronologically, for the most part.

I fancy myself a decent practitioner of the oratory arts, but the layout, the trees and weird parking lot are hard to describe. I'm tempted to draw you a map. You know what, fuck it. I'm going to get a pencil and a piece of paper.

As you can see there's lots of foliage and places to hide as you approach Rad Randy's. And remember it's on about a ten foot tall, man-made plateau to avoid flooding. The western door of the Cryptic Cavern section has a good vantage. Plastic-covered security lights perch on the few electric poles that cross the area kept everything lit in soft green. The dark foliage in the overflow ponds was covered by a patina of dust, creating an otherworldly effect as it reflected the glow from the security lights. It felt like the jungles of Vietnam were blending with West Texas dust, a fusion peculiar to Fort Smith, Arkansas in the summer.

Eh, I might be imagining that; there are plenty of areas along rivers that accumulate dust.

~

I slowly proceed out of the car and across the road. Instead of using the driveway, I cut through the woods. They aren't too thick, but enough to slow me down. As I come out the other side, now able to see Rad Randy's, I start to look around. There is about an acre of high grass between me and the parking lot proper. Then, I notice McGuinn to my right and up about fifty yards, along the line of trees under the bridge. He is squatted, keeping his head at about the height of the high grass. He still has the sword with him. I stop to watch him. He hides the sword behind a tree.

After he hides it, he crouch-walks a little longer until he gets out to where the high grass fades into gravel. There, he stands up and starts walking nonchalantly toward the door.

That's when I notice that three of the gangsters' low-riding, spoiler adorned Japanese sports cars with deep-tinted windows are parked in front of the Cryptic Cavern.

McGuinn puts his hands up in the air as a gesture of peace. One of the Yakuza walks outside, notices and screams something in Japanese. McGuinn responds in Japanese, in a placating cadence. The goon knocks on the glass door and yells. Four more Yakuza come out the door. They walk down and surround McGuinn and escort him inside at gunpoint.

I drop some caution and pick up speed, trying to get closer to the action. Fighting through the briars and brush, swatting the mosquitoes that are eating me alive, I make my way down along the transition between the trees under the bridge and the brush beside it.

I make it to where he hid the sword. I don't know why, but I was compelled to look at it in its hiding place. I wasn't thinking too hard about it, just doing. It didn't take me long to find it. It was in an easy spot. I held it, even gave it a little stab. Man, all that cultural cache makes it addictive.

I hear something. I squat down real quick to hide, then slowly peek up. McGuinn and the Yakuza walk back outside. One of them pops the trunk of the car to show McGuinn something: Kenny.

"AH AH AH" comes from behind me. My heart sinks. One of the Yakuza goons squeezes the back of my neck, grabs the sword, and yells with mirth to the other guys while walking me out of the high grass.

The entire timbre changes. The main one starts laughing. McGuinn breathes a sigh of defeat. The tides have turned. I'd messed everything up. They turn their guns on McGuinn and start talking some shit. He'd lost any leverage he'd had, and the Yakuza loved it. He walked me up to the building and pushed me into the wall. Honestly, it wasn't that bad, but I embellished like a basketball player trying to draw a charge. The main one from back at Kenny's house was there yelling instructions. One of the underlings grabbed some duct tape. I could tell where this was heading.

I saw Kenny bound and gagged. At least he was alive. We lost the sword, but my uncle was alive.

They opened the glass door to the Cryptic Cavern and pushed me in. The place was trashed, all the bookshelves turned over, all the glass busted. Daryl beaten and taped up, blood running from his face. "Hey," I say to him. He grunts, but I think he recognizes me.

I wasn't two feet past the door when I heard the gunshots. I dropped to the floor. The Yakuza escorting me darted out the door. A volley of shots raged outside. After twenty-five seconds, an eternity in a gunfight, the firing stopped.

I don't know why I was so stupid, but I poked my head out in curiosity. Two of the Kuz were down. Another three were working McGuinn over. Several were walking down to the high grass.

Soon they were yelling about a body. The leader yelled back, presumably about the one who got away. I didn't know it then, but the ambush was by Spaulding Meritacre and some mercenary he grabbed on the quick, a dishonorably discharged Marine Raider who no one has seemed to miss.

The merc died and Meritacre made a run for it. The price got too high for him, and he got the hell out of dodge.

The Yakuza were pissed. One of them slapped me and pressed me against and down the wall to the floor. Four of them commenced beating the shit out of McGuinn.

Car lights appear. Everyone looks up and gets their guns at the ready. The car quickly pulls a 180 and goes back out of the parking lot.

The leader starts talking, presumably about what to do with us. I'm pretty sure killing McGuinn and Kenny is on the agenda. Maybe even me.

More headlights. The Yakuza look up again. The two lights poke along cautiously, like they're thinking. Then, the engine roars like it's being pushed to the max. A decision has been made: ramming. The lights are getting bigger fast. No one is sure what to do. As it gets closer, maybe 20 yards, I recognize the front shape. Holy shit. A white Toyota Galaxy. It's not going to stop. Full speed ahead into the first car.

The Yakuza open fire. Blasting the windshield. The Galaxy turns up toward the mound, sending the gunmen flying to get out of the way. The Galaxy hits the building's concrete pad, peters out and rolls down to its right into the cars.

The Yakuza are confused. One of them goes and opens the door. Yep, and there's my grandpa, shot dead. As the gangster pulls him out, a million things run through my mind in an instant.

Shit Grandpa use your big brains . . . fuck. He spazzed. His wits failed him. All he did was slam it into them? The most clever, thoughtful man I've ever known, and this is what he came up with and this is how he died?[27]

27. I'll get to how he knew where to be.

I stand wide-eyed as one of them brings a baseball bat over to desecrate what's left of him. McGuinn grabs me, grabs the sword, and throws me through the door.

"Run. Hide," he screams. "Get out of here and don't look back." There was no hesitation. I took off running across the trashed Cryptic Cavern. The door to the main area was locked.

I kicked the door as hard as I could. The cheap door handle gave way in two kicks.

Then I hesitantly trotted through the large section, bumping into clothing racks, looking for a place to hide. There was a nightlight glowing somewhere, so I had a general shape of the confines. Plenty of places would have sufficed, but I couldn't decide.

There it was on the other side, highlighted with a faint glow. The highly restricted sex section. Perfect. I go through the thick red "NO ONE UNDER 18" curtain. Behind it is a black, folding security door. Luckily it wasn't locked, but it was hard for me to slide open.

I walk in. And after all I'd been through that day and would go through, this was arguably one of the most vivid moments of them all. Now, I had obviously been exposed to sex before; what California kid hadn't learned about sex? But since I was just shy of 13, none of it really stuck. Sexual information just doesn't compartmentalize well until you've hit puberty.

This room, too, had some kind of nightlight. I looked to my left, then stood, mouth agape at the northern wall, nothing but huge, unpackaged, cheap dildos attached to the racks with the little, glued-on, clear plastic eye hooks, priced with simple orange stickers. Like I said, I probably knew what a dildo was before walking in there, but man I was taken aback. These monsters were detailed.

I was brought back down to earth when I heard the folding gate move. I took off away from the wall and hid in the first place I could find, the center of a circular clothes rack of black leathers. I held my breath, afraid of what was coming through the door.

A henchman walks in. I hold my breath. He smirks at the wall o' dildos for a few moments, before a big scan of the room. My stomach is in knots as he takes his time, perusing the porno magazines and VHS tapes. He's done with that. He's moving closer to me. But first the tacky lingerie. He starts rolling the fabric of the panties in his fingers. Now, there's nothing left to distract him. Only the circular racks of leathers could be hiding me. He spreads open the first rack. Nothing. He walks over to the second and splits the hangers of leather chaps, nothing. He smirks. There's only one left. Game over, man. I squinched my eyes closed. He whistles and opens the leathers. There I am. Scared. I look up at him. He smiles. A jagged group of cigarette-ruined teeth. He points his Uzi at me. He laughs.

Violently. Instantly. He drops his gun to grope for the orange electrical cord that's wrapped around his neck. It's Scar. His knee is in the Yakuza's back. He pulls the cord without forgiveness. The goon's eyes are rolling back in his head. At the zenith of the henchman's resistance, Scar uses the goon's energy against him and spins him toward the cash register and slams his face into the checkout counter, shattering his teeth, upper jaw, and nose in one swoop. Then, Scar twirls him around and lets go of the cord at the perfect moment to send the goon flying into the rack of dildos, rubber dicks flying everywhere. Scar, holding one end of the three-foot cord fashioned for the purpose to which it was just deployed, looks at me, puts his finger on his lips and gestures for the exit.

GUNSHOT.

We both squat down. Scar creeps around the corner to figure out what's going on. He looks at me and waves for me to follow. Scar leading the way, we sneak back in the central section. Brenda is holding her .38 on McGuinn. He's holding the sword. There is a dead Yakuza.

"Hey! Same side!" I yell at them. They let down their guard; they suspected as much. I can faintly hear police sirens in the background.

SCREAMING IN JAPANESE.

Brenda reacts perfectly, swinging her pistol around the Yakuza leader's face, but his two henchmen have their fully automatic pistols aimed at us. We're outgunned in a Mexican stand-off.

Our backs are against the zodiac tapestries and shelves of assorted incense. Somehow a fire has started opposite us in the main room. One of the Yakuza not involved in our standoff tosses clothing racks into the blaze before coming over to reinforce their firepower superiority.

The glow of the fire increases.

This is the end, surely. Why don't they just kill us? They're not nice guys, but I guess they do need to get back to Florida or wherever they came from with as little attention as possible. They're not irrational.

McGuinn and their leader are blurting statements back and forth in Japanese. Over the sword, I'm sure. The sirens are picking up. Things are getting tense. The fire has evolved to a substantial blaze. The Yakuza standing in front of us are silhouettes against the orange glow. They scream "Weapons!" Brenda tosses her gun. McGuinn is standing his ground. I'm not sure why. We have no leverage. Pride and greed can do weird things to the mind, only exacerbated by stressful situations. Scar is ready for whatever.

But it doesn't matter.

A shuriken hits the Yakuza boss in the back of the neck between spinal discs; he drops to his knees, wide-eyed, one second of surprise on his face before he falls forward to the ground.

Every single eye darts to where it came from. The three Yakuza left are met with a barrage of highly skilled kicks. The first one gets a high kick to the face, dropping him immediately. The second a sweep. The third guy gets his gun ripped out of his hand before getting side-kicked across the room. It was fierce, beautiful, smooth, perfect, the stuff martial arts dreams are made of.

It is a thin man dressed in dark gray/near-black pants and

a thin rayon blend hooded shirt. His face is covered below the eyes with a neck gaiter. Comfortable, flexible clothes, providing maneuverability without looking too out of place.

He kicks the nearest goon in the face whose weapon hits the ground before being slid across the floor. The other goon throws his weapon away, wisely, and runs off. The third, the one he side-kicked and took his weapon, pulls out a knife and banzai charges the Shinobi.

The Shinobi parries the knife arm, simultaneously converting the energy into a judo throw (Ippon Seio Nage), sending the Yakuza over the Shinobi's shoulder. Before the Yakuza's ass even hits the ground, the Shinobi has his hands in the right place to take the knife and slit the Yakuza's throat in one smooth motion.

With all Yakuza dispatched, the Shinobi looks at McGuinn. The Shinobi holds out and closes his hand to signal that he wants the sword.

I stood transfixed. Man, I hope McGuinn doesn't piss him off. I mean, McGuinn does have the sword out of its scabbard, and it's not out of the realm of possibility that he puts up a decent fight. He is a knife fighting-guru, after all. But, is this the situation to find out if your skills translate well to Samurai swords?

I might be looking at the only motherfucker in the world bad enough to whip McGuinn and Scar at the same time.

The sirens are getting closer.

The Shinobi looks in his eyes. McGuinn reciprocates for a few seconds then looks down at me. McGuinn, with an eye on the Shinobi, reaches down for the scabbard. He sheaths the sword and hands it over.

The Shinobi bows and walks out past the fire.

I'll never forget his gait. Just a hint of bow leggedness, peculiarly high butt muscles. Everything about his casual strut out of the burning building screamed explosiveness. So light on his feet he could have vaulted to the ceiling on any step.

The heat from the fire let us know it was time to make our exits as well.

After a few steps we heard the roar of the ZX11 speeding away, fading into the night, masked by the approaching sirens. He nor the sword are ever seen or heard from again.

As we listen to it rip away, McGuinn looks at us, “You all take it easy. Sorry about everything. I better go too.” He takes off running out of the building.

Brenda, Scar, and I quick step past the raging inferno into the Cryptic Cavern where Daryl is still tied up. I ask Scar for his knife and begin cutting on the duct tape that has Daryl all bound up. I'm not too good at it, but we get it off. “What's up, Master Yamaguchi?” He rubs his wrists and doesn't say much.

We all walk outside to assess the damage. The lights of cop cars are shining from the bridge. Scar tosses Brenda the Subaru keys and takes off for the river. It's about thirty yards away. He jogs the distance. We watch him, illuminated by the moon in the east, swan dive off the elevated dirt bank into the Arkansas River.[28] He wasn't keen on dealing with the police either.

Shit! I just remembered Kenny. He was lying still right where he was left in the trunk, still tied up, unmoving. I sprinted down the mound to the car. His eyes were closed. I shook him. No response. My hands were wet. I brought them up to my face. In the green light, it looked like syrup, but I knew what it was. I looked at the car. It had been sprayed by gunfire in the melee.

I just fell backwards.

Brenda held on to me. Daryl stood near as the flames started coming out of the roof.

The cops finally arrived. Brenda told me to follow her lead. Not sure why. What did she know? It sounds like the cops were unbelievably slow, but it probably had only been 5-8 minutes

28. Remember what I told you about the Arkansas River?

since the first shots were fired.

It's all kind of confusing from the point Grandma and Rock got there. Grandma was distraught. Rock's attention was split between his burning building and the deaths of his girlfriend's boys.

So, there was a vacuum for Daryl and Brenda to fill. And they hammed it up nicely. The cops were pretty wound-up when they arrived on the scene, but once they saw the cars and the dead Japanese gangsters, they were sympathetic to us, even went so far as to have a fatherly feel when dealing with me. They didn't question me too hard, and I heard a lot of "Sorry you had to go through this, son."

Kelly Kincaid, star reporter of Channel 5 News, the pride of Fort Smith, was on the scene. Daryl, with still a little blood on his face and his pot belly stretching out his gray shirt tucked in his worn-out Rustler jeans, was ready to perform.

"A high stakes shootout took place across the River Valley this evening, leaving several dead and a building ruined. I'm here with local martial arts expert, Daryl Rudisill, employee here at Rad Randy's who witnessed it all. He says a Japanese crime syndicate was behind it all."

"That's right Kelly, the Yakuza, equivalent to our Mafia," Daryl says with a pedantic cadence.

"Can you tell us how it all began?" Kelly asks. Despite the sadness or trauma you might imagine I was in, Kelly Kincaid had me spellbound. TV reporting was a higher profile gig back then, and the misogynistic studio heads made sure their reporters were easy on the eyes, especially in the South. And, I'm not saying she was a bimbo either. Total package. Beauty, wit, class, intelligence. Our best and brightest seemed to go into TV journalism.

Anyway, Daryl tells her, "I was working on a *Warhammer 40k* landscape after hours when the toughs came in and asked in Japanese where the sword was. Fortunately, I speak the language fluently. I ascertained that they were after a legendary longsword, which, honestly, it's not uncommon for a guy like myself to be approached in this way. But I knew, since they called me Master Yamaguchi, one of my students was involved, so I acted cautiously, trying to glean as much information as I could without endangering one of my students any further."

"Amazing. And I can tell you were in a fight?" Kelly asks.

"Indeed, during our brief symposium on Masamune Samurai swords their sense of decorum quickly devolved, and I was attacked. Since I've been training martial arts my entire life, the eight to one odds were just about right. Unfortunately I was put in a spot where I had to choose between winning and the wellbeing of my students, since they mentioned having someone kidnapped."[29]

I saw firefighters pull the last two beat-up Yakuza from the wreckage. Kelly breaks from Daryl with less ado than he would have appreciated. She found a policeman to ask about body counts.

They got me to Brenda's pretty quick. The rest is a sad fog. Lots of sitting around. A child specialist grief counselor was there the next day.

29. I bet they just came in and beat his ass.

YOUR QUESTIONS

Okay, sorry I blew past you when you tried to ask questions. If we would have gotten derailed there, I would have never gotten back on track.

How did Grandpa know where to go? Oh, you think it is a deus ex machina, too convenient? Well, according to the police, his Motorola bag phone got a call from a Florida pay phone while he was at Hueco tanks, north of El Paso. His number, if you recall, was on a post-it note by Kenny's telephone. What was said on that phone call from Florida that dissuaded him from getting the law involved? Who knows? I can only guess. But he knew where to go and put close to 900 miles on the camper through straight desert and prairie in about twenty hours.

Huh? No, it wasn't McGuinn who called him. It was the Shinobi; he orchestrated it all somehow. What that phone exchange was like is an intrigue for our wildest imagination.

What? Why didn't the Shinobi stop us on the road? Probably because he wasn't sure who had the sword and needed us to lead him to it. He didn't want the cops to get the sword either.

The mercenary? McGuinn called Meritacre back in Florida. Meritacre picked up the merc on the quick and got to Arkansas. Sorry, all I know. Access to that world would be neat.

Brenda and Scar? I'm pretty sure they were the first car that came in and turned around. I thought it was obvious that she went down to Loo's to figure out what was going on and enlisted Scar for help. How did she convince him? Not sure. But he showed up ready to play. Worried about me or impressing Brenda? I go back and forth depending on the day, but I settle on a combination of both.

No, despite it being mentioned in the newspapers, no one in

the Fort Smith Police Department seemed to care that one of the Yakuza had a .38 bullet put in the back of his head execution style.

THE FUNERAL

WOOD-PANELED PHANTASMAGORIA

"You're Gonna Die" - William Shatner

Funerals are funerals.

There was hardly anyone there at the small auditorium, I'd say about 25' by 35', couldn't hold more than fifty people. The five of us, a handful of Grandma's long lost friends, and a few funeral parlor employees scattered around the place.

Faux-wood paneling, the kind with black quarter-inch indentions running north and south to give the impression there's space between the panels, I guess that's what they're for? The pews were a light brown. Worn-out maroon carpet. Two caskets up front. A wreath covered with a few photos. A service picture of Grandpa. A picture of the entire family when I was a baby. A picture of Kenny on the beach, 16-years-old or so, long haired even then, with his surfboard over his shoulder, the opposite hand flashing an "aloha" gesture. Then, a picture of him in his mid-twenties on an outdoor stage holding the green guitar with his tongue out.

Beforehand, I complained to Grandma that they should be buried in L.A. She understood my feeling but said we didn't have family out there anyway, and getting them both back out west would be hard. It just made more sense to bury them in Arkansas with her people. I didn't have a logical rebuttal. I kinda blamed location, projecting my embarrassment and anger about the fact that no one was there. Honestly, Grandpa wouldn't have had more than a handful of coworkers show up back in California, who knows Kenny's status with his friends back in L.A. It didn't matter one way or another, which was kind of the sad part.

Mom, Grandma, Brenda, and I were there in the front row.

Grandma and Rock had Mom on a plane from Portland, Oregon the moment they were able to get a hold of her.

Rock stayed in the back, rather solemn and awkward. Tough spot for the guy, but he was hanging in there.

The preacher, a heavy-set guy with a deep, southern accent, gave some words about separating the wheat from the chaff, his standard spiel. God's big plan, tragedies here on Earth are purposeful. The preacher sounded confident that there's a heaven and that they were there. I wasn't too receptive. My exposure to Christianity had been filtered through pop culture, no firsthand experience, just a nebulous idea. No deep thoughts about the big stuff. At the funeral, that is. The big stuff, the dark stuff, submerged into my subconscious to grow like a beast.

Then they put in a cassette tape; there was a thick, high-frequency hiss before "Go Rest High on That Mountain" started. We all sat there, reflecting, feeling sorry. "How Great Thou Art" was next. This was before the days of the Powerpoint picture montage.

I sat there and thought to myself that there was not a thing about this southern funeral that any way shape or form reflected these two men. Completely generic and unrelated to the unique personalities of the deceased. The pastor's comments could have been about anybody, completely interchangeable. No mention of petroglyphs, electrical engineering, traveling, music, the water. It really irked me. To me these guys were so cool and unique. Maybe they were, maybe they weren't. It's just a matter of perspective. But it happens to everyone, I guess.

I thought how much cooler it would be if I were running it. And how I was going to have to preemptively pick out a bunch of cool, meaningful tunes for my own funeral. A theme I would carry for years, telling my high school buddies to have a keg and weed at my funeral.

I have a lingering suspicion, an unformed idea bubbling up that maybe all judgments are ultimately aesthetic judgments. I really just didn't like the vibe of the funeral.

I've run it through my mind several times, trying to come up with a few lines in my head, the better lines, the perfect lines that describe their respective lives in totality, but the words keep slipping through my fingers. Maybe that's why we have generic funerals, personalized ones are just too hard to do, especially in a grief-filled rush. Or maybe, worse, we all live a lot more generically than we want to believe. Try putting into words what makes you unique. We all feel it. We all know it in our hearts, but it isn't exactly easy to express. Ask me to introduce myself in a group of people. "Hi! I'm Art. I'm into music, travel, and food." Oh yeah? Who doesn't like those things? Our sense of uniqueness may just go to the grave with us.

One of my favorite things I learned in all my stints of college was an examination of *Citizen Kane* in Introduction to Film. The three people who knew him best all tell different versions of Charles Foster Kane, which were all different from public perception. And he sees himself differently than each of those three do. So, who really has the final say on the totality of a personality? People have secrets, and people have blind spots, things about them others notice, but they don't know about themselves. And if you don't know yourself, what do you know? What can you know?

Diatribe. Sorry

I'm not sure that funerals have anything to do with the dead. Maybe some kind of ceremonial, symbolic truth that makes the living feel better? I don't know, but this one wasn't working— a father/son funeral, everyone's worst nightmare.

As it wound down, I had a bright idea. I walked back to Rock, and I sheepishly asked him if he knew how I could get in Grandpa's camper.

"You bet, bud," he says.

"Thanks. Can we go now?"

"Yeah, hop in the car. I'll tell them where we are going," he said, glad he could be of some help.

POST FUNERAL

"Foggy Jungle" - Windows96

Once again, riding in Rock's Caddy was awkward. No music. You could tell Rock wanted to be cool but knew there was nothing really to say to me. This wasn't what he signed up for when he started dating my grandma. But he wasn't feeling sorry for himself. He knew others had it worse than him. Just a dude trying to figure out how to be the best man he could be in a weird situation.

The impound lot, an inglorious affair, was about 100 yards behind the Sheriff's office.

We pulled up, parked, and started toward the lot. Eventually, a security guard emerged from a shack near the gate.

"Hey there," Rock hails as we walk up.

"No admittance," the unenthused guard says. He was a younger guy at the bottom of the law enforcement hierarchy.

"I know. I know. But we've got some special circumstances," Rock says as the guard just stares at him. Rock follows up, "I know everyone says that." Rock reaches for his wallet and then pulls a pen out from his shirt pocket. He writes on a card. And hands it to the guard. "One hundred dollars' worth free drinks at the Windjammer on me"

"Okay." The guard takes it suspiciously. I'm nervous.

"The kid just wants a few knick-knacks from his grandfather's Toyota Camper. They're burying him and the kid's uncle too. He's leaving to California tomorrow, won't have time to wait around for this to be all settled. It'd be mighty kind of you if you were to let him in for just a second."

"All right, don't get me in trouble," he said, sounding put-out.

"You got it, buddy!"

"Don't take anything," he says, "that's part of a criminal investigation."

"Yep. No problem."

The smashed up and burnt Galaxy was right there. I walked in and started to dig around. Rock stayed on the outside with his arms stretched out across the doorway.

Real quietly he said, "Don't take too much or he'll have to say something." I nodded. I wasn't sure what to pick. There were several books. I chose a green sci-fi paperback: Jack Vance's *Dying Earth,* the oldest, most beat-up book he had. Then, I grabbed his petroglyph notebook and his hand-built radio.

I looked around at everything. The stuff I traveled across the country with, the stuff I'll never see again. I walked out.

"You get something?" Rock asks.

"Yeah, some books and his radio," I said, worried the radio was too much. It was worth the risk though.

"Good deal," Rock said.

We walked back through the gate. It wouldn't take Rick Hunter[30] to see that something was under my shirt.

"Appreciate it," Rock says to the gate guard, "you stop on by any time now, ya hear? I'll take care of ya."

"All right. You watch, I'm gonna take you up on it," the guard says.

"You better," Rock said with a smile.

The conversation had an awkward tone, like I wasn't sure if the guard was being mildly facetious or he was going to actually show up at the bar in an antagonistic, demanding type of way.

~

We went straight back to Brenda's at my request. I was done with anything funeral related. We get there and the red Suburu Brat is parked in the parking lot.

30. Deep cut for the real OGs of late-night 80's re-runs.

"You know that car?" Rock asks.

"Yeah, it's cool," I said nonchalantly. My mind raced with wonder.

I get out, go through the gate, up the steps and I start to hear something. I hesitantly open the door. Then wave to Rock. He's old school, makes sure his guest gets in the house before he pulls away.

I walk into the trailer. Now, I'm pretty sure I'd heard people—well, my mom—have sex before, subtle squeaks of a mattress, maybe a light groan or heavy breathing here and there, but when I walked into that trailer that day . . .

PLEASURE SHRIEKS OF A BANSHEE! To this day, they were the most embellished screams of satisfaction I've ever heard. "Yes! Yes! Fuck Yes! Ugggggg!! Uggh!!!" As her cheap, tube metal headboard smacked the walls of the trailer like a jackhammer, shaking the house. I'd never been so close to sex in my life, and the way it was going I'm not sure I ever have. I mean, absolutely power slammed.

Every time I have sex, I feel like a small, diminutive figure in the shadow of Scar the sex god. Imagine doing it for the first time as an eighteen-year-old with your pants pulled down and your shoes still on, under the bleachers at a high school football stadium and expecting that kind of reaction.

Anyway, I stepped out of the house and sat on the porch for a little while. Then, I decide to walk down and see Loo. See what he was up to, maybe play some Nintendo. No one was home. I took a slow walk around the trailer park.

We flew back to Los Angeles the next day.

AFTERWARDS

"We Die Young" - Alice in Chains

I went back to Woodrow Wilson Middle School and continued my life. On with the show.

As you can imagine, the 1990 Regulski family Christmas wasn't exactly merry and jubilant, not even watching *Home Alone* in theater cheered me up. Rolling into 1991 was a weird time for me, hitting puberty while in deep mourning, all under the umbrella of the dramatic-at-the-time, constantly-reported-on Gulf War made for a curious combination of hormones and chemicals.

The next few years you could call my Alice in Chains phase. They debuted their first single *"We Die Young"* in July 1990, but I didn't hear it until I got back to California. The message and the aesthetics couldn't have better fit my emotional state. Ditching the Vanilla Ice flattop and growing my hair long in Kenny's honor, the next six or seven years would have a center, extending out to the obligatory Nirvana before The Smashing Pumpkins, Suicidal Tendencies, Sublime, and, yeah, Tool.

And my taste in comics followed right behind the music, getting grittier, grimier, and more excessive, culminating in my last unironic or un-nostalgic comic obsession: *Spawn*.

Same story with cartoons. No more noble, optimistic 80s heroes. On to *Beavis and Butthead* and *Ren & Stimpy*.

Yeah, the next few years were rough in their own way and magical in others, but that's the way the teenage years go for everybody. I had my issues from the big ordeal that may have manifested in different ways, but those are stories for a different time. I have no doubt that Kenny and Grandpa would want me to go on living the best I can, receiving fully the good, and toughing through the bad with as little wallowing as possible.

I didn't want much to do with the sword stuff for years. In my teens and twenties, I was concerned with being cool and having fun, being seen, desiring to be desired. Which all segued into that late twenties early thirties playing-catch-up phase, a preoccupation with making something of myself, moving up the hierarchy of importance—you know, distinguishing myself. But as I eased, or gingerly walked to avoid aggravating my lower back, into my mid-thirties, like many guys, I took interest in my family's past, and I researched and filled in some blanks of the story.

My mom is still chasing crazy dreams, but she's not crazy. Living in an apartment, cashing in her share of the Lockheed quarterly dividend checks. For years her concern for me was a little overkill. We clashed for a while, but I wouldn't have gotten along with anyone then. So, no fault to her for that. In fact, praise to her for putting up with me.

I'm now over forty, an age I never dreamed of reaching, and I am sitting around telling stories by the pool, playing some half-assed music here and there, starting and stopping on writing projects, bouncing around the country snagging the last disc jockey gigs. My mom would have been a parent for over twenty years at this point, and I've always gone and done whatever I want, whenever I wanted. I've never had to make the bitter compromises someone with big dreams and a kid out of wedlock has to, so I have no basis to get on a high horse about her. Quite the opposite; I'm supremely grateful I made it this far, and I sure hope she feels like she's had a good life and has done right by me. If I were to drop dead here in this spot, I'd have absolutely no room to complain. I've had a good life.

~

Soon after the fiasco, Rock and Grandma parted amicably. Neither of them were under any illusions about him being the kind of guy you ride out a heavy time with. She went back and took charge over her home in California, focusing on taking care of me and Mom.

Grandma is pretty old now, but all things considered she's doing well for a lady in her 80's. She's always carried some bitterness over the deaths, but it is what it is. Back in California, a few years later she married Bill Johnson, a semi-retired life insurance salesman, a solid man, a little too normal for my tastes, but he worked hard to do the right thing and was always real good to all of us, even when I was a pain in his ass, but he never let it bother him and was always there, unconditionally. May his tribe multiply. He, too, passed three years ago.

Grandma has a nurse coming to check on her every day for an hour or so and put her through a stretch routine. I try to visit her as much as I can. I'm sure my mom does at least once or twice a week.

Brenda died of lung cancer in 2008. We made it to Arkansas for the funeral. Got in and out without seeing anyone pertinent to this tale. There weren't too many people there. I guess she didn't have many friends toward the end. She either pissed them off or outlived them. They put her in the ground by her parents, not far from the other two; that was a little bit of a double whammy. The funeral parlor had been completely renovated.

After we buried Brenda on a rainy, cold February day, I drove to the nearby Long John Silver's, surprised it was still there. The blue and white pirate kitsch hadn't changed any since 1990. I ordered a bunch of beautiful, greasy food—hush puppies, clams, and the fish with batter sticking an inch off the side—and washed it down with a Barq's root beer. Talk about hitting the spot.

The only person in there, I slouched against the blue vinyl booth, looking out through the rain at that old part of Van Buren now ravaged by time. The area lost traffic when Wal-Mart closed and moved to the other side of town in the form of a "Supercenter."

I hadn't even noticed there was music playing over the little PA system. Then out of nowhere came a double shot of Steely Dan, first "My Old School" then "Deacon Blues." It was perfect.

So unlikely it might have been divine intervention. I'm sure the ultra-hip and cynical Walter Becker and Donald Fagen would bristle at the thought of a Long John Silver's/Steely Dan aesthetic and emotional synthesis, but for some reason the juxtaposition worked like a dream on that rainy, cold afternoon.

I'd heard Steely Dan on many occasions since riding around with Rock, but this time ignited a passion. People scoff at nostalgia, rightfully so, but this was different. Déjà vu isn't the right word, but a tunnel was opened to the past, a past that may or may not have actually existed, but told me about who I was, like tapping into the mother lode of my psyche, a figurative heart that pumps blood into the veins of my existence, a life force I didn't know I had. That occasion, that music, that location, that ambiance, that instance let me know myself, a defining moment. I was cool with who I am, and glad I had the chance to experience it all.

I sure hope Brenda had some similar moments.

Sitting there, high on sentiment, I decided to hunt ol' Rock down, say hello and check on him. I searched out one of his bars, the Windjammer. The old place on Midland boulevard hadn't seen a renovation in 40 years, God bless 'em. Unfortunately, the bartender, a short lady named Barbara, barely knew who Rick Young was. She said she thought the current owner bought it in the late 90's. I pressed the old gal and asked her if she'd call the owner and ask. She said she knew he was too busy to talk. I ordered a Miller High Life, gave her a twenty and told her to keep the change. A few minutes later she came out of the office and told me Rock sold everything and moved to Galveston, Texas.

I'm tempted to Google him, see what happened, but I'm afraid it might make me sad. In my dream world, Rock, the eternal bachelor, is out on a sailboat in the Gulf of Mexico, listening to music, enjoying nice drinks, giving a new lady the time of her life, a week of adventure, passion, attention. Who knows? Maybe you'll look him up and tell me.

After that, inspired, I grabbed a sixer of Milwaukee's Best and drove out to where I thought Scar's chicken shed was. I looked all around up there northwest of Van Buren and never found the spot. Nothing was familiar.

~

McGuinn is living in quiet anonymity, humbled, atoning for his sins. He said he put up vinyl siding for a while, saving up to start a new traditional Kempo Gojo Ryu Karate dojo along Main Street in Watertown, Wisconsin, where his mom's people are. He teaches kids behind a big open glass window with red-outlined yellow block letters spelling "Karate."

He charges students a modest amount and teaches them all the basics of self-defense, but I have a feeling they're getting a great role model, coaching them on duty, accountability, respect, integrity, restraint, discipline, humility, magnanimity, charity... All the good stuff of character building, the true value of being a part of a dojo.

When I was in high school, he sent me his first black belt as an apology. He said the best years of his life were spent as a poor kid training at the dojo late into the night listening to music or in the snow beating up on phone books taped to fence posts, all while dreaming of girls, money, and karate championships.

I imagine him as the kind of guy nowadays who lets a kid keep coming long after their dues are delinquent.

GRANDPA

North Korea, Nov 28, 1950, 30 degrees below zero, windchill unfactored. Army Tech Sergeant Norman Regulski lies in the snow on a small hill holding an M-1 Carbine looking out into the blackness of a moonless windy night. He and a handful of his fellows from the radio squad wait for an army that outnumbers them twenty-to-one. Before they left their tent and headed to the embankment, the words "World War III" were hitting the air like little bolts of electricity.

The intense, nervous atmosphere crescendos to a legendary pitch as the horns and gongs start. Mixed with the strong winds bashing against jagged, snow-covered hills, the cacophony portends to something of epic, biblical proportions, the trumpets opening the seventh seal.

~

Let's start from the beginning.

After the pitiful end of my Deadhead phase (I use the term loosely; I followed all the jam bands in the festival circuit), I was staying back at my Grandma's in L.A. And one day I hit up some thrift stores and brought home full VHS collections of *China Beach* and *Tour of Duty*. A marathon binge led to a sentimental mood, inspiring me to figure out what my grandfather did in the Army.

I had never really let it sink in that my grandfather was in the Army. Most of my life I thought the military was the lamest thing ever. Not out of any high-minded pacifist ideology, just aesthetics, didn't like the feel of it. Seemed boring, square, drab, wound-up.

I started quizzing Grandma about it. All she could tell me for certain was that he was in the Army in the Korean War. She didn't think he saw direct combat since all he did was repair electronic devices. He specifically never made a big deal about it, and rarely would he talk about war with friends, even when directly probed.

I did an archives.gov search with my mom signing the next-of-kin stuff, and found out his pay grade upon leaving service was E-5, that he was a 39 Echo (military Occupational specialty code for small electronics repairmen), and that he was 7th signal company, 7th Infantry Division, U.S. Army. I don't know if he showed a proclivity for electronics in entry testing, it was just luck that they threw him in there, he asked for it, or he had general intelligence that was applied to a specific thing.

I was able to find out that his unit was at the battle of Chosin Reservoir, "The Frozen Chosen," something about which I knew next to nothing, but with a heavy, catchy epithet like that, my interest was piqued. In my initial burst of enthusiasm, in classic Arthur Regulski style, I plowed through all the documentaries and read a few books, getting to the point where I considered myself a Korean War buff.

From there I searched for people online who might have served with him, nosing around obscure forums and abandoned pages, researching and networking until I found a guy who had served with Grandpa and was willing to meet me.

In all the books, there wasn't any mention of radio repairmen, so I didn't have any expectations. I was honestly a little afraid I'd hear something embarrassing or dishonorable that would shake up my strong opinion of my grandpa, but I'd have to take that chance.

The big day. I drove out to Southern Arizona, Fort Huachuca, to meet Michael "Sarge" Binghamton. He was particularly curt online, but I pushed the envelope since I wanted it so bad.

I was to meet him at 8 a.m. at the little MWR (Morale Welfare and Recreation) golf course. I was on time, but neither one of us anticipated the obvious problem that I couldn't get on base without a military ID. After dealing with the gate guards, I turned around, parked, and called him.

Sarge wasn't too adept at operating his flip phone. It took me three tries of hearing him breathing hard and grunting in frustration trying to get the phone answered (he didn't realize opening the phone instantly started the connection). And boy was he pissed. You could almost hear the steam coming out of his ears when he realized he'd have to get back in his car and come after me.

I left Grandma's car at the strip mall outside post, and got in his perfectly maintained, immaculately clean mid-90s Mercury Grand Marquis. He barely even looked at me, just gripped the steering wheel in his leather driving gloves as we made our way back to the golf course. He was mumbling under his breath and cussing at other drivers. "Fucking go! You goddamn idiot," when the car ahead of him hesitated at the left green arrow.

The word cantankerous was invented for Sarge. I usually can't handle that kind of negative energy, but I wasn't going to pass up a chance to talk to someone who served with my grandpa.

Hardly saying a word to each other, we got seated in the club house diner, a small, old fashioned affair with a handful of tables, a waitress and a short-order cook. Since this was like the second time I'd ever been to a golf course, it was in the morning and it was only a few hours after my bedtime, I thought I'd have a little sugar to get the day going. So, I'd order the famous, or at least the thing I associated most with golf clubhouses, Arnold Palmer. I'm always trying to get in character. When in Rome.

He scoffed and shook his head before whistling the waitress back over and said, "Bring him an MGD. Thanks, hon." Then he looked at me and said, without a hint of humor, "Don't drink that bullshit fairy stuff around me." I just nodded. Then he said, "I gotta go pee. Prostate the size of a fucking football helmet."

While he was gone, the waitress brought our Miller Genuine Drafts. "You with Sarge, huh? Craziest asshole around here. People get away when he's coming."

I laughed.

Big pee stains down the front of his stretch-waist khakis pants, he walked back to the table and said, "That's the problem with your generation; they don't have good hobbies like golf and fishing. Spend your lives behind screens, rotting your brains." This was an allusion to me telling him in our e-mail correspondence that I didn't golf.

"You need to get a haircut too. Look like a damn sodomite." I just sat there. I didn't know what to say. He looked at me and sensed I was disappointed in the way this was going.

"All right, Korea." He took a swallow of beer and started to think. "I thought cockroach cunt-Christ Truman was an idiot, but he's a goddamn sight better than that fucking weaselly ass bag of rotting dog shit, moron fuck we have in the office now." He took a bitter breath. The dude strung profanities together with such originality and rhythmic ease. It was a privilege to listen to such a wordsmith improvise.

"Truman lost his nerve. Sure as hell didn't do those North Koreans a favor. Look at the difference between North and South Korea. If that won't convince you the superiority of the American way of life, nothing will. We shoulda burned Pyongyang to the damn ground, and claimed the whole peninsula, cost be damned. Drive the red trash all the way back to the Great Wall of China."

"I didn't think that was a practical option, was it?" I asked with hesitance and deference. The last thing I wanted to do was antagonize this guy.

He just looked up into the sky, twitched his lips, and dropped it. Maybe I was right? A stalemate and two Koreas was a workable, low-cost outcome for all parties? Maybe he was worn out from arguing it his whole life?

"So you're ol' Seagull's[31] boy, huh?"

"Grandson. He's my mom's dad."

"Ah, thought he might have been getting after it in his old age."

31. A play on ReGULski.

I chuckled. "Nah."

"I respect the hell out of ol' Seagull. But it took a while. I thought he was a reclusive little fuck. We'd always be cutting up, playing cards, talking shit, talking about girls we'd chase when we got home. He'd sit on his bunk reading his geeky little magazines."

"What kind of magazines?" Little things like that fascinated me, what type of young man was he as far as the minutia was concerned.

"I didn't trust him. Too quiet. Not unfriendly or uncooperative, just weird. I didn't like him. And I let him know too. But he never took the bait when I was looking for a fight, so I thought he was a pussy."

"Damn. Um yeah he wasn't a confrontational guy. Can you tell me what he was reading? Sorry, I know that's a nerdy thing to ask. I'm just curious."

"Chip off the ol' block huh?"

"Yeah."

"*The Dying Earth* is one queer ass title I'll never forget. I thought reading dumb books about a dying earth," he sneered, "was the lamest use of a man's time. Little green men . . ."

"No kidding?" That's the book I recovered from his camper if you'll recall.

"I'll never forget that as long as I live, weirdest thing.[32] Reading is boring enough as it is, but to be reading degenerate shit like that, damn."

I shrugged my shoulders. He decided it was time to give me something.

"I thought he was a dweeb, an outsider. But don't get me wrong. I can't think of a single time I saw him shirk a task. And I'd be lying if I told you I was better at fixing radios than him. I knew he'd shit himself if the crunch ever came. I was wrong. I'll give him that, I'll give him that, never begrudge him that. Buddy,

32. Dude doesn't get out much.

take that to your grave with you; take it back to your family name. Regulski wasn't a pussy."

"I know." I said matter-of-factly with a tear in my eye. His death came to my mind. I guess the asshole could tell. Read my mind.

"How did he die anyway?" He asked. I told him a simplified version, strategically leaving out the weirdest stuff. He took a minute to think.

"He was put in a spot that his only option was to put his foot on the gas and hope for the best. It's like that sometimes. You look up to us old fucks like we have all the answers, and sometimes we just don't," he said.

I shrugged. "I know the feeling."

"We were kids surrounded by death."

~

I'm going to paraphrase his story. We did a lot of clarifying and went off on tangents about nuances that just aren't the most interesting threads.

All poetic liberties belong to Sarge...

~

"We were with the 7the Signal company, part of the 7th infantry division, U.S. Army. The 7th infantry along with the 1st Marine Division formed X(tenth) Corps, the force led with cautionless zeal by General Ned Almond into North Korea. It was a force hell bent on pushing all the way to the Yalu River, the Chinese border. General Douglas MacArthur, based in Tokyo, commander of all the forces in the Pacific, had already guaranteed President Truman complete and total victory in Korea. The peninsula would be unified and the boys home for Christmas. Truman met MacArthur in Hawaii to talk about the war. He looked MacArthur in the eye and asked, 'Is there any chance the Chinese get involved?'

'Zero, Sir,' Macarthur told him.

X Corps pushed through the rugged mountains far faster than was prudent. In fact, Oliver P. Smith, commander of the storied 1st Marine division, argued that it was downright dangerous and reckless. Almond told Smith to press on, get to the border at all costs, we have this thing won, the Chinese won't enter the war.

So, the two divisions were spread thin on the dirt roads that cut through the rugged, precipitous mountains, often one lane, and if a vehicle broke down the entire convoy was delayed. Once they reached the southern tip of the Chosin reservoir, the two divisions split up. The Marines went to the west side, the Army to the east. The headquarters elements, including 7th signal, bivouacked at Hagaru, a small collection of buildings you could barely call a village in a small plateau valley, the only place that had any promise as a command post.

We were glad to stop. It had been so cold the past few weeks, below zero, and it only got colder as we climbed in altitude. The plan was to set up a quick command area there with a runway for delivering supplies and getting the wounded out to Japan.

After nightfall, our signal platoon finally got our tent set up, a pain in the ass anyway, but hell in three foot'a snow. About the time we got to sit back and enjoy a good cup of army percolator coffee, pure hell broke out over the radio. Calls for fire. Casualty reports. Human waves, thousands of attackers were surrounding our boys from all sides. They fuckin' did it. The Chinese brought 120,000 men across the border under the cover of darkness, aiming at our total annihilation. If the Chinese got involved, the Russians might be right behind them: World War III.

The hills rang with full-tilt volume of fire.

Me, your granddaddy and the rest of our signal platoon were just sitting there in awe, drinking our coffee and rubbing our hands. We were cold as could be; we felt sorry for the poor bastards out in the snowy mountains on a night like this.

Then the good Sir, Lieutenant Lionel Bostich, the pride of

Rumford, Maine, the dorkiest college boy son of a bitch I've ever met, returned from the command tent, the one with the head honchos. 'Two minutes! Get your carbines, bayonets, and put on all winter clothes you can find. Form up out front.'

Our stomachs hit the floor. We didn't say anything as we all scampered to get the right gear. We formed up outside, eight of us from the signal platoon.

LT Bostich was waiting there, practicing his speech in his head. Over the sound of our sniffling, he started. 'All right men, as you know our boys up north and the Marines are surrounded. It's just a matter of time before we, too, are surrounded and attacked, probably by tens of thousands. This base is the linchpin. If it falls, X Corp is doomed. I'll let you think on the ramifications of that. So every man one of us will be on those hills. Everybody here, everybody back home, and all freedom loving people around the globe,' he was getting worked up on the grandiosity and momentous sentimentality of it all like any good officer should, 'are, whether they know it or not, counting on us, looking at us to rise to the occasion.'

Bostich was probably only twenty-four or so. 'Men, as we depart for this line. I want you to know that I have the utmost respect for each and every one of you.' We were shaking and shivering, putting our hands over our mouths, too cold to care about what he was saying. 'Treat this like your finest hour. Thank you. And God bless the USA. Get in line at the ammo tent.'

By the time he was done with his speech, we were dying to go back inside. The coldest we'd ever been.

The marine handing out the ammo talked a little shit. 'You little doggies make every shot count.' His friend added, 'What are you talking about? These doggie pogues can't shoot.'

I bowed up to his ass, 'Fuck you, you goddamn son of bitch. I'll whip your fucking ass!' LT got involved in his cheesy-ass way. 'Save it for the commies,' he yelled. Seagull just rolled his eyes. He never appreciated that kinda thing.

We were headed to the west side perimeter of Hagaru. The two of us probably wouldn't be here if me and Seagull were sent to the now-famous, bloody, East Hill. All sides needed covering though. Luck of the draw.

On our way out there, LT Bostich did something I'll never forget. A Marine Captain was walking by. You could tell he was a grizzled old veteran. Definitely fought in the Pacific. Lame ass Looey (Bostich) yelled for him, jogged up to talk to him and I quote, said, 'Sir, I'm a signal platoon leader, and we don't know what to do.' I was so embarrassed. I know what to fucking do. You point the gun at the [unrepeatable racial epithet] and you pull the fucking trigger.

The big, tall Captain America Marine looked down at Bostich for a moment, considering him with a slight hint of annoyance, and said, 'Lieutenant, you did the right thing. You and your men follow me.'

We followed him about 300 yards to the perimeter. He told us to hang tight. He came back with a Marine sergeant and told us to take our cues from him. The sergeant looked tired and mean, like he had seen it all. The kinda guy that was old enough to be a gunny, too troublesome to promote, too fierce a warrior to kick out.

Getting lined up on the western side wasn't too hard. We just laid in the snow about five foot apart, trying to keep our heads low while still looking for the enemy. LT Bostich tried to make small talk with the Marine sergeant. "You've seen lots of action?"

All the sergeant said was "Okinawa" before he sat up on his haunches, staring off into the dark, sipping whiskey, not inviting anyone else to it. Never caught his name, with all of our cold weather gear on it was hard to see name and rank.

Goddamn it was cold. Reports from different locations in the region vary from -20 Fahrenheit to -70 windchill. You could hear the Marines up the way fighting. We just stayed in the snow and listened to the hell that would soon be coming our way.

Then it happened: the horns and gongs started. It's how they communicated and coordinated attacks. They were here. My right hand resting under the trigger well started uncontrollably slapping the side of the weapon."

~

At this point in the story, back in the clubhouse, lost in thought, Sarge just started staring out at the course lit up by the 9 a.m. sun.

~

"Hours. Pitch black. Freezing to death. Waiting for a hundred thousand mindless commie rodents to come down the mountains and overrun us.

We heard the first gunshots on the opposite side of us, the East Hill. All hell broke loose. Total war. The Marine sergeant told us to sit tight and stay alert. We'd get our turn. Seagull never showed any emotion. He kept his eyes forward and didn't complain.

Despite the cacophony coming from the opposite side of the base, we were to remain at our positions. Some Marine platoons got pulled over, but we were the ones who got left on the west. It wasn't because we were signal either; they had bakers, mechanics, the 1st Marine Band, whoever they could find covering that east Hill, fighting their guts out.

All through the night we listened and waited for our turn. Dawn came. We were still alive. If you were to look out over the hills from the east side, you could see thousands and thousands of dead. They came in waves, mindlessly, without tactics or guile. Historians say otherwise, but they must have been doped out of their gourds to keep coming like that, dying in windrows, running straight into our fire.

We didn't get to sleep. The next day was straight work, mostly carrying the wounded to the overcrowded field hospital and taking ammo on the return trip. Your grandpa had a sweet gig for a little bit, working on jammed rifles in a warm tent, well, warm enough for him to take his outer gloves off and not get frostbite.

The next night was going to be worse. The Chinese had taken the road to the south, so we were surrounded. A hodge-podge of 300 men led by the British 41st Marine Commandos were trying to cut through the Chinese encirclement and join us. They left early in the morning. The general sentiment was that we'd be deader'n a doornail if we didn't get reinforcements. By nightfall, they hadn't made it. Bad news. "Get to the line."

Same spots as the night before. Colder. Right on schedule, the gongs and bugles started. Shortly after, the attack. Once again, our side only saw light action. But we could hear fighting to the south as well this time; our reinforcements were down there somewhere scrapping for their lives.

At 1 a.m. they made it. The debonair Lieutenant Colonel Drysdale, adorned in his green beret, strolled into Hagaru like a hero, leading troops who had been marching and fighting through hell for the past sixteen hours to get to us.[33] The whole outpost applauded.

We made it through another night. The reinforcements took our place on the line. But honestly, I'm not sure being detail rangers on the post was a better assignment. I don't think me and your old man slept more than an hour altogether in four days. Goddamn, what you can get out of scared young men."

~

I'm gonna cut it off here, I think. You're getting tired, and I know you didn't come here for a military history lesson from a guy like me,[34] but I think it's an awesome part of the Regulski saga. A full exploration of the nuances of this frozen festival of carnage would take an entire other night to tell it well with its due respect. Get with me when you're in the mood for the details. Maybe we could meet up in the winter around a campfire? Put some corned beef and hash on the skillet. I'll bring a corncob pipe

33. Look up Hellfire Valley. 900 left that morning. 300 Made it to Hagaru.

34. The art/music/film scene might surprise you once you're dealing with people older than thirty. If you want to talk all night about war, guns, financial discipline, and the fall of California, find an open-mic blues jam.

and wear olive drab fatigues. If not, do yourself a favor and look into it—interesting, horrifying, and inspiring. Even if you're not into war, you'll be amazed at what people—military and civilians of both sides—were able and unable to endure. Morbid absurdity.

Cliffs for the rest of the story:

- High-stakes scraping away at the ice and frozen dirt through the night under floodlights to create a life-saving landing strip, cheering as the first plane to take away the wounded barely made elevation in time enough to get over the mountains.
- Sarge and G-pa had to carry wounded from the line, including soldiers burnt-black from poorly aimed American napalm. Haunting.
- The famous Chew En-Lee marching the stranded 7th Marines into Hagaru singing "The Halls of Montezuma" in lockstep. A glorious moment. "We might make it out alive after all."
- "Retreat, Hell!" They spent a sleepless week as a part of one of the greatest withdrawal maneuvers in the annals of military history.
    - When the bulldozers cut through the snow and ice on the southern border of Hagaru, the sides looked like aspic[35] or pimento loaf with all the dead bodies frozen under accumulated snow.
    - 155mm Howitzers forced to open up on encroaching infantry at close range.
    - Under duress and racing against time, engineers built a bridge over a several-hundred foot pass.

~

Sarge got worn out telling the story and made a snide comment to the effect of "Don't worry about the bill; I can tell you need the money." I thanked him for meeting me, and he slapped me on the shoulder before he headed out to the golf course. I sat there

35. Look that up.

thinking, ordered a few more MGDs, and eventually some hot links for lunch before calling a cab back to my car off post.

~

Norman Regulski, born in 1928 Central California at the height of the depression to a single mom, Anna Regulski, who immigrated from Poland while pregnant, with a five-year-old Joseph Regulski holding her hand. Specific circumstances unknown, her precarious journey was probably commonplace but still unimaginable to a modern person. Risking it all to raise little Americans, and, by God, she did.

After working as a hotel maid for thirty years, Ann Regulski died in 1961. Grandpa's older brother, Joseph, a sailor in the U.S. Navy was killed at the Battle of Midway aboard the battleship *USS Hammann* in 1942.

~

Yeah, trust me, I'm second guessing why I was telling you this horrific stuff. Total downer. But it's kind of a "Be thankful for what you got" thing. He could have been one of the abandoned wounded waiting to catch a bullet between the eyes. But he made it out and went on to live a good, humble life full of love and interesting hobbies.

Everyone I've ever met who survived the depression is frugal as hell, but not him. He'd buy his kids any candy or soda they wanted, fully supported their hair-brained dreams, and never took anything too seriously. As a wise man once told me, "The sun shines, the moon beams, and we'll all eat chocolate ice cream." The only time he ever even mentioned Korea was in off-hand remarks when cold weather was brought up.

When I compare his twenties to mine, with all the good-timin' and adventures, it can feel shameful. If it weren't for men like him, there couldn't be guys like me, so I owe it to him to live the best life possible. Milking the freedoms and privileges for all they're worth, best thing I can do to honor their legacy.

THE KEY LARGO SUNSET

"Key Largo" - Bertie Higgins

1.5 ounces of Malibu coconut rum, 1 oz vodka, 2 oz pineapple juice. ½ oz grenadine. Generous splashes of lime juice, lemon sour, and agave nectar. My attempt at recreating the marvel.

Did you enjoy it? Sorry I forgot to ask.

~

Hauling ass across the Kansas prairie, somewhere outside of Colby, with no AC in my old car, damn near broke, I was desperate for a drink. I'd been driving since I woke up and turned in my hotel key in Denver at 10:55 a.m. The longer I went without seeing a place to stop, the thirstier I got. Until finally, like a desert mirage in an old Popeye cartoon, I saw this little bar that could have passed for a tool shed.

A cheap beer and a stretch here I come. If I'm real lucky they'll have some complimentary bar pretzels.

The place was dusty and had a few racing culture posters on the wall, babes on muscle cars. I sat down at the bar, and just before asking for whatever their cheapest beer was, I saw they had a mix-drink menu made of laminated 3 x 5" yellow index cards held together by a key ring. There was a drink called the "Key Largo Sunset." It was way more than I should have been spending.

At that point, I hadn't thought about Key Largo in years. I said, "Key Largo Sunset," to the old bartender in a leather vest who moved like it took everything he had to get from one side of the bar to the next.

"You got it, buster," he said before he made the drink, taking his time, doing it right.

Trying to make small talk, I asked him if he'd ever been to Key

Largo. He said he had and didn't elaborate.

As he continued to labor in the creation of the drink, opening up various refrigerators and coolers looking for all the ingredients, l sat there watching the dust float in front of the window.

He sat the drink down, told me to enjoy, and I gave him all the money I had, the tip less than a dollar. I apologized and explained my financial situation before taking the first drink.

The most beautiful sip. In a time and place for tossing square bales of hay on to a flatbed trailer, I was whisked away to the Keys.

MEETING LOO

Around 2012 I was able to find Loo on Facebook after years of periodically searching for him. I wasn't surprised that he wasn't a social media type of guy. However, it wasn't a personal page I found, but a "Fans of Loo Dang" page. Interest piqued! He was now a well-regarded guitarist and composer. He had gone to Stanford, majored in music, and hit the ground running as a guitar gunslinger, traveling the world as a highly skilled mercenary for backing bands, short-term ensembles, and one-offs with the likes of greats like Steve Gadd, Jay Graydon, Donald Fagen, Dweezil Zappa, Chester Thompson, Herbie Hancock and Gary Burton to name a few. God, what a resume.

Using the fan page and following leads on how to get a hold of him, I finally found his email. We exchanged pleasantries and made some awkward catch-up conversation. But I was on the move at the time, and he seemed busy, so we couldn't connect.

I did get on his newsletter, and I watched from afar as he started branching out on his own, sliding into the namesake/front man role and playing originals. I was there for all of it, swelling with pride from the first note I heard. He was doing something special. So I started promoting his music like it was my job, buying all his stuff and trying to give him as many online views as possible.

Then one day when I was outside the Bay Area doing some temp work, I noticed he'd be performing at a San Jose convention center in a few weeks. I wrote a quick email with an obvious heading: "ART REGULSKI COMING TO A SHOW." Hoping maybe I could shake hands with him backstage or something. He replied a day or two later and said he and his fiancé would love to take me out to dinner the night before.

At their suggestion, we met at a swanky, intimate, dimly lit wine bar, just right for talking to people without seeing their blemishes. Each table had its own alcove for conversational privacy, tasteful joint. The smell of Silicon Valley money seeped out of even the smallest design decisions.

Since I had watched videos of live performances, his current look didn't surprise me. But seeing him up close after all these years was striking. So much had changed, my little bamboo sprout was now mighty. He had ditched the thick brow-bar glasses and cotton shorts somewhere along the way, and now looked like he was a model for upscale men's wear (tailored, dark blue jeans and a gray sports jacket, sleek black glasses). And he owned the look. It wasn't some situation where you can tell someone is dressing up and out of their comfort zone.

His fiancée, Sarah, though, is on another level, the modern half-Asian Jackie O. Absolute thoroughbred. You could tell she grew up in a tidy house with big expectations, definitely a sorority girl. And I don't mean that pejoratively, impeccable social skills and a million-dollar smile, maintains eye-contact and interest, engaged and focused when talking to you, brushing off any social faux paus without embarrassing the offender. A black belt in grace.

I started off a little shy, feeling outclassed, hoping to keep the conversation off me, too embarrassed to talk about my failed art projects and shoddy work history. I made small talk by asking him about video games. Said he hasn't played one since college. I told him I have mixed feelings about that. "Me too," he replied.

They could tell I was being reticent, not giving good conversation. Disappointed in myself, I searched in my mind for a palatable topic, and I decided on Grandpa. My quest for his life may be my most respectable endeavor; he was someone who I felt I could be proud of in any company. So, I told them about my research into his war efforts, his history, and my attempted UFO story. Loo remembered the radio. The radio segued into me telling him about Rock taking me to get the books. They nodded along, thinking it was all nice stuff.

By the time I was done stumbling through the grandfather

spiel, I started my third glass of Cabernet, and the real me started to come out. I asked him if he remembered the girls' titties in Panama City Beach, and he smiled, "Oh man." I retold the story to his girlfriend, and she absolutely loved it, died laughing. He blushed but was happy for our amusement. Seems like he grew up to be the kind of guy who gets embarrassed around sexual conversation. Good for him. But they shouldn't have encouraged me.

They're a stunningly classy couple; I couldn't be prouder. I was sitting across from the American dream. They are the type of flawless you see around Christmas in car commercials where the woman comes out of the snow-covered house to see a luxury sedan tied up with a ribbon and bow.

Then, angling to move to music, I told him about the sad day inside of Long John Silver's after Brenda's funeral and my subsequent passion for Steely Dan. He nodded with a sly smile and said he was familiar with the Steely Dan catalog.

"Speaking of The Dan, in the middle of the night, late Summer, Stillwater, Oklahoma, I was walking through Wal-Mart in my girlfriend-at-the-time's old cheerleading shorts looking for a coaxial to HDMI converter so we could get the cable TV going again. Not even drunk or stoned, just a moment of post-coital clarity, 'Do It Again' came on and it was a euphoric piece of perfection out of a Hunter S. Thompson story; I was at peace with who I am and the unorthodox adventures that constitute my life. I was part of it all."

"Wait, what?" Sarah said, intrigued, leaning her head forward for confirmation.

"What?"

"Why were you in cheerleading shorts?" Sarah asked.

"I forgot to pack lounge wear, and they were the only clean shorts around." I shrugged my shoulders in honesty, "Is that weird?"

With an ear-to-ear, brow-raised, tight-lipped smile like she was holding something back, "You walked out in public like that?"

"Yeah, a 24-hour Wal-Mart. I wasn't the weirdest person there. It's not that big a deal . . ." I couldn't hear myself over her laughter. I smiled. I love to make people laugh even when I'm the butt of the joke.

I was completely loosened up and unselfconscious at this point. Humored with myself, realized that my shtick was working, my eccentricity an experience for all to enjoy.

Laughing at myself, I told him about my multiple dead fetuses of musical dreams. The failed bands, both the grunge country act and the stoner hair metal band, and about how heartbroken I was when the drummer quit right when we were about to turn the corner. We commiserated with the cliché about how the worst part of the music business is the musicians.

I told him if I were to try it again, I'd go with a sci-grunge band, reminiscent of Alice in Chains making the soundtrack for Blade Runner. He said he'd gladly play on or provide some soundscapes with one of his badass synthesizers like his ARP Odyssey, the Roland Juno-6, or the Yamaha DX-7, all of which are killer synths that defined the 80s, nice collection.

But I told him most of my effort is currently going into a modern cyberpunk novel called *Slipstream of Sensation: Memories-Dreams-Dust and Deja-Vu*. About a company's new scientific process/business model where you can relive any moment of your life, but the cost? You lose the memory like it never happened at all. To relive is to lose. That's the kernel. But plots are hard. William Shakespeare and Stanley Kubrick both had problems coming up with original plots. Is what it is—difficult work. A tight, interesting plot is as elusive as a pop melody.

I need to find some additional drama. Maybe the company is secretly harvesting the memories and selling them on a secondary market, with wisemen accumulating them for knowledge and a creative studio strategically pumping their artists with memories in hopes of coaxing certain aesthetics. Or maybe big government compassionate collectivists mandate the mass reliving of others' traumas for empathy, "Perfect memories = perfect people." Potentially take it in a self-help, psychologist direction where memories are managed like drugs: big sports win for serotonin boosts for those with low self-esteem. Or go raunchier—the promiscuous and sexually powerful selling their romantic experiences with subsequent privacy and jealousy concerns.

Then I backtracked to my attempt at screenwriting. Told him I lost my interest in film, but that I'm still trying to shop two of the screenplays I wrote: a post-apocalyptic mercenaries on acid story and my whiskey-fueled, Vietnam War, Native American long range reconnaissance patrol team adventure. Even if they don't sell, writing those was a fun time.

Loo didn't have much writing advice, but he assured me I've got enough creative ability and life experience to make something truly rich and unique if I fully commit myself. Sarah said she has good friends from college in the publishing industry she can hook me up with. Thanks, but I don't know.

He asked what McGuinn was up to. I told him about the karate school. If we were going to memory lane, I was going to ask the million-dollar question: "What happened to Scar?"

Loo was quiet for a moment. Knowing he was about to disappoint me, he said, "I don't know. " He felt bad and followed up, "My mom finally got Dad to move to California in Junior High, and I never looked back."

"Man. Did he ever tell you about Scar?" I ask Sarah.

He said he had. His tone should have signaled to me it was time to let it go, but there was too much momentum in my mind. I thought about the orange electric cord and wondered if Loo knew about that, wondered if Scar was the type to brag about his exploits. But some vague poetic notion of life, some sensibility in me, told me not to bring that up. That is going to be between me, you, and Scar. However, there was one story about Scar worth repeating. A creepy, obnoxious smile came to my face . . .

Pounding my right fist into my left hand and using my decent ability to impersonate a woman screaming, I recreated the scene of me going to Brenda's and seeing the Subaru there. I was loud enough to draw looks from across the restaurant, unamused attention.

Faux pas numero uno.

I didn't get the laugh I'd hoped for, but they played it cool, not encouraging me, but not making me feel bad.

"Man, badass dudes like Sao make me proud to be an American," I reflected, tilting my head up in admiration. You could tell that tickled Loo a little. He viewed Scar from a completely different angle, but for a second you could tell he let himself see Scar through my eyes.

I thought we were done asking how people were doing, but he had one more he had to know about. "Ever hear from Chad?" Loo asked.

I gave him my exaggerated frown with a clucking, sucking sound in my right cheek.

"You sure? We're having fun," I said. I knew it would be a downer, a vibe killer.

"I have to know now that it's a thing," he said.

I scrunched up my face and bobbed my head to the left and right with indecision, giving him one last chance to back out, "It's not good."

He took a resigned, understanding breath, "Let's hear it."

I told him about how I tracked him down the best I could—internet, phonebooks—until I found a Chad Jackson obituary. Loo nodded. From the obituary, I was able to track down a cousin from whom I learned that Chad had died of an Oxycontin overdose about ten years ago. He had a back injury that put him in deep pain, topped off with complications from type 2 diabetes. The cousin didn't give me much peace of mind. Chad's adult life didn't go too well. Lots of welfare and disability. Depression. Obesity.

Loo Looked off into the distance. I thought I saw a tear form in his eye. He got up and left the table.

"I hope I didn't ruin the night," I said to Sarah before I explained what Chad was like and how he and Loo bonded despite initial distrust, revealing how shy and skeptical Loo used to be.

That was a good conversation. She absorbed every word. I pretty much finished off the second bottle by myself and ordered the third.

The alcohol was blasting from my kidneys into the bloodstream with reckless abandon by the time she asked me about my love life, and I devolved into a rambling fool.

"You should meet the type of girls who swipe right on itinerant disc jockeys." I wink at her. "Honestly, you can get a long way with the skills of being able to give undivided attention over a bottle of wine and, when needed, spin an entertaining story."

Then, somehow, I got on about how my love life is defined, maybe recalled is the better word, by aesthetic periods. My first for-instance was my *Garden State* soundtrack-themed romance in the fall of 2005 in the semi-rural outskirts of New York City. Or my New Wave revisitation in Chicago around 2010 with a woman ten years my senior.

I segued into my spiel about going to airports just to meet women, make friends, and hear stories. "Dude . . . you want to meet girls? Get laid? Whatever you need: The Airport. First, buy the cheapest one-way ticket you can and then go through security to the airside. It sounds expensive, but you can stay there as long as you want, and it has everything you need. You'll see the beautiful and interesting people. The doers. The travelers. The adventurers. The movers. The shakers. All killing time, all drunk, excited or bored. They assume you can't be too big a loser if you're flying. It's a status voucher. Seriously, the upside and 'what if' factor is worth a $75 Southwest Airlines ticket to Phoenix."

I don't consciously self-sabotage, but sometimes I just say

stupid stuff. I told that terrible "screenwriter and the Polish girl" joke. Ugh. It came to my mind. One part of my brain was like "don't tell it; it never works; it's in bad taste." The other part of me said, "It might land this time." It didn't.

She squeezed her lips together for a forced smile. I had found the limits of her cool. She picked up her phone and texted something, probably telling Loo to hurry up and get back before I did something we'd all regret. She knew it was time for the check.

Ugh. I wasn't built for this world.

Instead of taking the feedback and retreating, I went full speed ahead, telling my joke idea about starting a new system of etiquette in which we send gift baskets to our lover's ex-lover when our current lover shows great aptitude for oral sex. Her lack of amusement wasn't dissimilar to the responses I've received from my last two girlfriends.

Talking about sex will either ruin a party or take it to another level. What can I say? My drunken self is a riverboat gambler.

She really didn't have to address this one; Loo came back right in the nick of time. They had some loaded non-verbal communication and started wrapping things up. They'd realized I turned out as crazy as you might expect, but they weren't mean about it.

Despite my half-ass insistence that I would pay for my fair share, they were adamant about picking up the tab, especially once they saw the unkempt, sweaty wad of cash and stack of credit cards I pulled out of my pocket and saw me begin to start tallying up how much credit I could scrap together from all the cards.

As we shook hands on the way out, he looked me in the eye and said again, "Be sure to stay until the end."

"Of course! Do I seem like a guy who bails early to beat the traffic?" He smiled, and I continued, "I'll be bullshitting with roadies all the way through the end of the load out."

Sarah pulled around in their tidy, maroon, Honda

Accord—tasteful, safe, not too flashy. They both waved as I waited outside the entrance for my cab.

God knows what he tells her about all us weirdos when they're lying down at night.

I went back to my cheap motel, the Space Station Inn on the seedy outskirts of town. I could have stayed in a safer mainstream place like Motel 6, but there is something about cheap motels, bed bugs be damned, that brings out the creative juices. I did some of my best thinking after midnight at the Knights Inn outside Shreveport, Louisiana. A revolver to the right of my mouse, I felt like I was Ernest Hemingway as people I assumed to be prostitutes and gangsters roamed the walkways outside, talking shit, pecking at the door and in hushed tones asking if I needed anything. My little attempt to be like a character in a Warren Zevon song.

THE SHOW

The San Jose McEnery Convention Center. There isn't a slope to the room, just tables and chairs. It's not meant to be exclusively for shows. They might have benefit dinners and bingo festivals for large civic organizations. Maybe even double as a ballroom for galas and upscale weddings. It wasn't like the usual low-brow rock concerts or weeded out reggae fests I am used to. Nor was it a demure jazz club. But, despite the whatever-they-could-find-that-was-the-right-size room that didn't have any aesthetic juju whatsoever, there was a rock band level of anticipatory energy. Maybe not Van Halen excitement, but it didn't feel like a stuffy, academic show either.

We, the crowd, were one from many subgenres and niches: City pop fans, retrowave-listening computer nerds, fusion junkies, Jazz heads, and prog rock snobs. I wouldn't be surprised if the cheapest ticket in the 1,000-seat house was eighty dollars. Everyone there took their music seriously.

They had me up toward the front with the high rollers. Being at a table by myself is a type of awkward I can handle, no problem. I didn't look too hard for a date, but I was hoping to use my status that night to find one. Hey, I may not be as handsome as I once was, but it wasn't a far-fetched notion. I even went above my normal attire of Hawaiian shirt over a band t-shirt with jeans, tucking my black and pink abstract, geometric shirt, one of the coolest things I own, into short khaki shorts for a Thomas Magnum look, albeit a shorter/fatter one.

Oh, and my drinks were on the house. They didn't mention a price limit, but I tried to keep it under $100 a bottle. Tried. The more I drink, the more I want.

I was early, so I walked up to look at all their gear. Yamaha-sponsored, the guitars, drums, and piano all looked tasteful and clean—soft, beautiful, low-gloss grays, blues, and greens.

I had knocked a few glasses back by the time the lights dimmed and the performers walked out on stage. There he was, my boy, the cotton shorts kid, in tailored slacks and sports jacket, waving to the crowd with a huge, warm, gregarious but humble smile as he picked up his guitar.

He let the crowd die down a bit, but every crowd has a jokester who squeezes in a last whistle and scream.

The drummer tapped in a 1/2/3/4 and hit a snazzy one-measure drum fill that led the bassist in with a thick groove. The rhythm section's pocket was so deep it had the gravity of a black hole, even the stiffest among us couldn't help but fall into a vortex of foot tapping and head nodding. Then came Loo with a perfect lead note, a slide to a twelfth-fret, third string G, sustained with perfectly tasteful vibrato.

From then on, the show was an absolute blast. They rocked. Each note was exactly where it should be, utter luxury in their tone, pieces, and performances. LD is a consistent professional, but he was inspired that night. His backing band were all world-class musicians, all enthused and proud to be at the top of their game, doing what they do best and getting appreciated for it. The set itself was like a song, starting up-beat, sliding up and down, an emotional journey from one person's most intimate thoughts to the edge of the galaxy, a saga of the human spirit and the grandeur of the cosmos.

I would have died a happy man at the end of that show. My cup runneth over. I loved everything about it. We were in the presence of greatness, "IT." Excellence. Peak performance. The stuff dreams are made of. Inspiration. Invigoration. Inoculation.

Then, Loo walked up to the microphone and said, "This next one is a cover, a tribute to Arthur Regulski, one of the biggest inspirations in my life, one of the coolest, most interesting guys in the world." He looked at me and gestured for me to stand, "Everyone give him a big hand. You can catch him DJing for KMIT Paradise Radio out of Stockton, and it's just a matter of time before he writes the great American novel." All thousand people look at me for a second before Loo stops pointing and begins clapping. The people take their cue with aplomb; a roar of applause takes over the hall. Red-faced, I take an awkward, circling bow and sit back down. The applause keeps going, until, like a lion tamer, Loo slashes across his body and puts a finger to his lips.

The crowd stops dead. Silence.

A beautiful BMajor13 from the keyboard. I knew exactly what it was: "Aja" by Steely Dan, arguably their best, most refined song. Loo and the band absolutely nailed it note for note like the studio version. Their keyboardist did the heavy lifting of the main vocal part, but Loo came in on some backup vocals. The drummer even nailed the original Steve Gadd Mozambique drum solo. I don't know if they had that in their pocket as something or learned it that day, or a little of both. Neither equally impressive scenario would surprise me.

The song ended. The crowd roared. He looked at everyone with an appreciative smile as they stood in ovation. He waved to the crowd as the band walked off stage.

The crowd went wild. I'm clapping as hard as I ever have, even more than Ween in '99. So proud. The experience was completely and unfalteringly phenomenal. Everyone knew they were witnessing peak Loo Dang. Fans that didn't even know each other were double high fiving. Others had their hands jolted in the air like it was a Sunday night at an East Texas Pentecostal Church. It all evolved into a chant for an encore.

"Aja" was my big surprise; I was feeling good. High on life. One of the best, most memorable moments in my life.

Then Loo comes back on stage wearing the highest quality retro Jose Canseco jersey and carrying a Neon Green Charvel San Dimas, an exact replica of Kenny's guitar, pink geometric paint job and all, I mean exactly right, drawn by hand from memory. Wow, flooded with emotions, a beautiful mixture of happy and sad.

He holds the guitar up for me to see. "Art knows who this one is for," he put his hands together and did a little bow while looking to the sky.

He took a breath, turned around, and looked at his drummer who proceeded to tap them in.

It started out beautifully. All right. I dig it. Something I'd never heard him play before. But after about thirty seconds in: a kaleidoscope of cascading of Déjà Vu. I knew what was up. I was picking up what he was putting down. He was covering the Japanese Jazz fusion Kenny would play on vinyl.

Out of the gate, they went hot and uptempo: The Katsume Horii Project's "Cruising Boy," high energy, intensity, the whole band together play the main theme before the saxophonist builds on the momentum and intensity with an electrifying 32 bar solo with a scorching climax before a sultry resolution as the band dies down evenly behind him. The solo continues melodically, carrying everything by himself for a few measures.

"Steve Jackson, Milwaukee, Wisconsin" Loo introduces him as he continues his ultra-sexy, suave solo, before the band comes back with matched intensity, but not a second too late, timed perfectly to give the audience just the right amount of repetition but keeping it exciting and unexpected. The rhythm section drops out and the rest of the band holds-out the last note as long as their respective instruments can, creating a smooth ambient cloud that slowly dissipates across the room.

From the void, slowly, faintly— rumors, hints, whispers begin to emerge—dings, bings, boings, clacks. The auxillary percussionist, a real nerdy fella wearing a turtleneck and thick glasses who looks like he should be running a chemistry lab in the 70s, overseeing all the esoteric gear on the backline, works our imagination with the weird sounds, inserting just a little more every few measures. Loo announces him: Werner Wartenburg, Berlin.

Then, from the subterranean nether worlds, the bassist brings in the ultra-dank bass riff from Ryo Kawasaki's "Bamboo Child."

Unadulterated punch. The pocket on this riff is so deep, no one can escape.

"Reginald Littlejohn. Port Hedland, Australia." Everyone applauds as LD announces.

The clicks, beeps, and bops continue to crescendo over the bass line as the trap kit guy, "Floyd Thomas, Little Rock, Arkansas," starts to insert tasteful cymbal accentuations until he fully enters with a slick, understated fill, leading into a bomb of a groove that sits perfectly with the bassline. He pushes the groove into the red, but nothing too gaudy; Floyd is way too cool for that, such a pure, smooth drummer. A young African American guy with his baseball cap turned around backward, he has a fluid, natural, graceful athleticism about him, strength and power, but in a never-touched-weights-in-his-life kinda way. Playing the drums is so easy for him, like he'd been doing it a thousand years, reincarnated as a drummer every life, playing the same songs. I'm more likely to screw up picking my nose, in which I am well practiced, than he is to miss a beat. Made me proud to be a quarter Arkansan.

They pushed the intensity of the percussion, but they stopped it soon in a surprising, but planned spot. I'm telling ya, this band is tight.

After just a brief silence, Floyd comes back in with a simple, but sizzling little drum beat that starts up Hiroshi Suzuki's "Romance." Donna Debosier comes in with the clean, majestic trombone solo. Loo introduces her—Temple, Texas—then she adds a minute of beautiful improv onto the tail of the original.

She mellows it out, then Werner comes in with a glissando that cools everything way down until the piano player, Michael "Silki" Cho, earning his nickname, takes over with a more classical Jazz sounding Ryo Fukui "Scenery" piano solo that was so beautiful, so graceful, so delicate, so enchanting it relaxes everyone and takes them slow dancing on a mahogany floor in the finest of clothes.

After a minute or two of the elegant piano, Silki brought the tempo and intensity back down to zero. Everything was perfectly set up for the man, the hero, to take over. He had been in the shadows for a while, but then the stage crew shined a small spotlight on him. Masayoshi Takanaka's "Crystal Memories."

Werner started working some wind chimes, Silki put a nice melody over it, Floyd came in with the simple beat, then guitar heaven. Listen to the original to get the gist, but Loo was unreal. No words could describe the majesty. What a fucking song . . . the smooth guitar virtuoso masterpiece culminated with an intense assault by the whole band, locked-in, note-for-intricate-note.

It ends. The band, covered in sweat, had played their guts out. They took just a moment to catch their breath. Meanwhile, Loo talked to the audience.

"We're tired, but we've got one more, and we're going to give you everything we've got. You might have heard this one before."

He starts with a guitar solo. Everyone is quiet. Listening intently. What's he doing? Then you hear someone cheer. Then another. People are starting to pick up on some familiar sonorities. Before long, everyone is stretching their legs and backs as high as they'll go, trying to get closer to the action. In our lust for greatness, in our bacchanal frenzy, we can feel it but can't name it. We subconsciously know what's coming, yet we plead and beg for more.

Then BAM!

"Children of the Neon Bamboo," his biggest, best, most cherished, most ambitious song. The crowd started going absolutely crazy. They were there. They were witnessing greatness. A rollicking epic, full of hope, mystery, grandiosity, fun, excitement and wonder for life.

In the middle they slowed it down and added an other-worldly ambient section. Floyd did kind of a slow beat, Werner added embellishments on tamas and octobans to give it an exotic hint of antiquity. Over the top of it, Loo used his floating Floyd

Rose tremolo like a master, adding two minutes of controlled chaotic atmosphere that was both ambiance and music at once. Enraptured. Taken from our bodies in an astral projection, a sailboat on the seas of time and space. All was right. Peak consciousness. Connection. Unity achieved.

But our trip through the heavens wasn't over yet. They started to pick up the pace. Then, the whole band got in sync, playing for speed, but not just any speed. Speed that made you think we were star pilots soaring through space to defend Earth from invaders. A battle against all that is dark, culminating in triumphant orgasmic frenzy, before finishing off with a few bars of light lead playing as the band slowed, staying in sync, until the last cymbal quit ringing.

They put their instruments on the rack, met in the middle of the stage, locked arms over shoulders, bowed to the standing ovation.

"Thank you. Good night!"

They walked off the stage dripping with sweat and pride. Hugging each other in camaraderie.

I was clapping. My night was made. My year was made. My decade was made. All was right in the universe. But, it gets better.

As the band left for the green room, Loo grabbed the Charvel and walked to the front edge of the stage holding the green guitar high in the air for the roaring crowd with both hands like a sword. Pumping it in the air, he brought them to a fever pitch of jubilation and excitement. He lowered it, took it by the neck and handed it down to me. After I took possession, he took a long respectful bow. The whole crowd looked at me and roared as he walked off.

We all had two hours of our life during which all worry, longing, and discontent was banished.

I walked back to my car with a tear in my eye and a guitar in my hand. Kenny would have been so proud.

~

Nowadays, I try not to bother him too much. We are cool, but in different worlds. He's got a lot going on, married with twins on the way. No need to force anything and risk upsetting what's already perfect. Asking any more from him or the universe would be greedy.

RAMBLE ON

I've had about 30 summers since that one. Some of them okay, some of them downright miserable, but that one was a good one. It's carried me through some of my darkest times knowing that me not living well, not sucking the marrow out of life, and especially killing myself, would disappoint those two.

Yeah, part of me is a sanctimonious goober who asks myself how I could sentimentalize 1980's consumerism. Fuck it. Pizza Hut, Pepsi, Sega, and *Ninja Turtles* made my childhood awesome. Don't let the perfect be the enemy of the good. Billions of people have had it way worse than we did. Those greedy corporate folks were giving the kids and their families exactly what they wanted, a good time, a break from the suck. Yeah, we had problems. We were an unorthodox family, not Leave-it-to-Beavers, but we had a good time, our time. We may not have had it all, but we had something.

I could have ended up on the Soul Asylum "Runaway Train" super sad video about missing kids, "Arthur Regulski last seen July 18th 1990."

~

You look beat. I reckon it's time to call it a night. If I were to get any drunker, I'd talk your leg off worse than I already have.

Just leave the stogey unless you want a plastic bag to save it for later. I'll pick up the glasses and cans tomorrow; Mike's pretty lenient about trash and dishes up to a day or so.

You can sleep on the old couch in the studio den if you're too tired or drunk to drive. The couch has definitely had its share of vagrants and varmints. Cum stains. Blood stains. Sweat stains. You name it. It was nasty the first time I came to this studio five years ago. God knows where all it's been.

I'll just sleep on the floor in there. He's got blankets in the closet. But I warn you, I have to have the TV on to fall asleep. We can see which Michael Dudikoff classic is on the action channel or dial-in *Magnum P.I.* on the nursing home station. But the mesothelioma settlement and prostate supplement commercials get old and depressing quick, so we could throw on this old Scuba-Dive-Mexico VHS. It has an amazing South American themed ambient backing track, so soothing when combined with sounds of the ocean.

Keep the shirt if you like it. If not, leave it here. I'd rather you give it back than take it home and throw it away. Vintage classics aren't cheap these days.

No, I will not tell you where I've hidden the guitar, and, yes, I would go to Tarantino-esque lengths to get it back.

If you're still here on Tuesday, they do half-price Queso until 4pm down at the strip club.

SAYONARA

"Keep Safe" - Astral Tales

Be happy it ever happened at all.

THANK YOU

Casey Clare Fraser

Dylan Garringer

Eowyn Garringer

Joseph Heck

Crystal Kimmey

Kim Kimmey

Heather Marinics

Jeanette Mirll

Jon Pham

Madison Roberts